LITTLE NEMO
RETURN TO SLUMBERLAND

ERIC SHANOWER
GABRIEL RODRIGUEZ

COLORED BY
NELSON DANIEL

LETTERED BY
ROBBIE ROBBINS

EDITED BY
CHRIS RYALL & SCOTT DUNBIER

EDITORIAL ASSISTANCE BY
MICHAEL BENEDETTO

PUBLISHER
TED ADAMS

COVER BY
GABRIEL RODRIGUEZ

COLLECTION EDITS BY
JUSTIN EISINGER & ALONZO SIMON

COLLECTION DESIGN BY
ROBBIE ROBBINS

BASED ON THE BRILLIANT WORKS OF WINSOR MCCAY

Little Nemo: Return to Slumberland created by Eric Shanower and Gabriel Rodriguez

ISBN: 978-1-63140-322-4   18 17 16 15   1 2 3 4

Ted Adams, CEO & Publisher • Greg Goldstein,
President & COO • Robbie Robbins, EVP/Sr.
Graphic Artist • Chris Ryall, Chief Creative
Officer/Editor-in-Chief • Matthew Ruzicka, CPA,
Chief Financial Officer • Alan Payne, VP of Sales •
Dirk Wood, VP of Marketing • Lorelei Bunjes,
VP of Digital Services • Jeff Webber, VP of
Digital Publishing & Business Development

IDW
www.IDWPUBLISHING.com

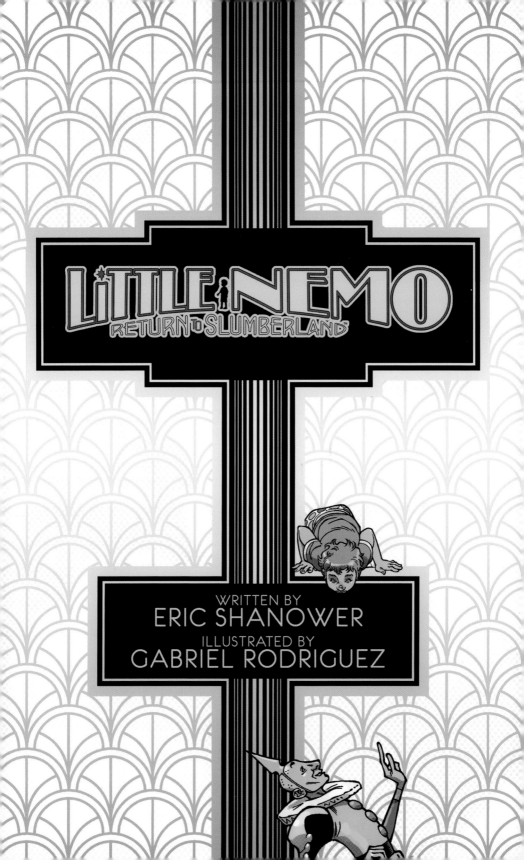

LITTLE NEMO
RETURN TO SLUMBERLAND

WRITTEN BY
ERIC SHANOWER

ILLUSTRATED BY
GABRIEL RODRIGUEZ

CHAPTER ONE

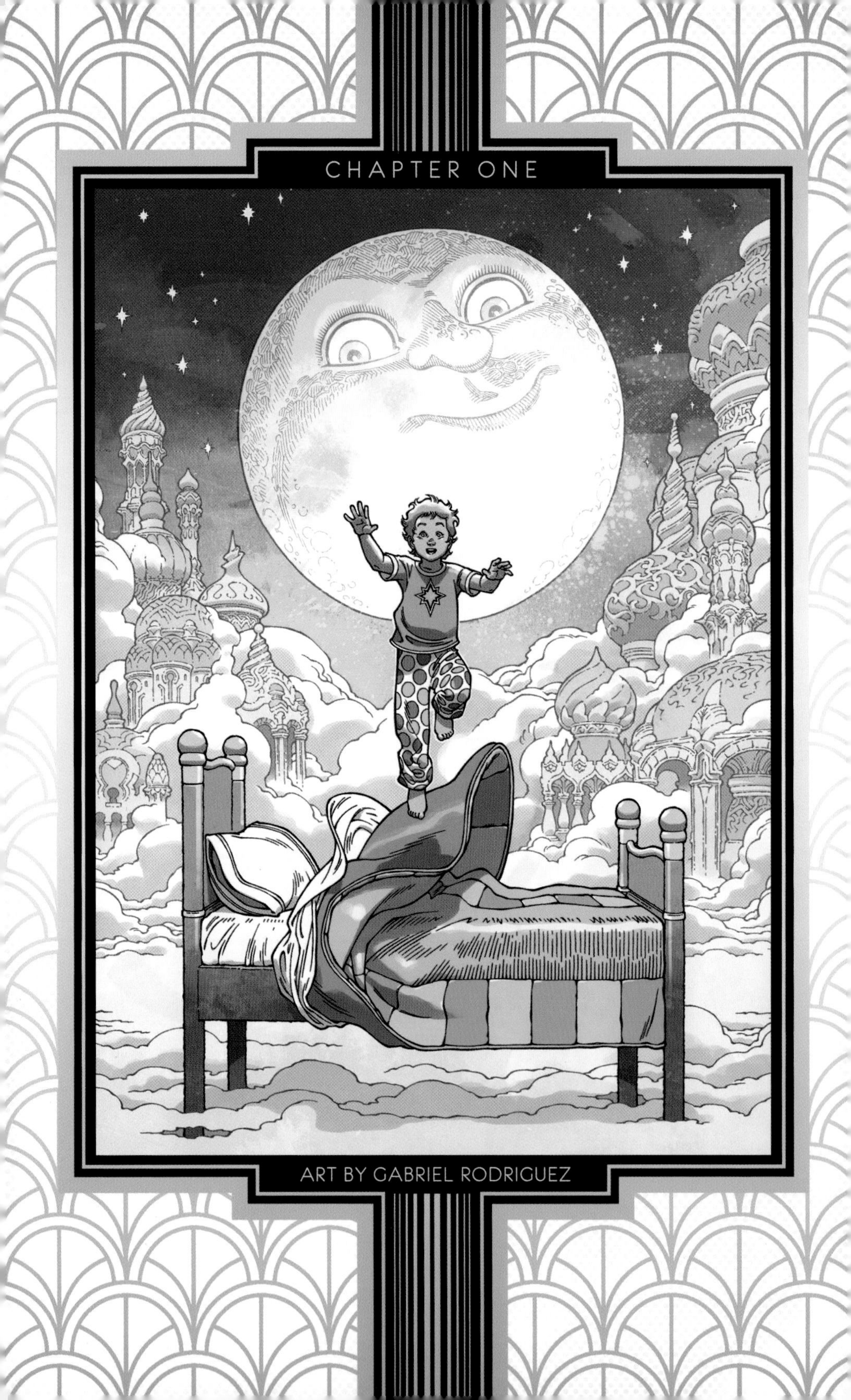

ART BY GABRIEL RODRIGUEZ

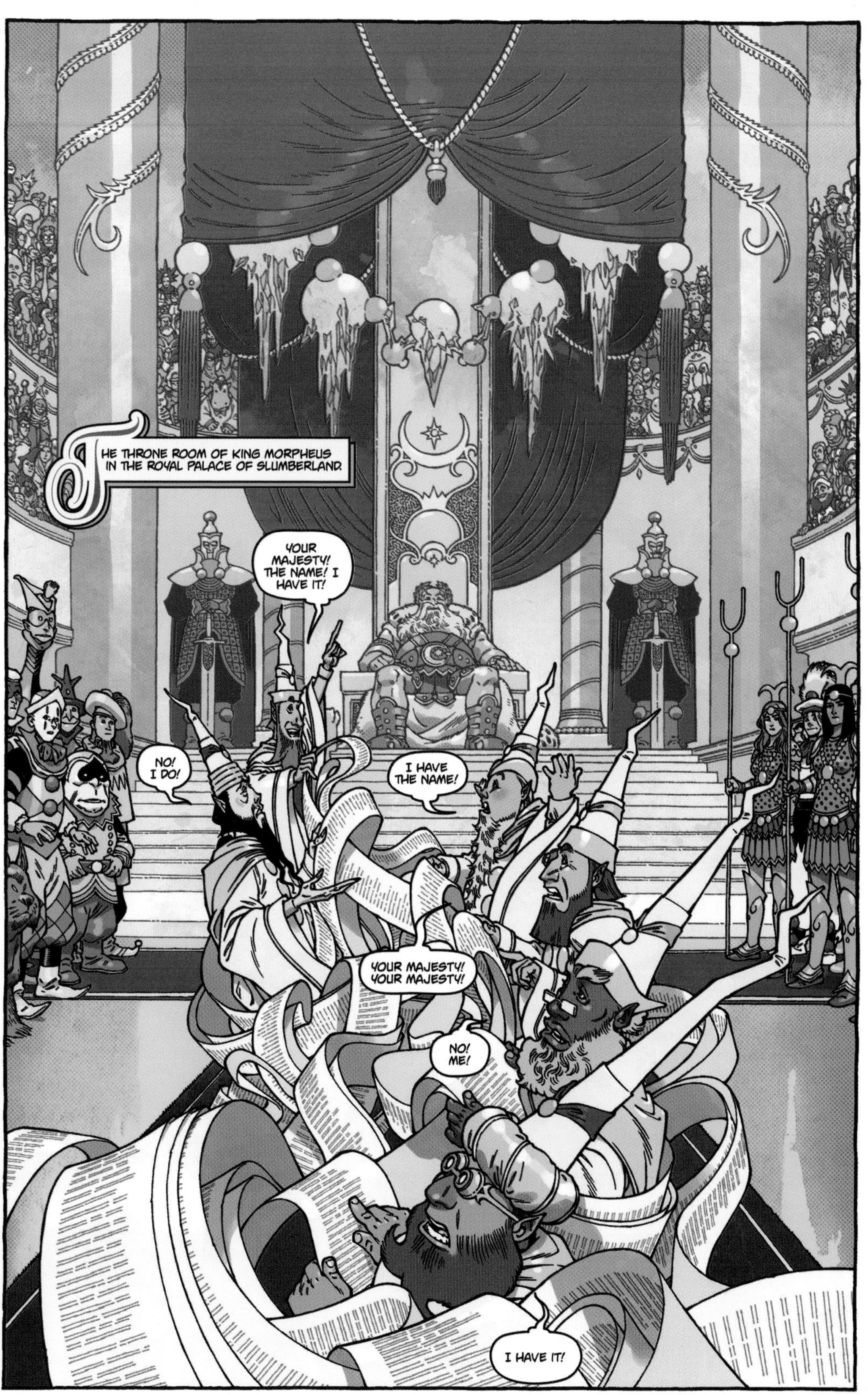
THE THRONE ROOM OF KING MORPHEUS IN THE ROYAL PALACE OF SLUMBERLAND.
YOUR MAJESTY! THE NAME! I HAVE IT!
NO! I DO!
I HAVE THE NAME!
YOUR MAJESTY! YOUR MAJESTY!
NO! ME!
I HAVE IT!

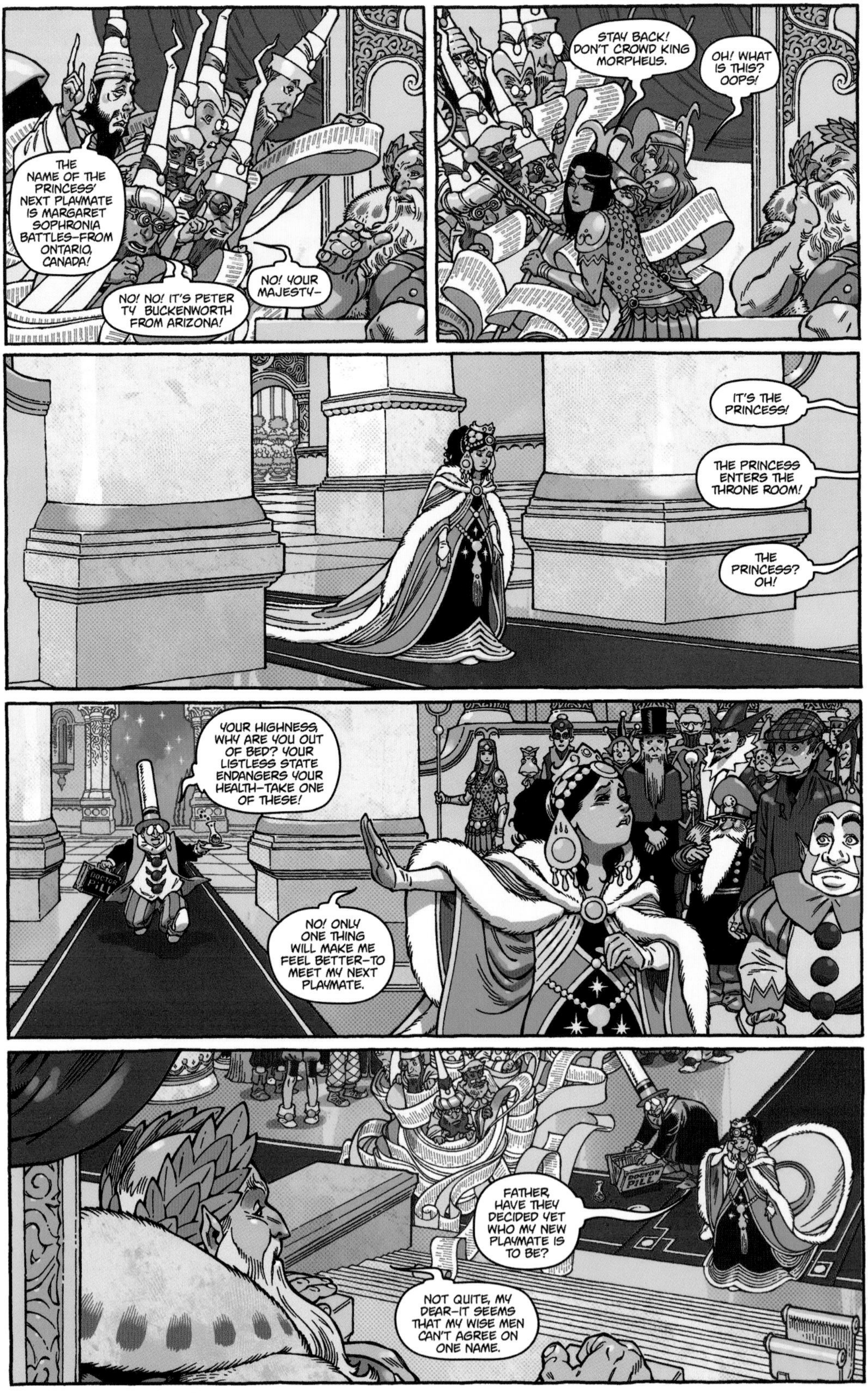
THE NAME OF THE PRINCESS' NEXT PLAYMATE IS MARGARET SOPHRONIA BATTLES—FROM ONTARIO, CANADA!
NO! NO! IT'S PETER TY BUCKENWORTH FROM ARIZONA!
NO! YOUR MAJESTY—
STAY BACK! DON'T CROWD KING MORPHEUS.
OH! WHAT IS THIS? OOPS!
IT'S THE PRINCESS!
THE PRINCESS ENTERS THE THRONE ROOM!
THE PRINCESS? OH!
YOUR HIGHNESS, WHY ARE YOU OUT OF BED? YOUR LISTLESS STATE ENDANGERS YOUR HEALTH—TAKE ONE OF THESE!
DOCTOR PILL
NO! ONLY ONE THING WILL MAKE ME FEEL BETTER—TO MEET MY NEXT PLAYMATE.
DOCTOR PILL
FATHER, HAVE THEY DECIDED YET WHO MY NEW PLAYMATE IS TO BE?
NOT QUITE, MY DEAR—IT SEEMS THAT MY WISE MEN CAN'T AGREE ON ONE NAME.

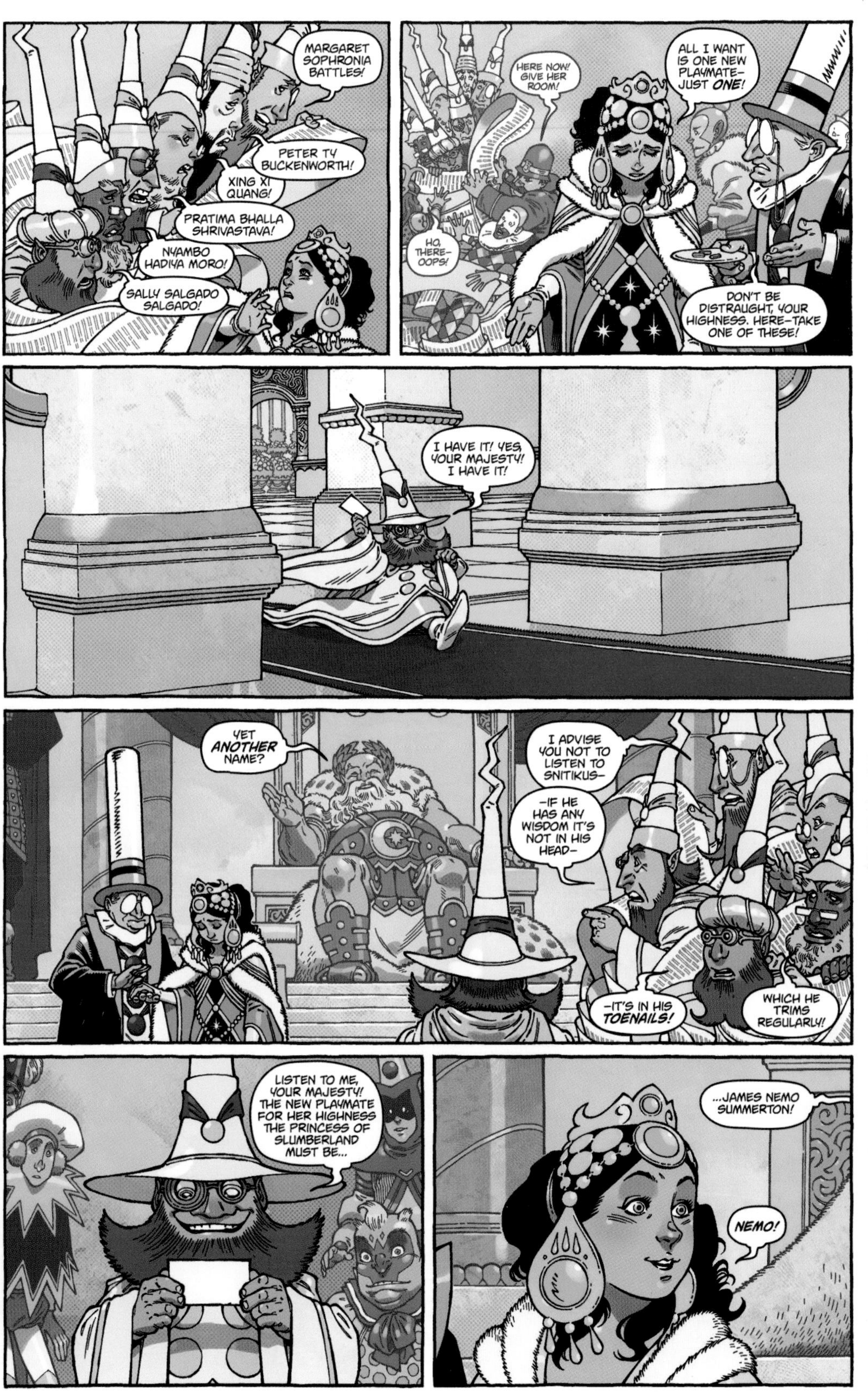
MARGARET SOPHRONIA BATTLES!
PETER TY BUCKENWORTH!
XING XI QUANG!
PRATIMA BHALLA SHRIVASTAVA!
NYAMBO HADIYA MORO!
SALLY SALGADO SALGADO!
HERE NOW! GIVE HER ROOM!
ALL I WANT IS ONE NEW PLAYMATE– JUST ONE!
HO, THERE– OOPS!
DON'T BE DISTRAUGHT, YOUR HIGHNESS. HERE–TAKE ONE OF THESE!
I HAVE IT! YES, YOUR MAJESTY! I HAVE IT!
YET ANOTHER NAME?
I ADVISE YOU NOT TO LISTEN TO SNITIKUS–
–IF HE HAS ANY WISDOM IT'S NOT IN HIS HEAD–
–IT'S IN HIS TOENAILS!
WHICH HE TRIMS REGULARLY!
LISTEN TO ME, YOUR MAJESTY! THE NEW PLAYMATE FOR HER HIGHNESS THE PRINCESS OF SLUMBERLAND MUST BE...
...JAMES NEMO SUMMERTON!
NEMO!

OH, FATHER! HE'S THE ONE—HE *MUST* BE! HIS NAME IS NEMO!

WE WERE ALL VERY FOND OF THE LITTLE NEMO WHO WAS YOUR PLAYMATE LONG AGO.

SIMILARITY IN NAMES MEANS NOTHING!

LISTEN TO ME!

NO! NO!

WE MUST ADHERE TO STRICT GUIDELINES!

SNITIKUS KNOWS NOTHING!

I HAVE THE CORRECT NAME!

NONE OF MY PLAYMATES SINCE NEMO HAS BEEN AS WONDERFUL. THIS IS THE ONE, FATHER.

SEND FOR MY CRYSTAL GAZER AND WE'LL TAKE A LOOK AT THIS NEMO.

HERE I AM, YOUR MAJESTY! I JUST WASHED MY CRYSTAL BALL IN SCALDING WATER AND I CAN HARDLY HOLD IT—BUT HERE I AM!

STOP JIGGLING THE BALL!

IT'S STILL HOT!

NO! NO!

NEMO! SHOW US NEMO!

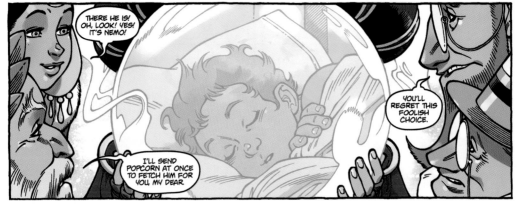

THERE HE IS! OH, LOOK! YES! IT'S NEMO!

I'LL SEND POPCORN AT ONCE TO FETCH HIM FOR YOU, MY DEAR.

YOU'LL REGRET THIS FOOLISH CHOICE.

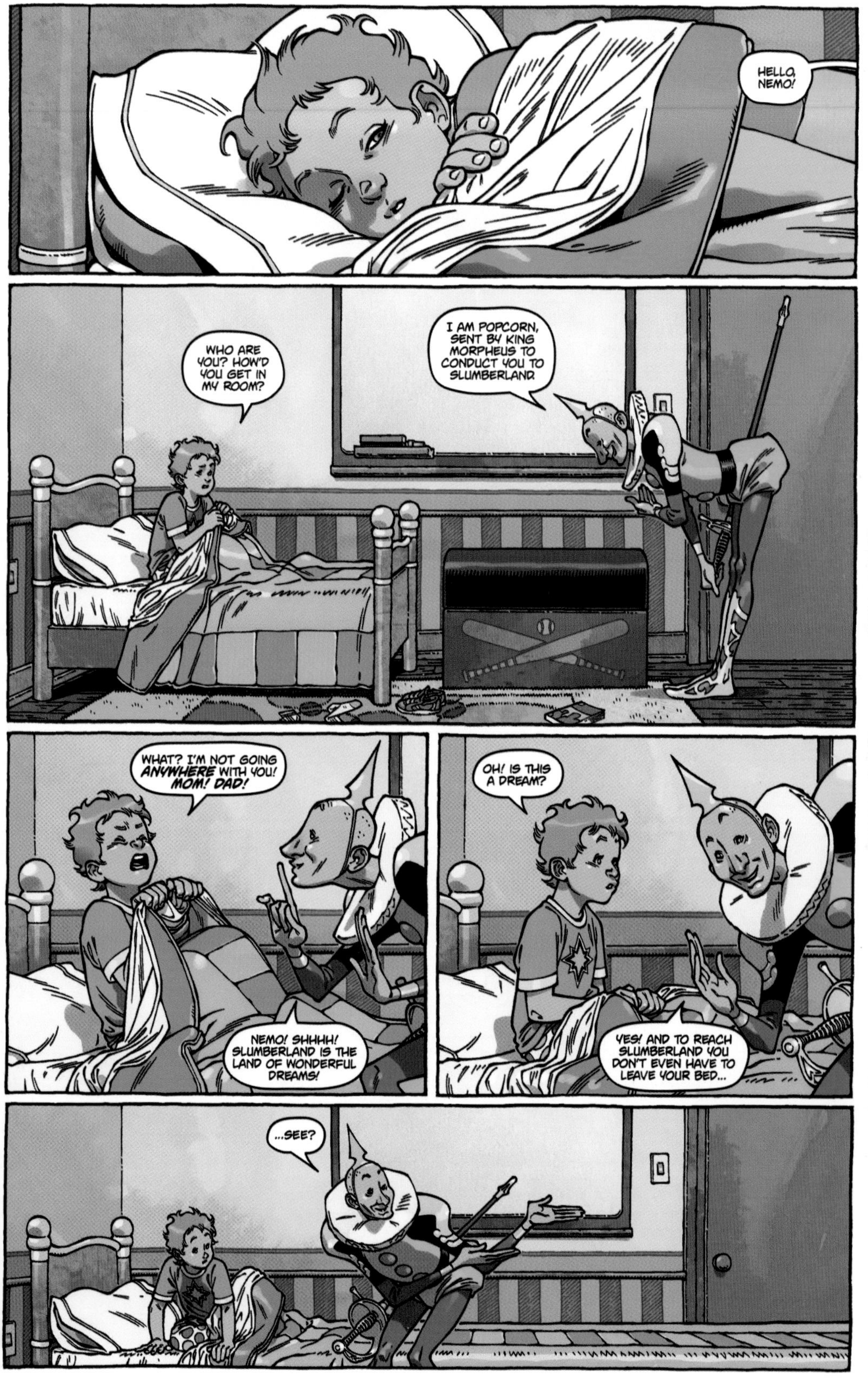
HELLO, NEMO!
WHO ARE YOU? HOW'D YOU GET IN MY ROOM?
I AM POPCORN, SENT BY KING MORPHEUS TO CONDUCT YOU TO SLUMBERLAND.
WHAT? I'M NOT GOING **ANYWHERE** WITH YOU! **MOM! DAD!**
NEMO! SHHHH! SLUMBERLAND IS THE LAND OF WONDERFUL DREAMS!
OH! IS THIS A DREAM?
YES! AND TO REACH SLUMBERLAND YOU DON'T EVEN HAVE TO LEAVE YOUR BED...
...SEE?

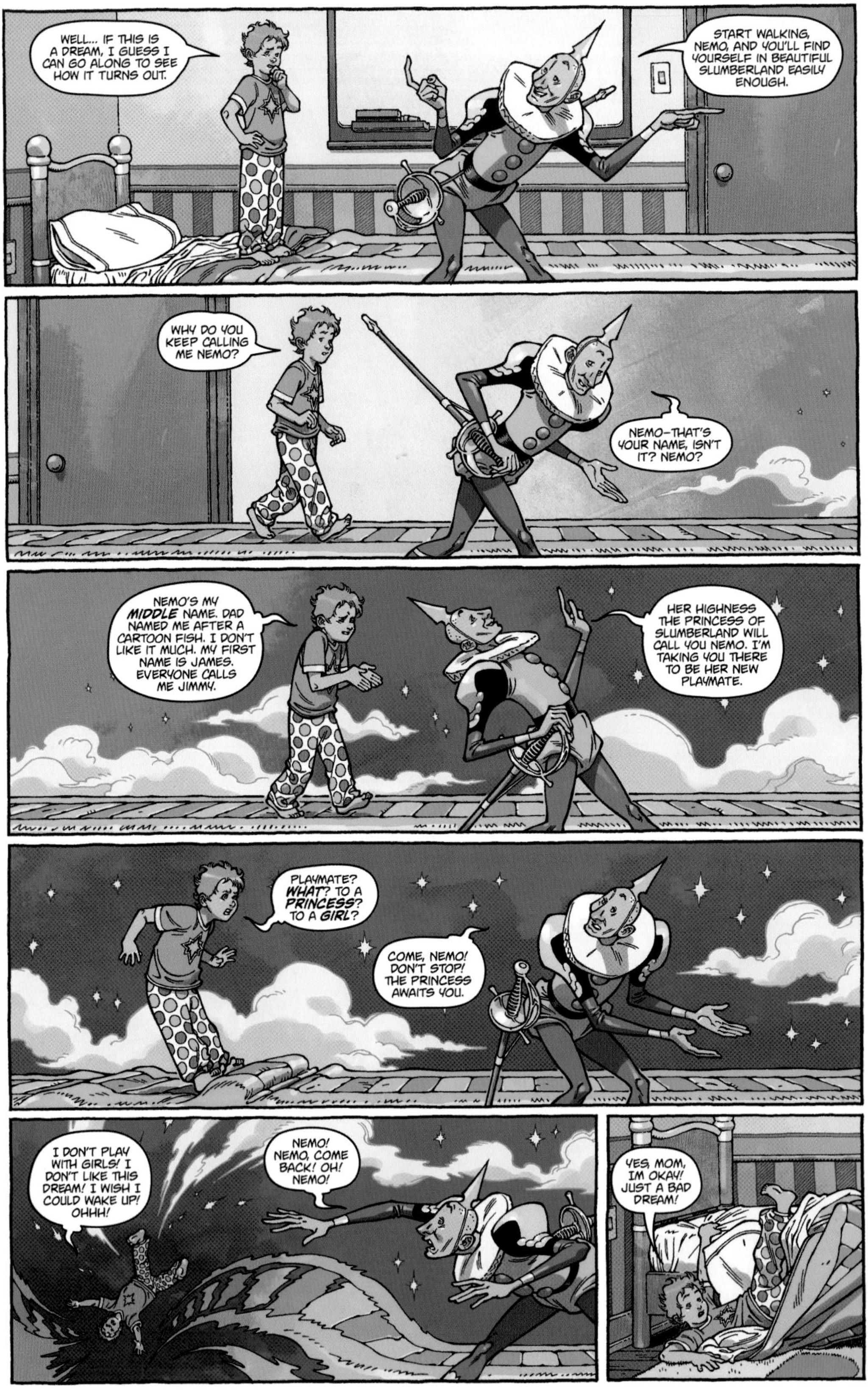
WELL... IF THIS IS A DREAM, I GUESS I CAN GO ALONG TO SEE HOW IT TURNS OUT.
START WALKING, NEMO, AND YOU'LL FIND YOURSELF IN BEAUTIFUL SLUMBERLAND EASILY ENOUGH.
WHY DO YOU KEEP CALLING ME NEMO?
NEMO—THAT'S YOUR NAME, ISN'T IT? NEMO?
NEMO'S MY *MIDDLE* NAME. DAD NAMED ME AFTER A CARTOON FISH. I DON'T LIKE IT MUCH. MY FIRST NAME IS JAMES. EVERYONE CALLS ME JIMMY.
HER HIGHNESS THE PRINCESS OF SLUMBERLAND WILL CALL YOU NEMO. I'M TAKING YOU THERE TO BE HER NEW PLAYMATE.
PLAYMATE? *WHAT*? TO A *PRINCESS*? TO A *GIRL*?
COME, NEMO! DON'T STOP! THE PRINCESS AWAITS YOU.
I DON'T PLAY WITH GIRLS! I DON'T LIKE THIS DREAM! I WISH I COULD WAKE UP! OHHH!
NEMO! NEMO, COME BACK! OH! NEMO!
YES, MOM, IM OKAY! JUST A BAD DREAM!

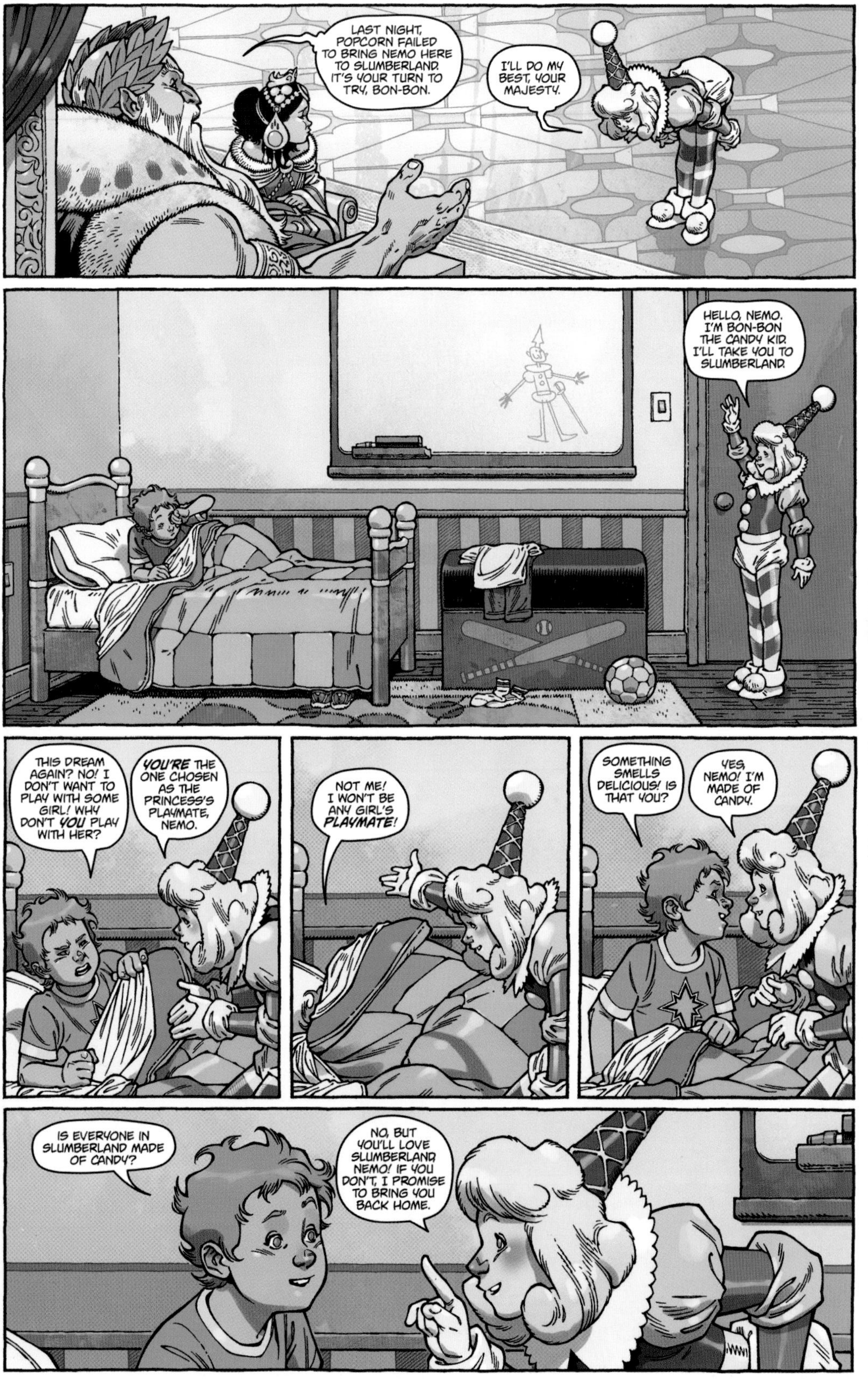
LAST NIGHT, POPCORN FAILED TO BRING NEMO HERE TO SLUMBERLAND. IT'S YOUR TURN TO TRY, BON-BON.
I'LL DO MY BEST, YOUR MAJESTY.
HELLO, NEMO. I'M BON-BON THE CANDY KID. I'LL TAKE YOU TO SLUMBERLAND.
THIS DREAM AGAIN? NO! I DON'T WANT TO PLAY WITH SOME GIRL! WHY DON'T YOU PLAY WITH HER?
YOU'RE THE ONE CHOSEN AS THE PRINCESS'S PLAYMATE, NEMO.
NOT ME! I WON'T BE ANY GIRL'S PLAYMATE!
SOMETHING SMELLS DELICIOUS! IS THAT YOU?
YES, NEMO! I'M MADE OF CANDY.
IS EVERYONE IN SLUMBERLAND MADE OF CANDY?
NO, BUT YOU'LL LOVE SLUMBERLAND, NEMO! IF YOU DON'T, I PROMISE TO BRING YOU BACK HOME.

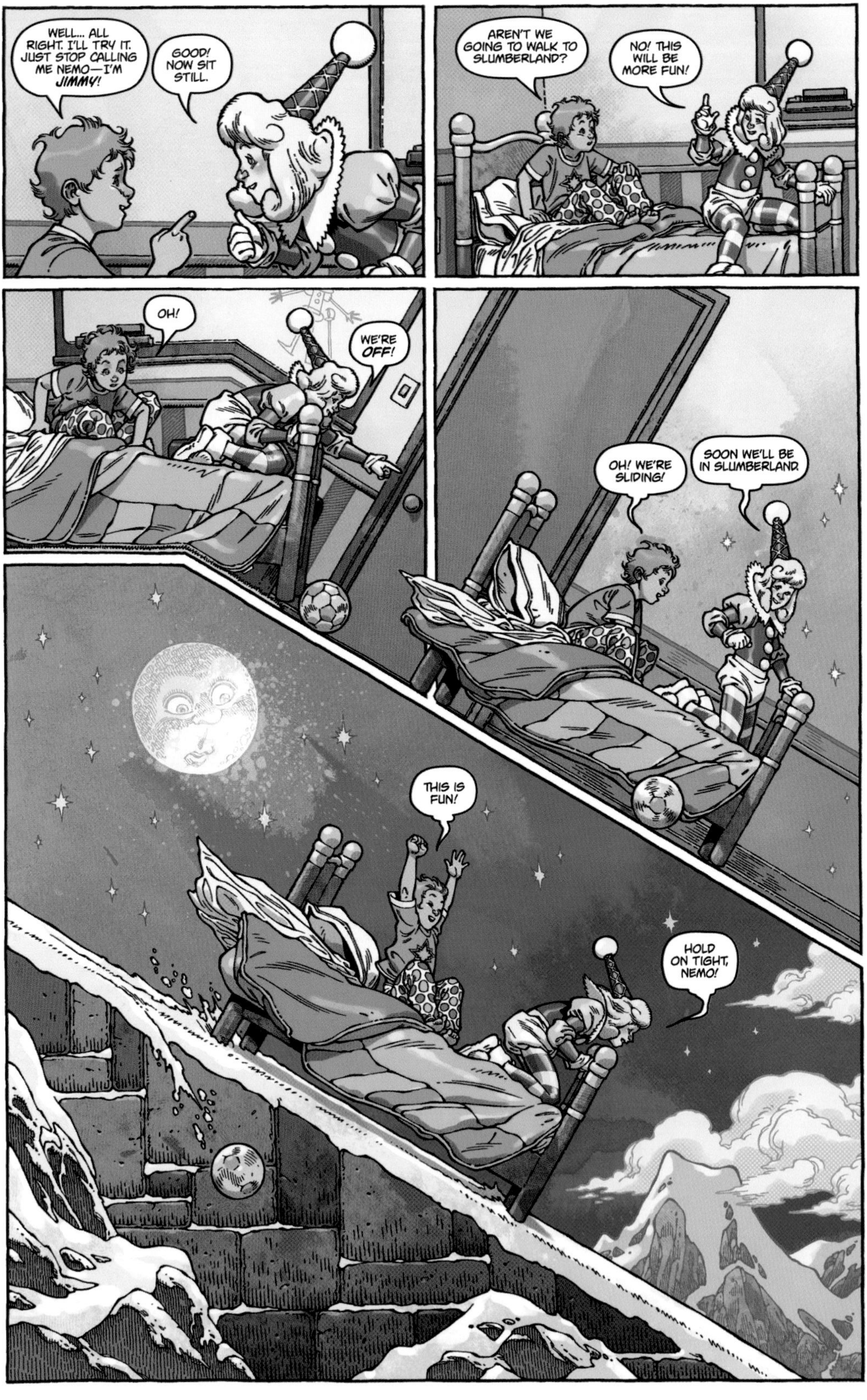

WELL... ALL RIGHT. I'LL TRY IT. JUST STOP CALLING ME NEMO—I'M *JIMMY*!
GOOD! NOW SIT STILL.
AREN'T WE GOING TO WALK TO SLUMBERLAND?
NO! THIS WILL BE MORE FUN!
OH!
WE'RE *OFF*!
OH! WE'RE SLIDING!
SOON WE'LL BE IN SLUMBERLAND.
THIS IS FUN!
HOLD ON TIGHT, NEMO!

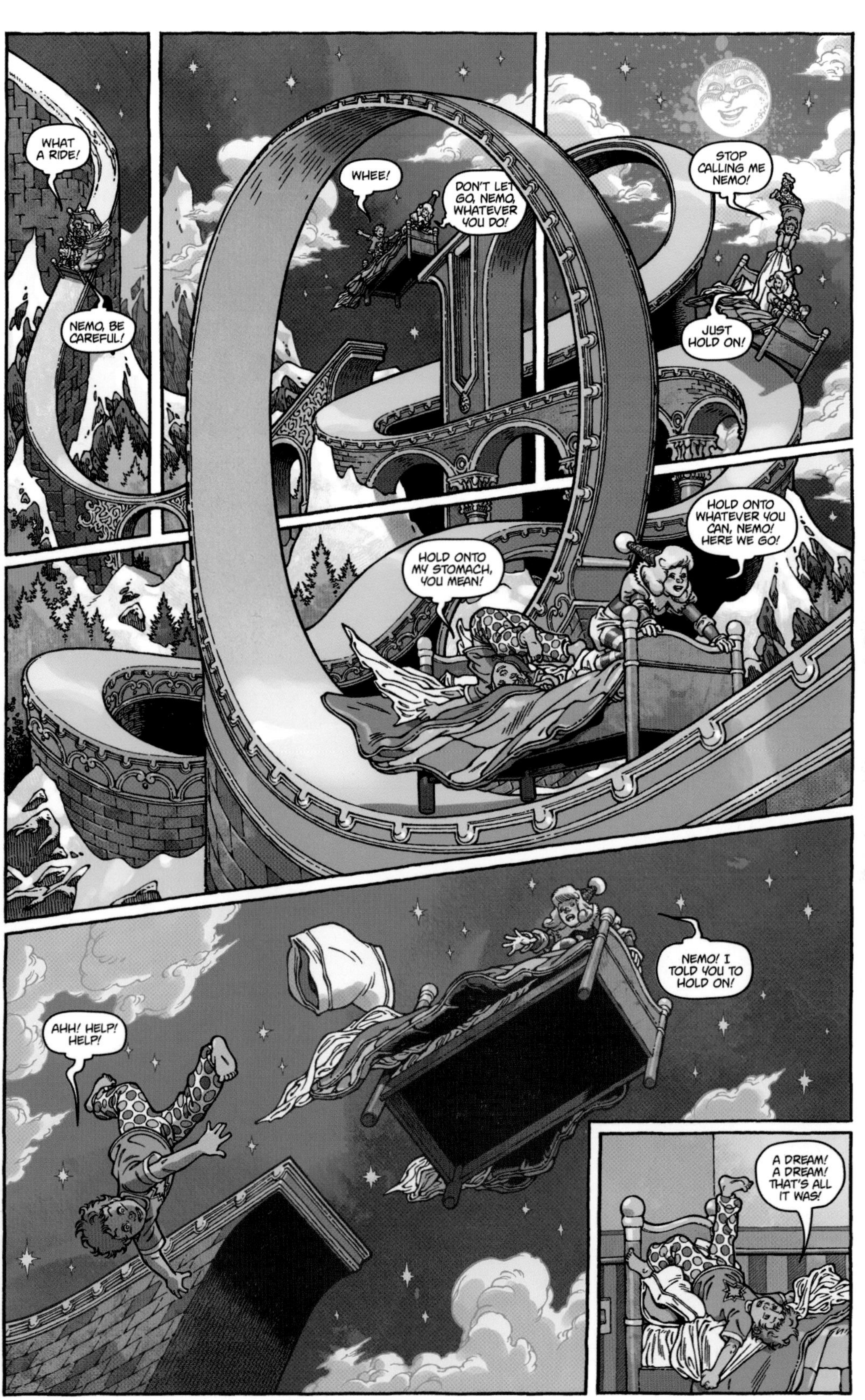
WHAT A RIDE!
NEMO, BE CAREFUL!
WHEE!
DON'T LET GO, NEMO, WHATEVER YOU DO!
STOP CALLING ME NEMO!
JUST HOLD ON!
HOLD ONTO MY STOMACH, YOU MEAN!
HOLD ONTO WHATEVER YOU CAN, NEMO! HERE WE GO!
AHH! HELP! HELP!
NEMO! I TOLD YOU TO HOLD ON!
A DREAM! A DREAM! THAT'S ALL IT WAS!

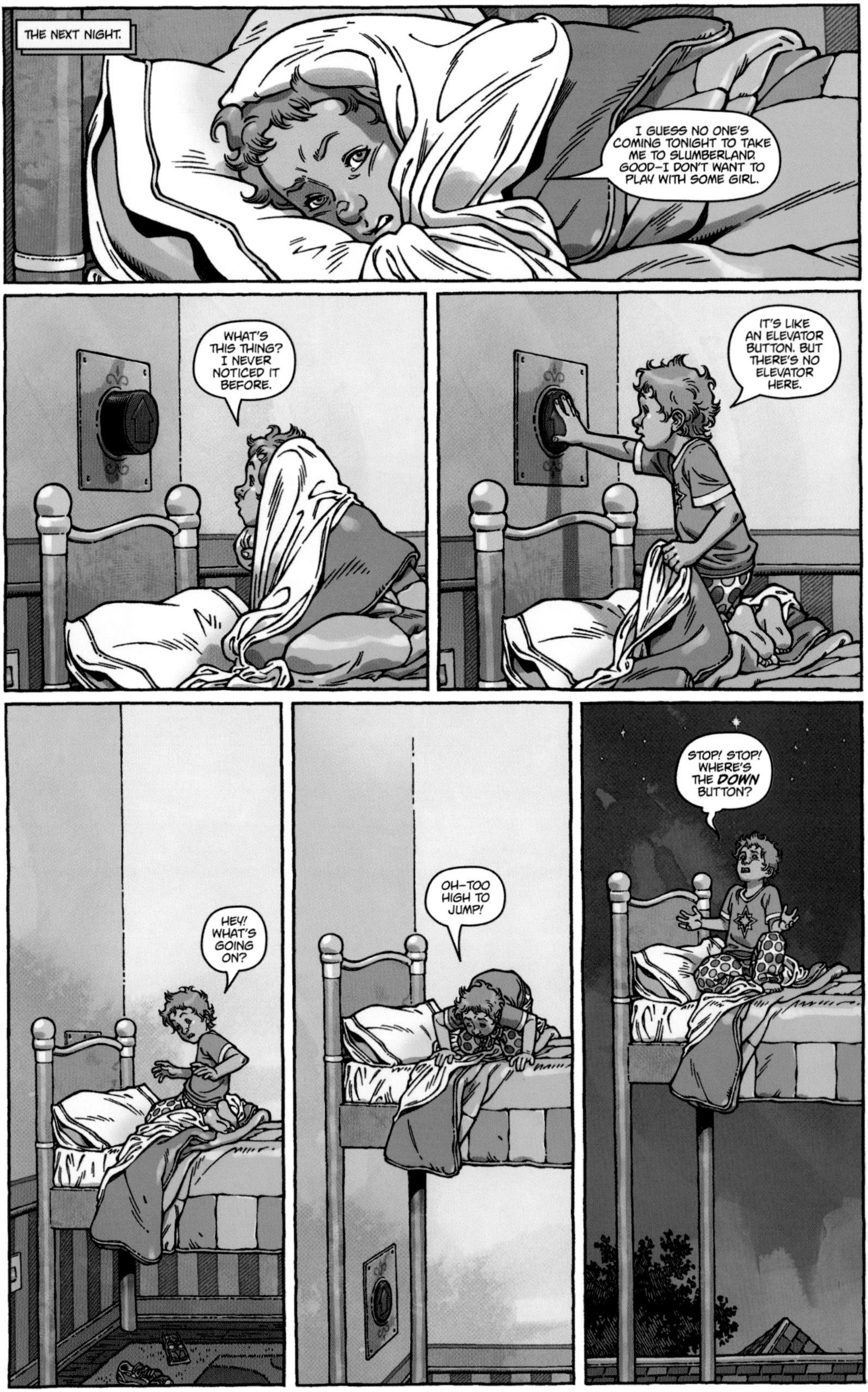
THE NEXT NIGHT.
I GUESS NO ONE'S COMING TONIGHT TO TAKE ME TO SLUMBERLAND. GOOD—I DON'T WANT TO PLAY WITH SOME GIRL.
WHAT'S THIS THING? I NEVER NOTICED IT BEFORE.
IT'S LIKE AN ELEVATOR BUTTON. BUT THERE'S NO ELEVATOR HERE.
HEY! WHAT'S GOING ON?
OH—TOO HIGH TO JUMP!
STOP! STOP! WHERE'S THE DOWN BUTTON?

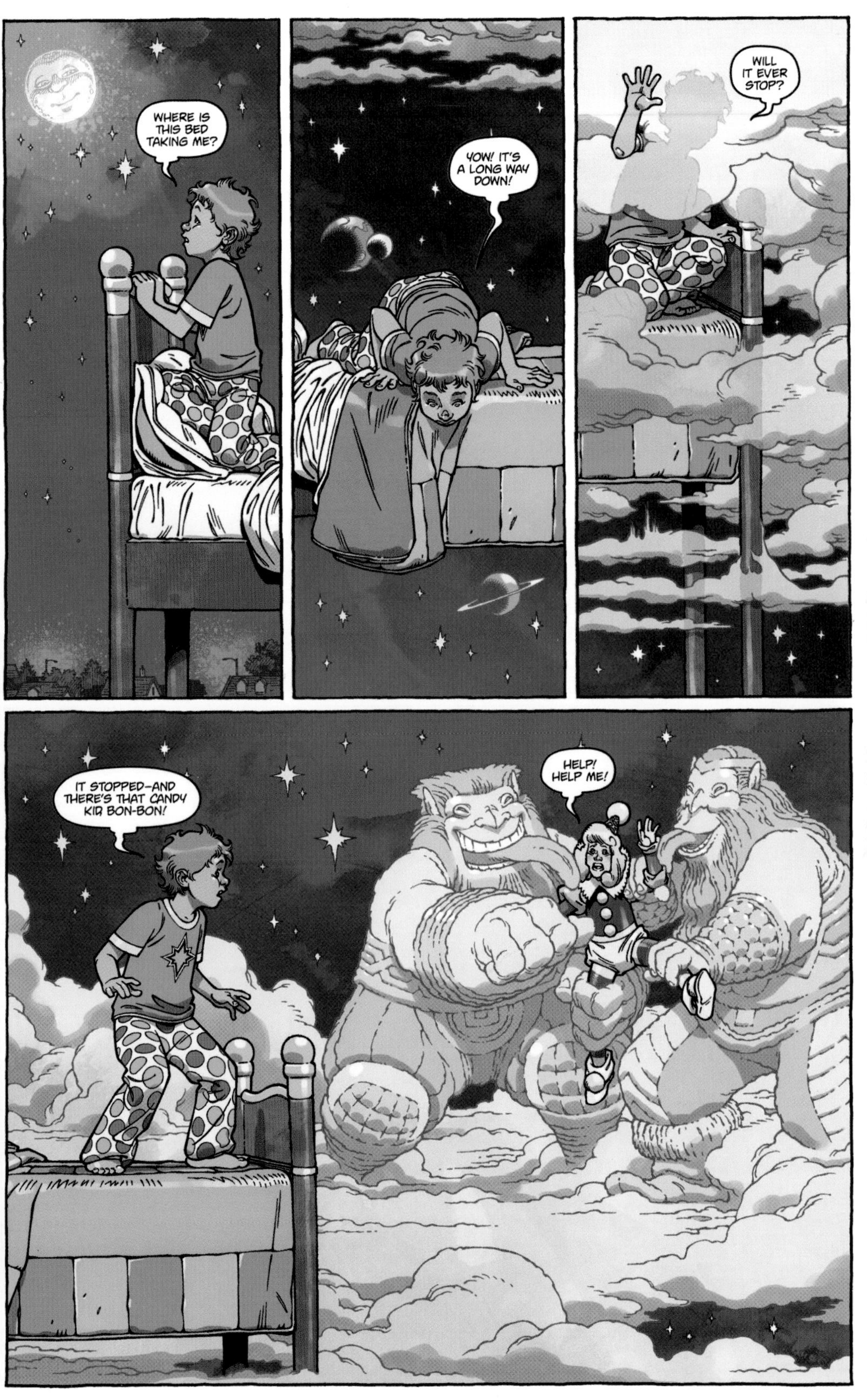
WHERE IS THIS BED TAKING ME?
YOW! IT'S A LONG WAY DOWN!
WILL IT EVER STOP?
IT STOPPED--AND THERE'S THAT CANDY KID BON-BON!
HELP! HELP ME!

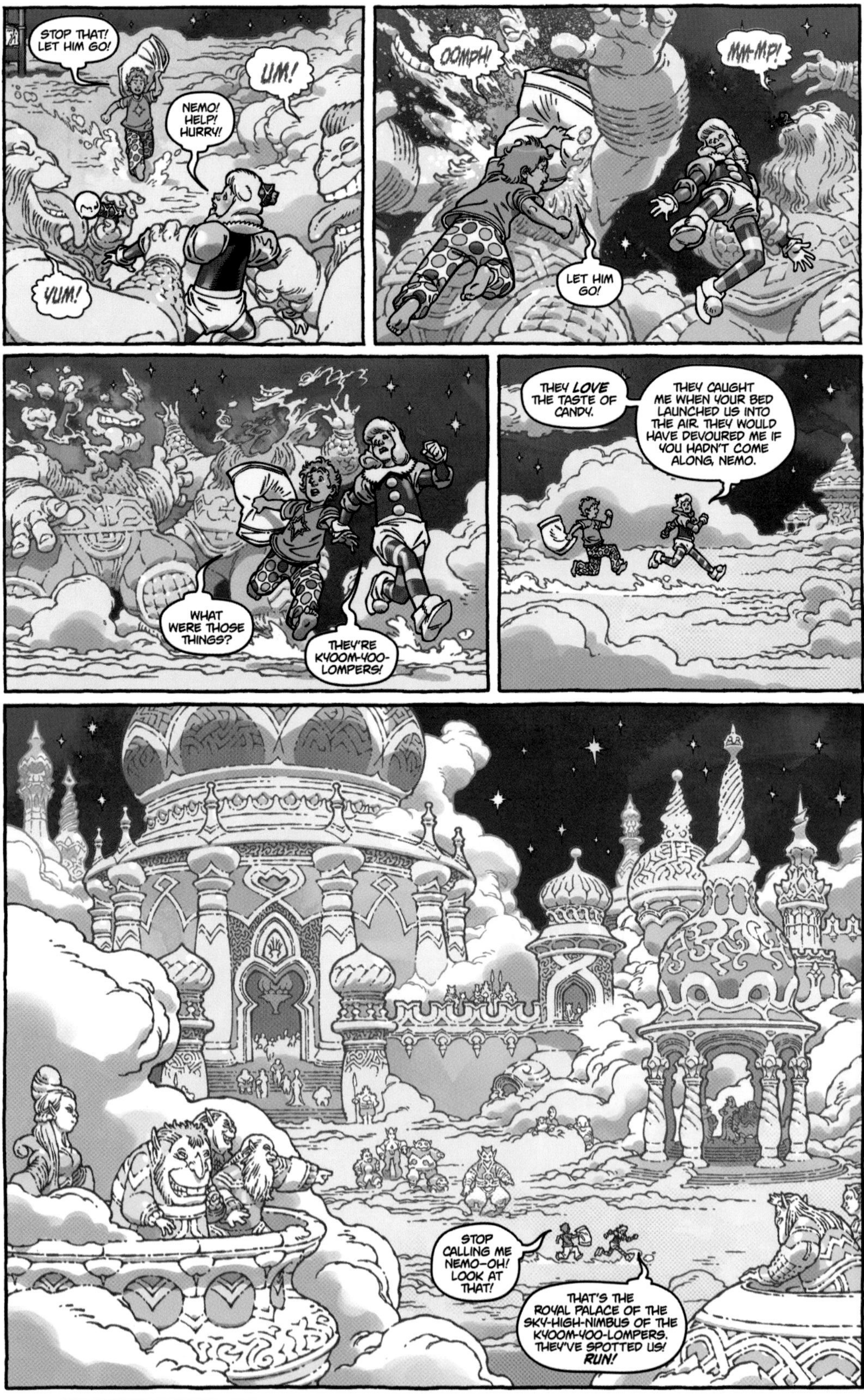
STOP THAT! LET HIM GO!
UM!
NEMO! HELP! HURRY!
YUM!
OOMPH!
MM-MP!
LET HIM GO!
WHAT WERE THOSE THINGS?
THEY'RE KYOOM-YOO-LOMPERS!
THEY LOVE THE TASTE OF CANDY.
THEY CAUGHT ME WHEN YOUR BED LAUNCHED US INTO THE AIR. THEY WOULD HAVE DEVOURED ME IF YOU HADN'T COME ALONG, NEMO.
STOP CALLING ME NEMO–OH! LOOK AT THAT!
THAT'S THE ROYAL PALACE OF THE SKY-HIGH-NIMBUS OF THE KYOOM-YOO-LOMPERS. THEY'VE SPOTTED US! RUN!

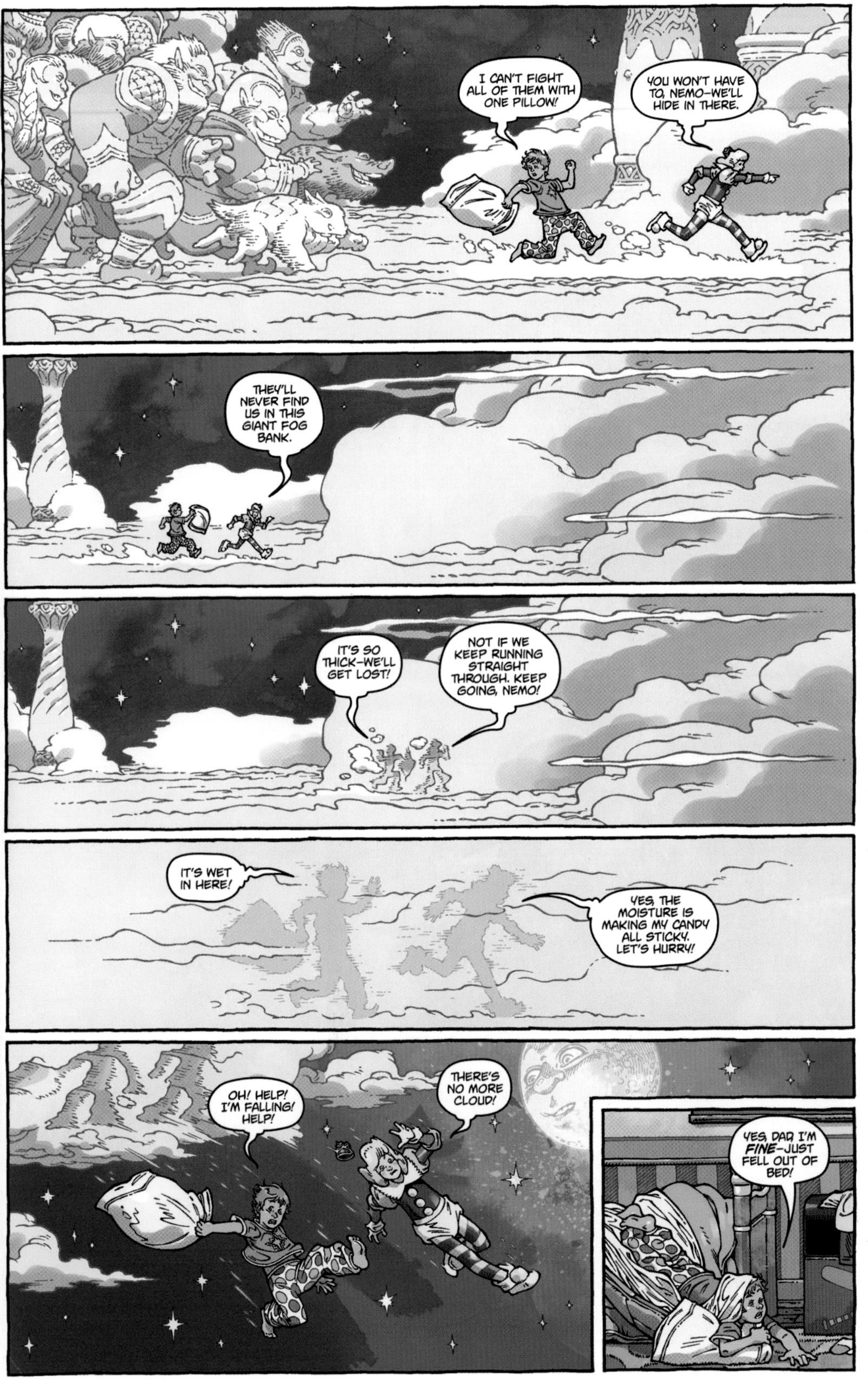
I CAN'T FIGHT ALL OF THEM WITH ONE PILLOW!
YOU WON'T HAVE TO, NEMO—WE'LL HIDE IN THERE.
THEY'LL NEVER FIND US IN THIS GIANT FOG BANK.
IT'S SO THICK—WE'LL GET LOST!
NOT IF WE KEEP RUNNING STRAIGHT THROUGH. KEEP GOING, NEMO!
IT'S WET IN HERE!
YES, THE MOISTURE IS MAKING MY CANDY ALL STICKY. LET'S HURRY!
OH! HELP! I'M FALLING! HELP!
THERE'S NO MORE CLOUD!
YES, DAD I'M FINE—JUST FELL OUT OF BED!

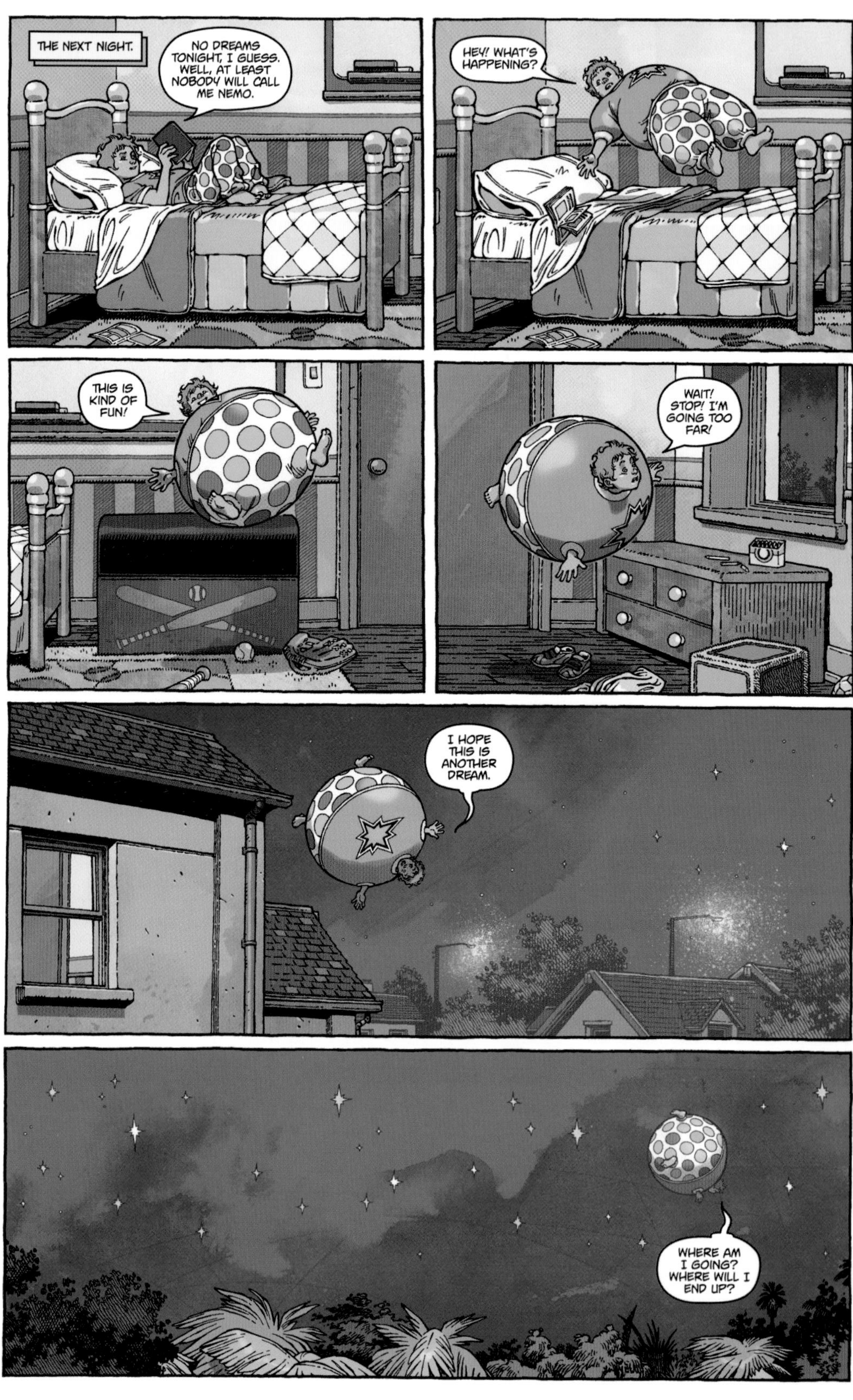
THE NEXT NIGHT.
NO DREAMS TONIGHT, I GUESS. WELL, AT LEAST NOBODY WILL CALL ME NEMO.
HEY! WHAT'S HAPPENING?
THIS IS KIND OF FUN!
WAIT! STOP! I'M GOING TOO FAR!
I HOPE THIS IS ANOTHER DREAM.
WHERE AM I GOING? WHERE WILL I END UP?

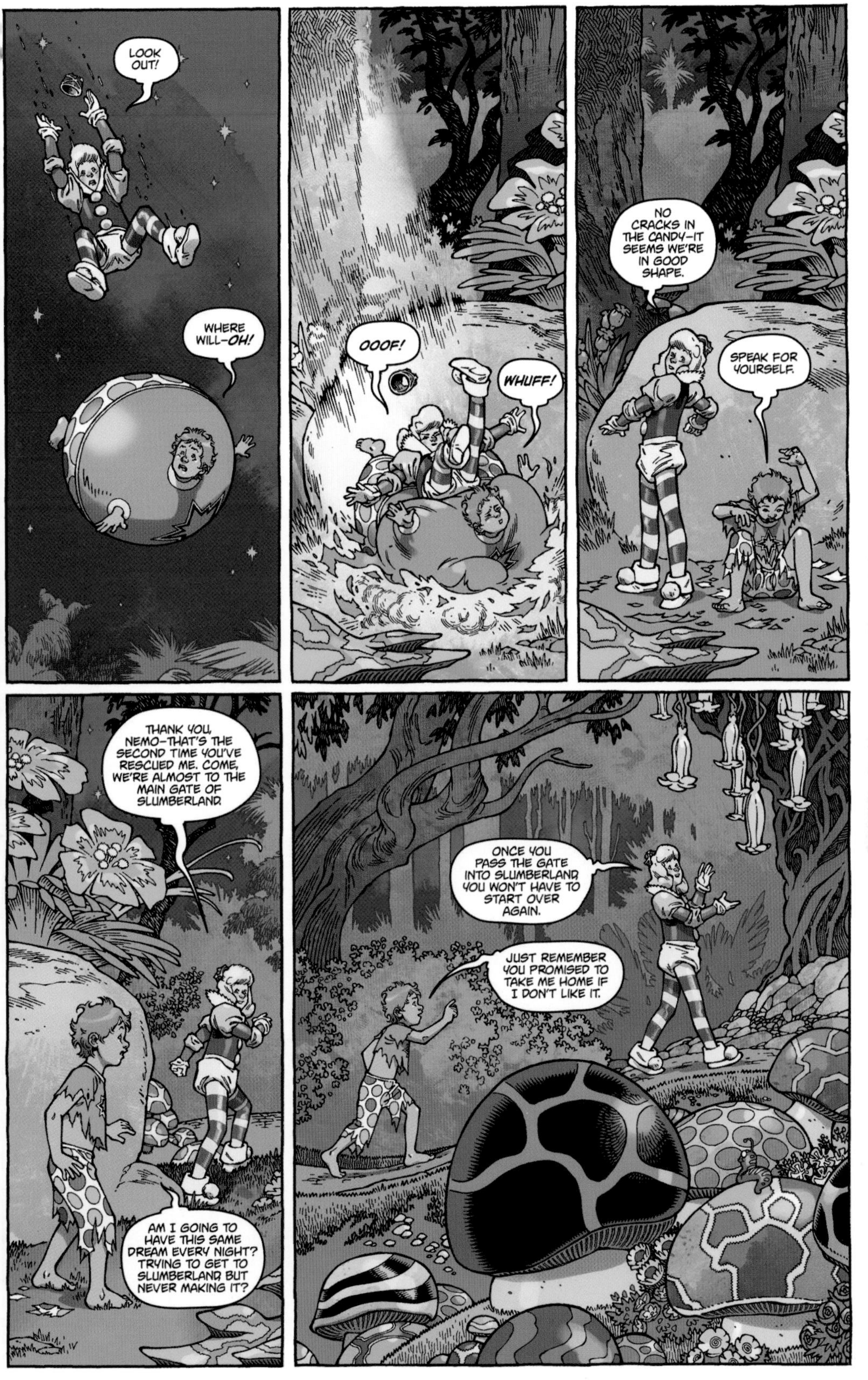
LOOK OUT!
WHERE WILL–OH!
OOOF!
WHUFF!
NO CRACKS IN THE CANDY–IT SEEMS WE'RE IN GOOD SHAPE.
SPEAK FOR YOURSELF.
THANK YOU, NEMO–THAT'S THE SECOND TIME YOU'VE RESCUED ME. COME, WE'RE ALMOST TO THE MAIN GATE OF SLUMBERLAND.
AM I GOING TO HAVE THIS SAME DREAM EVERY NIGHT? TRYING TO GET TO SLUMBERLAND BUT NEVER MAKING IT?
ONCE YOU PASS THE GATE INTO SLUMBERLAND YOU WON'T HAVE TO START OVER AGAIN.
JUST REMEMBER YOU PROMISED TO TAKE ME HOME IF I DON'T LIKE IT.

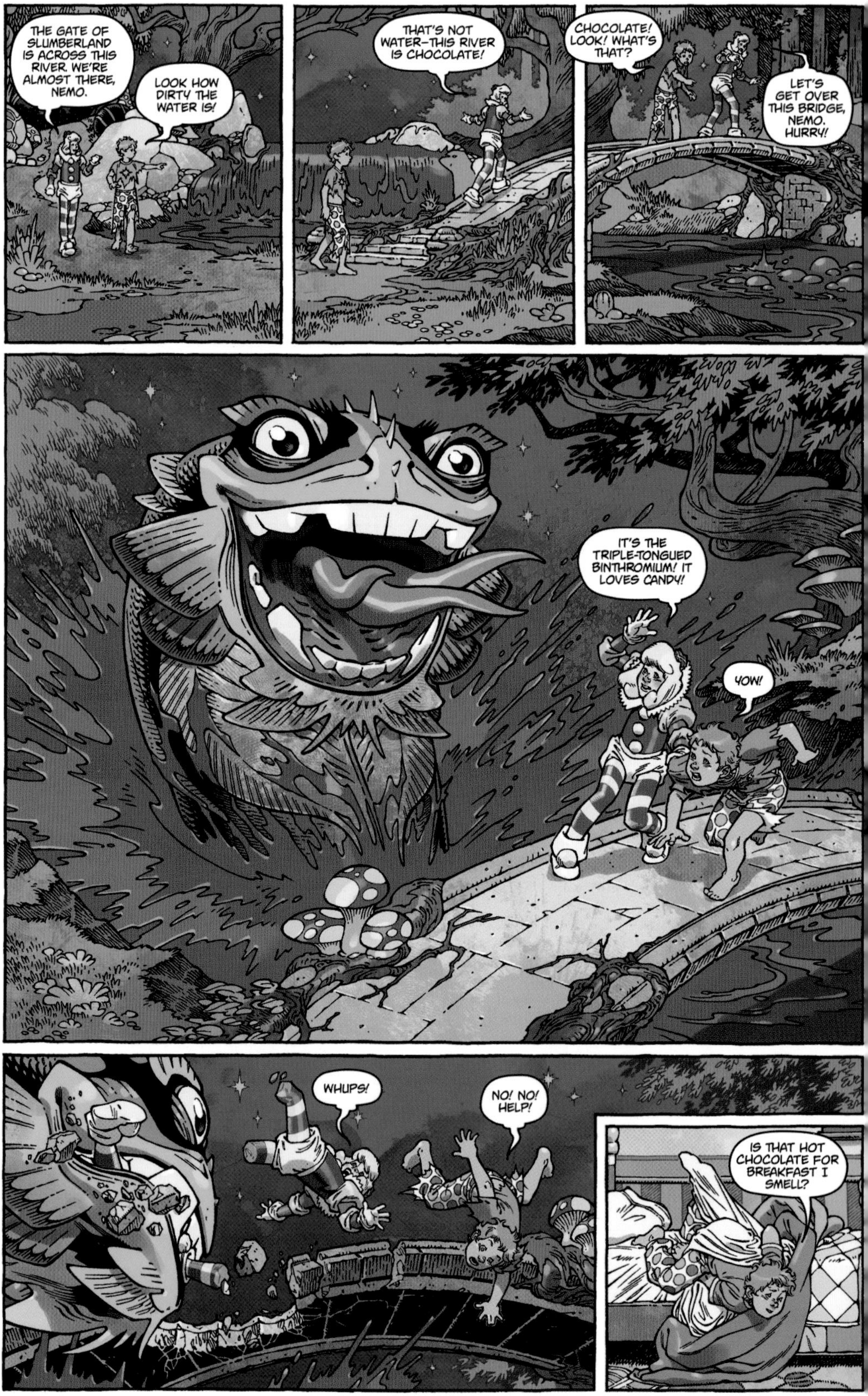
THE GATE OF SLUMBERLAND IS ACROSS THIS RIVER. WE'RE ALMOST THERE, NEMO.
LOOK HOW DIRTY THE WATER IS!
THAT'S NOT WATER—THIS RIVER IS CHOCOLATE!
CHOCOLATE! LOOK! WHAT'S THAT?
LET'S GET OVER THIS BRIDGE, NEMO. HURRY!
IT'S THE TRIPLE-TONGUED BINTHROMIUM! IT LOVES CANDY!
YOW!
WHUPS!
NO! NO! HELP!
IS THAT HOT CHOCOLATE FOR BREAKFAST I SMELL?

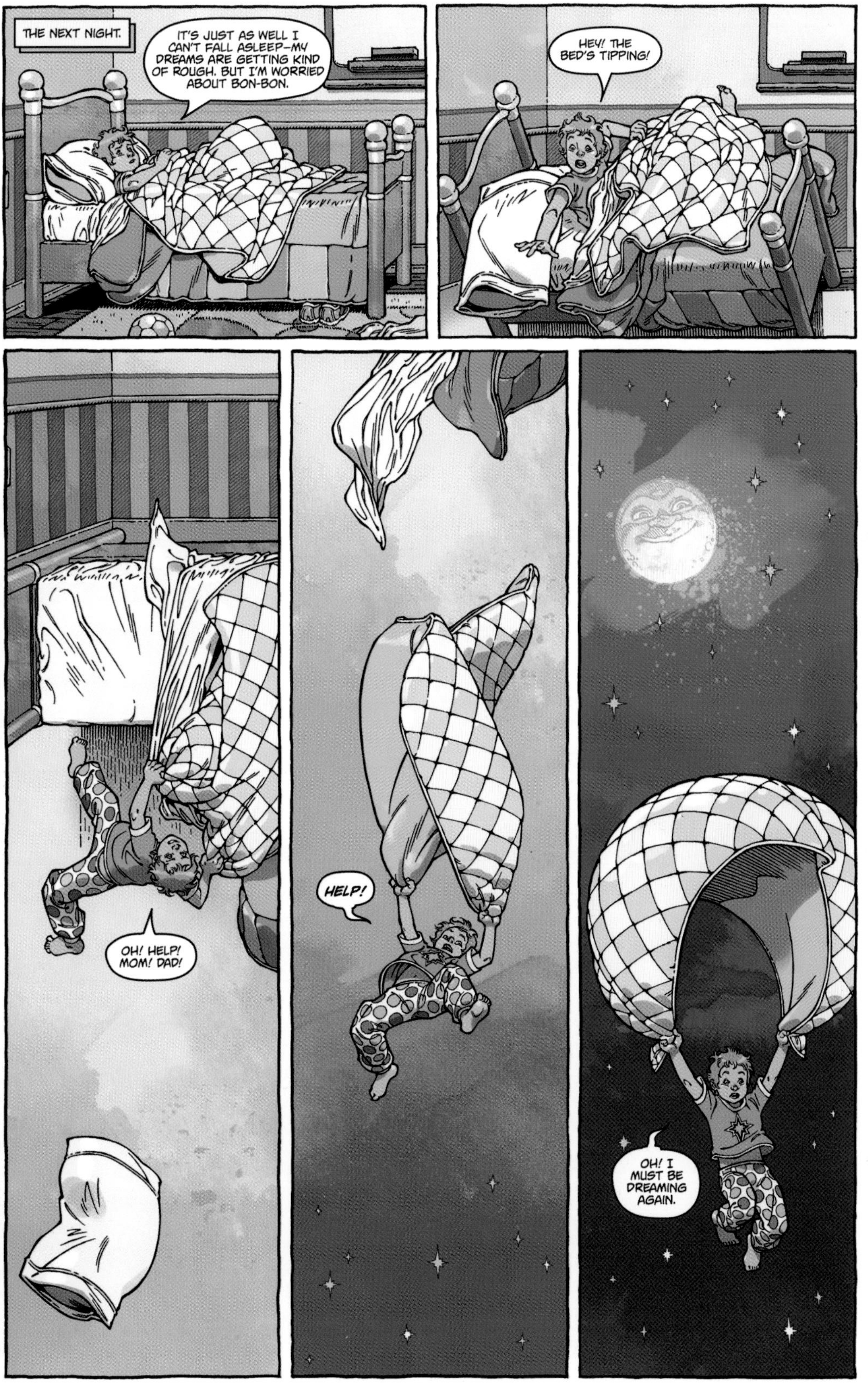
THE NEXT NIGHT.
IT'S JUST AS WELL I CAN'T FALL ASLEEP—MY DREAMS ARE GETTING KIND OF ROUGH. BUT I'M WORRIED ABOUT BON-BON.
HEY! THE BED'S TIPPING!
OH! HELP! MOM! DAD!
HELP!
OH! I MUST BE DREAMING AGAIN.

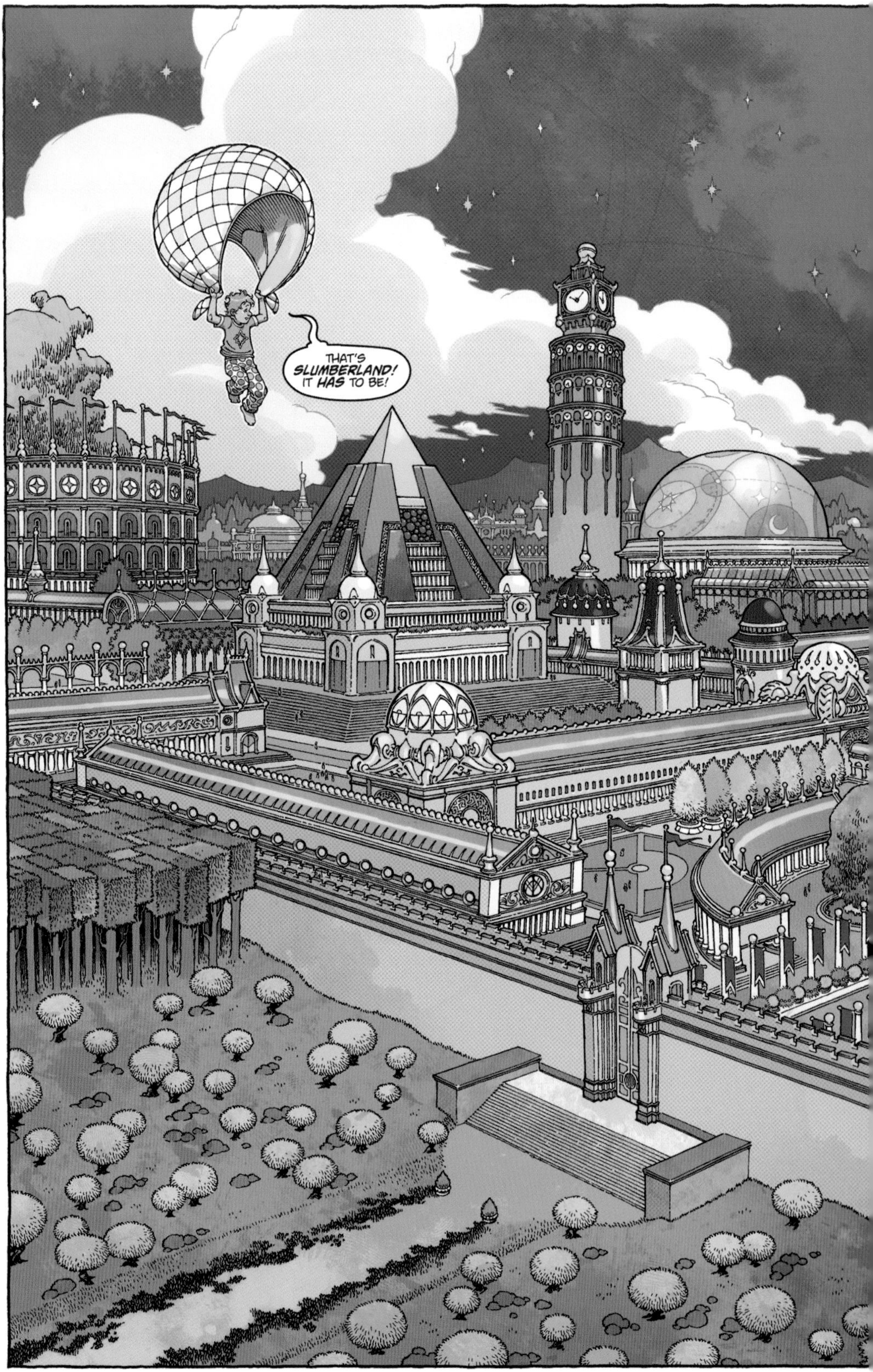
THAT'S SLUMBERLAND! IT HAS TO BE!

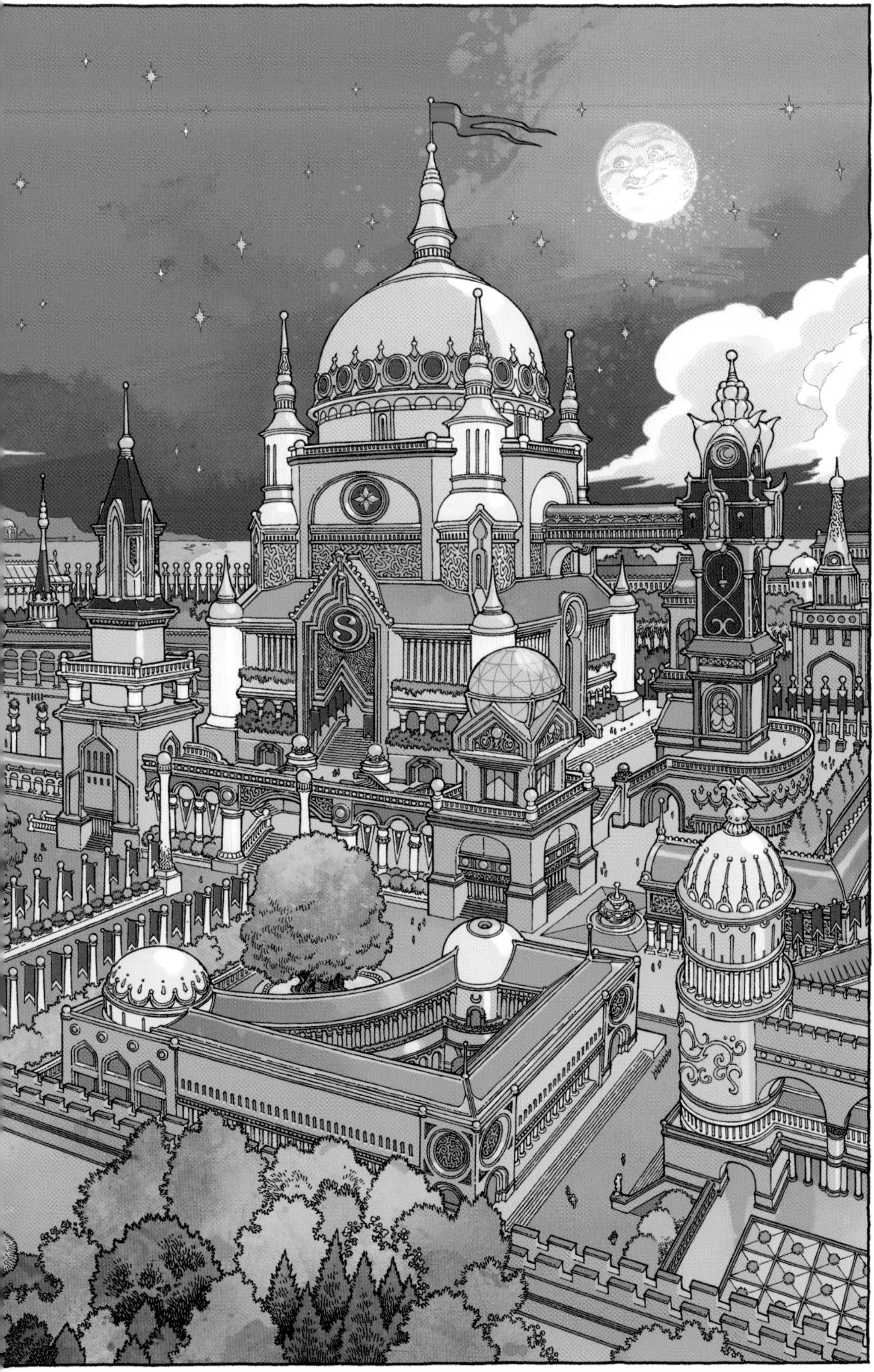

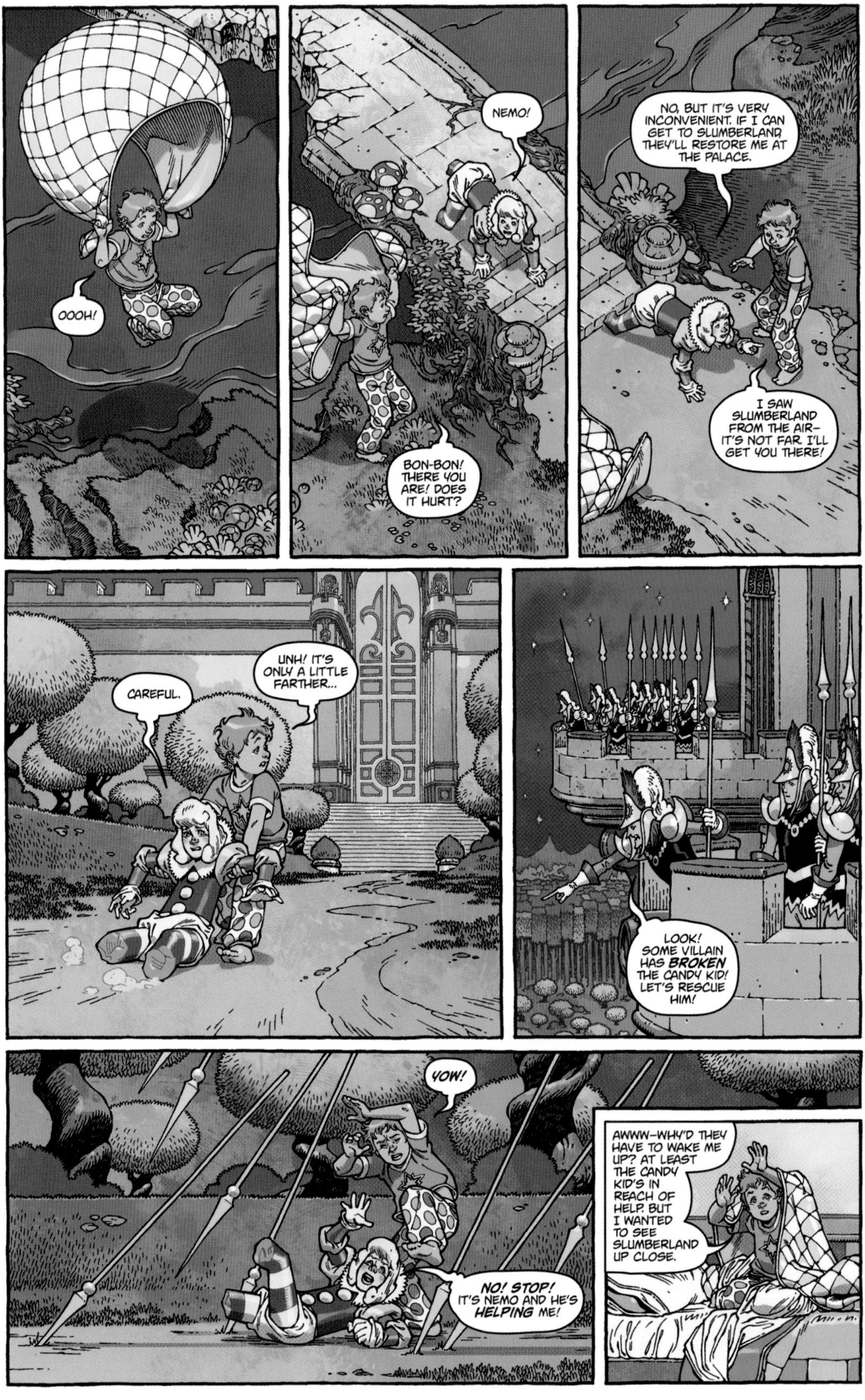
OOOH!
NEMO!
BON-BON! THERE YOU ARE! DOES IT HURT?
NO, BUT IT'S VERY INCONVENIENT. IF I CAN GET TO SLUMBERLAND THEY'LL RESTORE ME AT THE PALACE.
I SAW SLUMBERLAND FROM THE AIR-IT'S NOT FAR. I'LL GET YOU THERE!
CAREFUL.
UNH! IT'S ONLY A LITTLE FARTHER...
LOOK! SOME VILLAIN HAS BROKEN THE CANDY KID! LET'S RESCUE HIM!
YOW!
NO! STOP! IT'S NEMO AND HE'S HELPING ME!
AWWW-WHY'D THEY HAVE TO WAKE ME UP? AT LEAST THE CANDY KID'S IN REACH OF HELP. BUT I WANTED TO SEE SLUMBERLAND UP CLOSE.

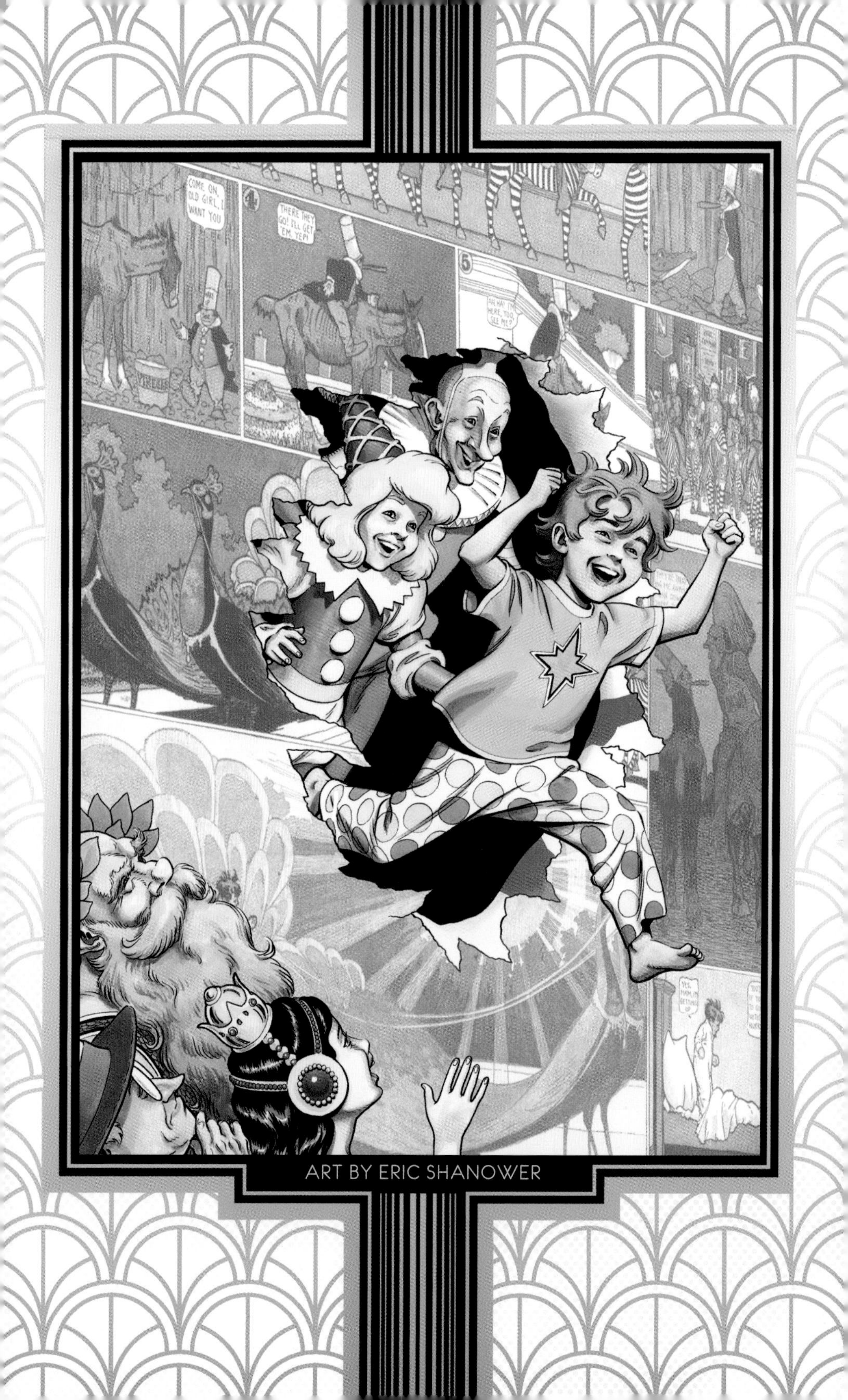
COME ON, OLD GIRL, I WANT YOU
THERE THEY GO! I'LL GET 'EM, YEP!
AH HA! I'M HERE, TOO, SEE ME?
YES, MAMA, I'M GETTING UP

ART BY ERIC SHANOWER

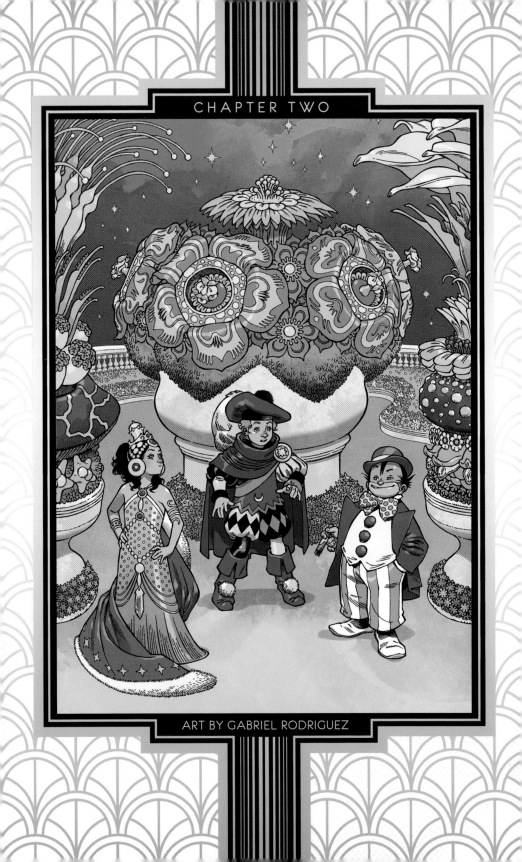

CHAPTER TWO

ART BY GABRIEL RODRIGUEZ

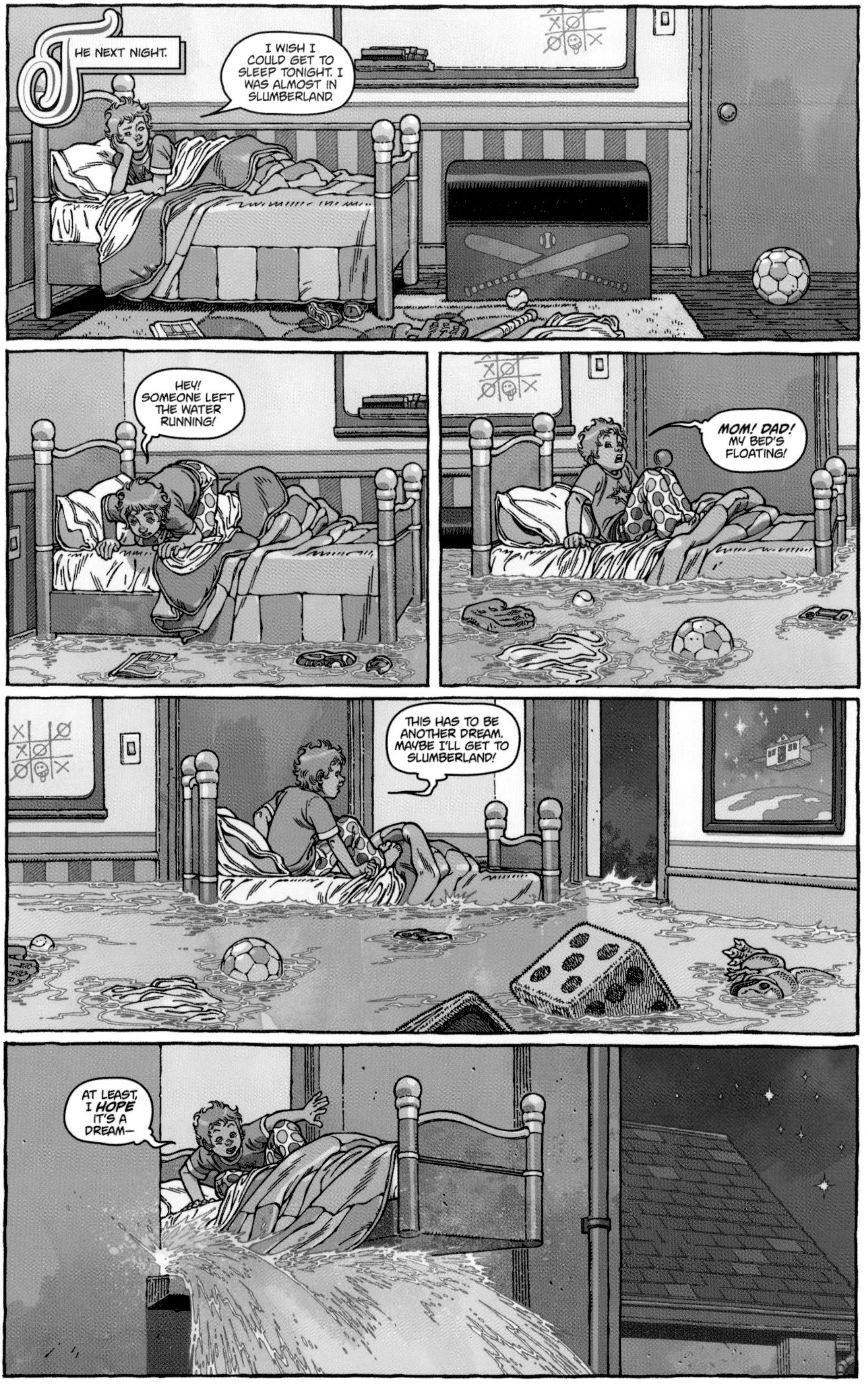
THE NEXT NIGHT.
I WISH I COULD GET TO SLEEP TONIGHT. I WAS ALMOST IN SLUMBERLAND.
HEY! SOMEONE LEFT THE WATER RUNNING!
MOM! DAD! MY BED'S FLOATING!
THIS HAS TO BE ANOTHER DREAM. MAYBE I'LL GET TO SLUMBERLAND!
AT LEAST, I HOPE IT'S A DREAM—

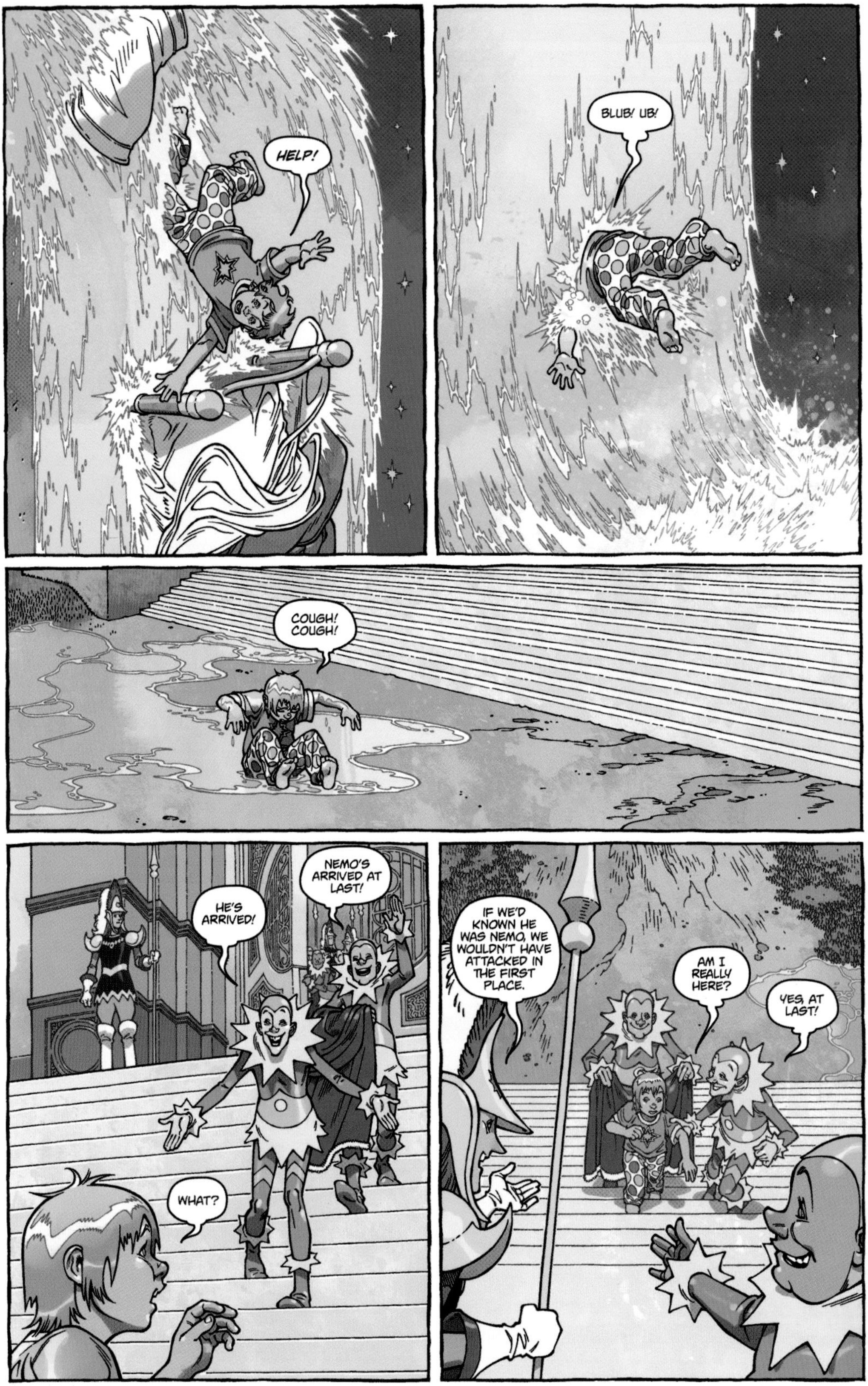
HELP!
BLUB! UB!
COUGH! COUGH!
HE'S ARRIVED!
NEMO'S ARRIVED AT LAST!
WHAT?
IF WE'D KNOWN HE WAS NEMO, WE WOULDN'T HAVE ATTACKED IN THE FIRST PLACE.
AM I REALLY HERE?
YES, AT LAST!

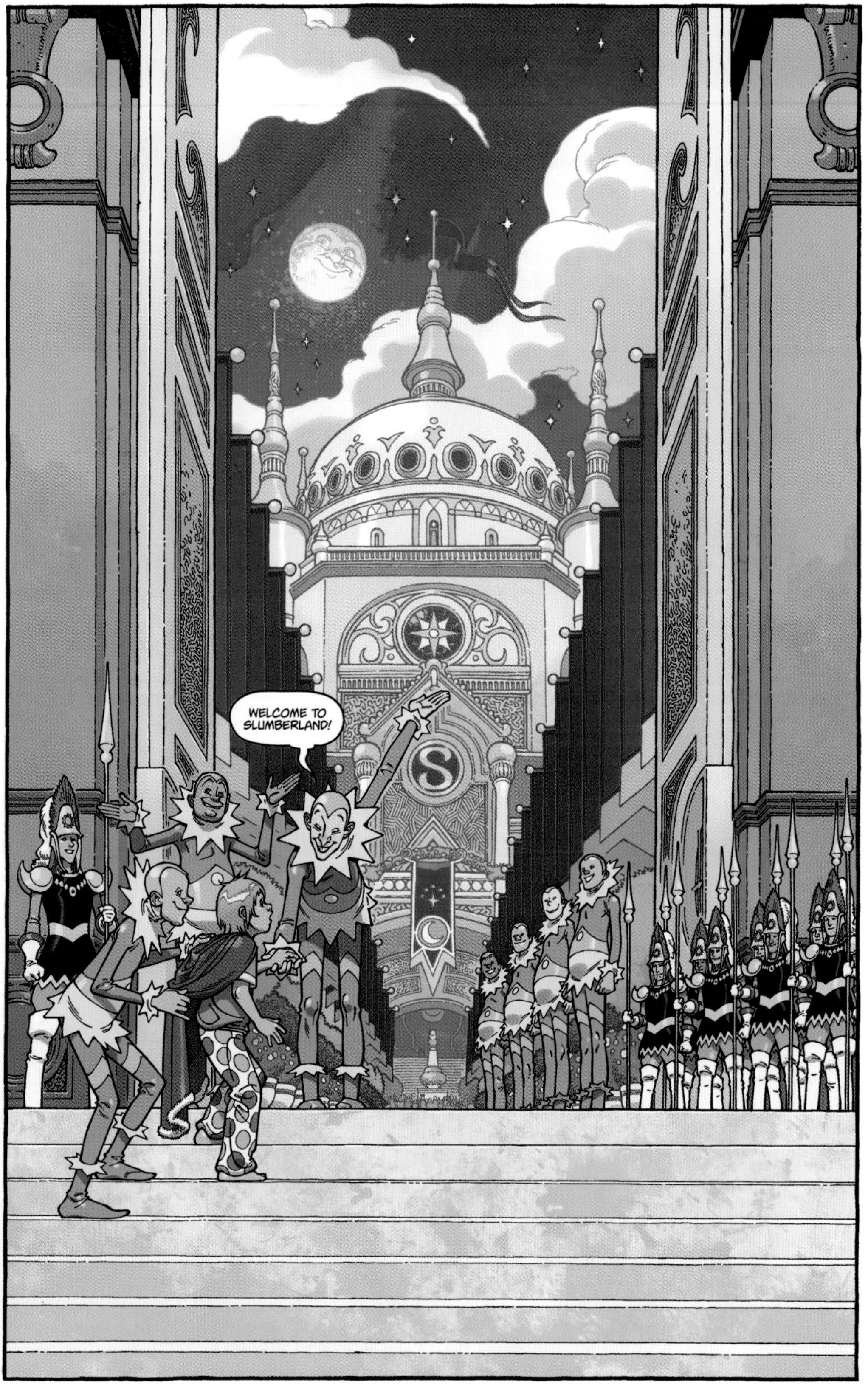
WELCOME TO SLUMBERLAND!

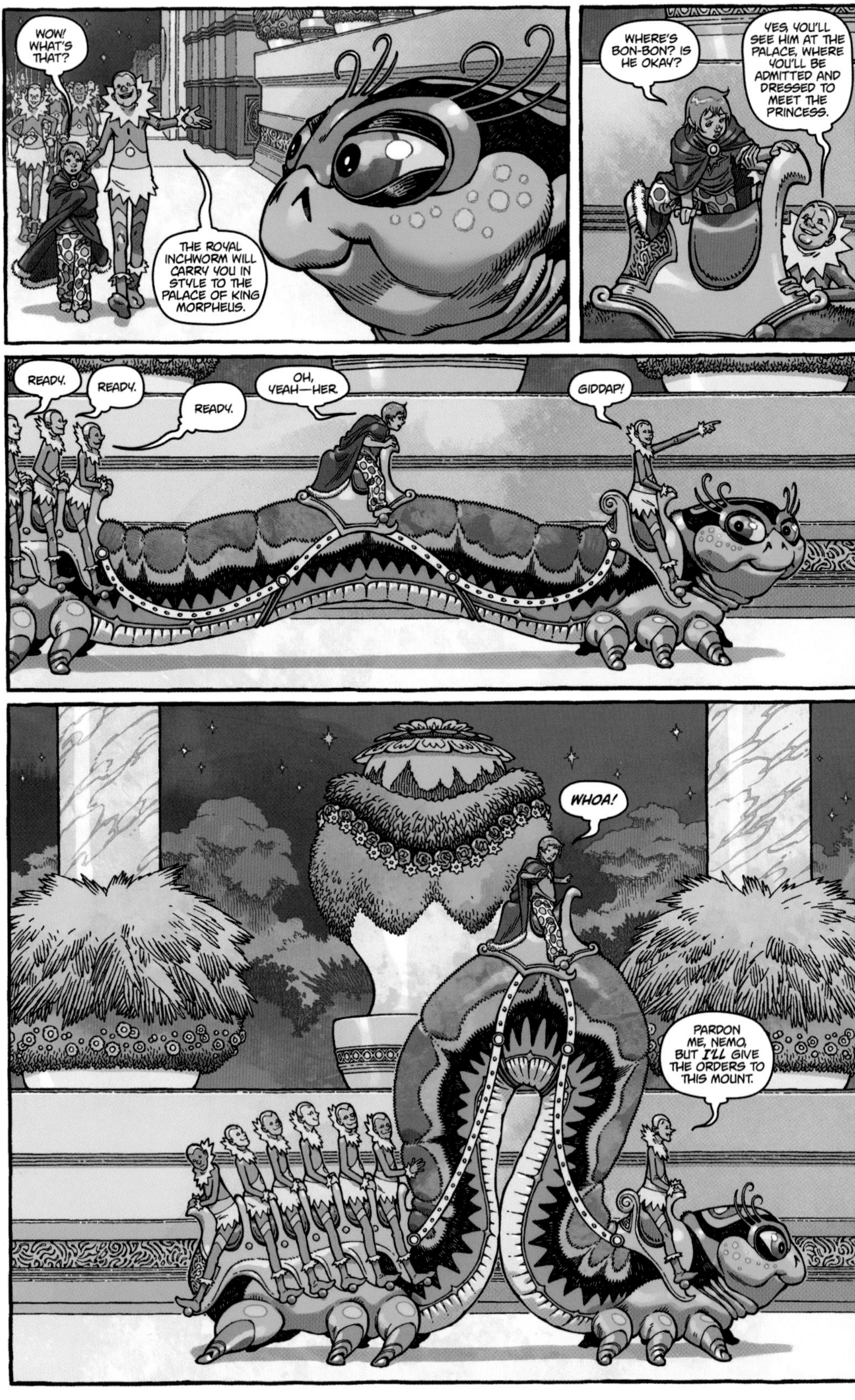
WOW! WHAT'S THAT?
THE ROYAL INCHWORM WILL CARRY YOU IN STYLE TO THE PALACE OF KING MORPHEUS.
WHERE'S BON-BON? IS HE OKAY?
YES, YOU'LL SEE HIM AT THE PALACE, WHERE YOU'LL BE ADMITTED AND DRESSED TO MEET THE PRINCESS.
READY.
READY.
READY.
OH, YEAH—HER.
GIDDAP!
WHOA!
PARDON ME, NEMO, BUT I'LL GIVE THE ORDERS TO THIS MOUNT.

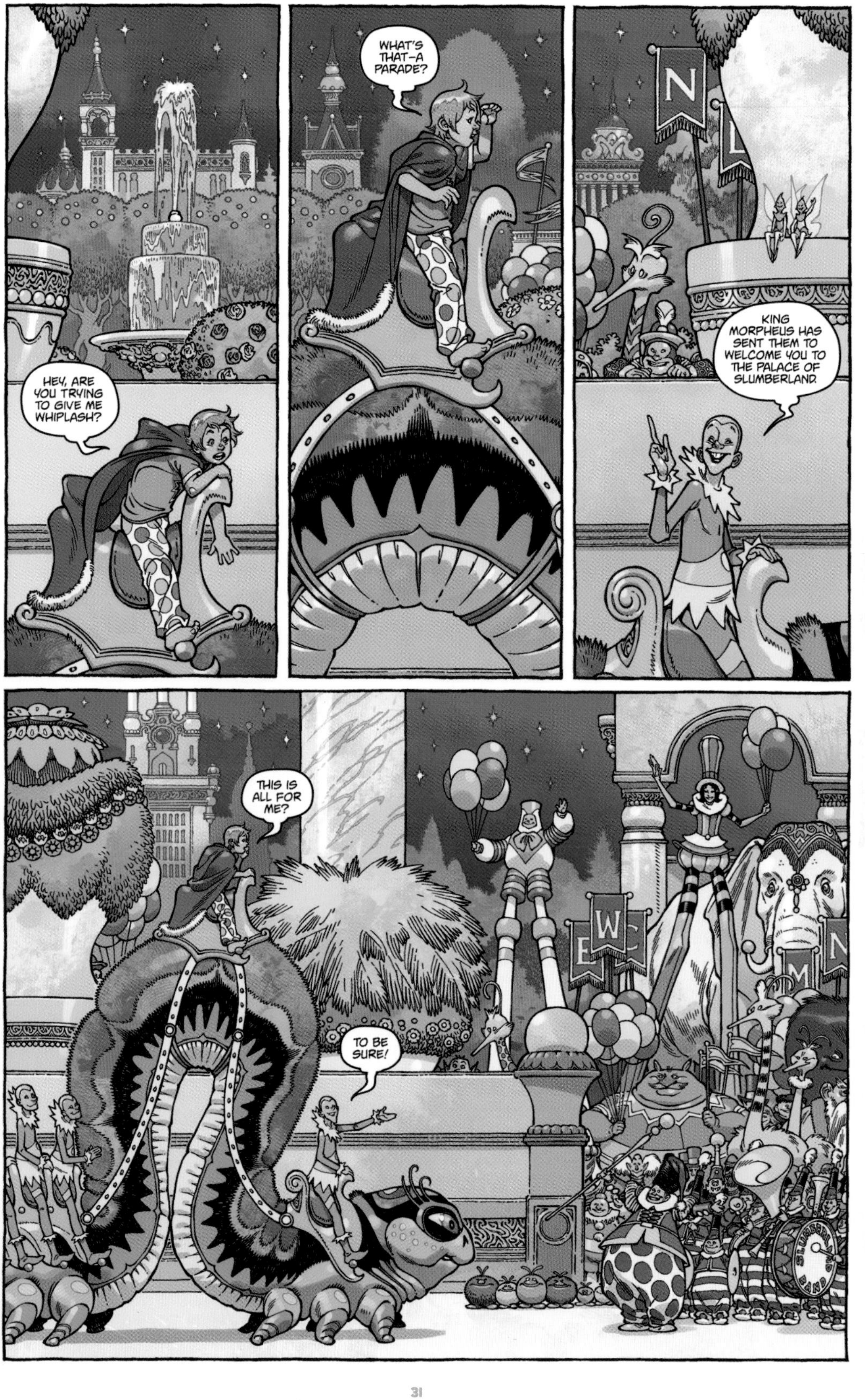
HEY, ARE YOU TRYING TO GIVE ME WHIPLASH?
WHAT'S THAT–A PARADE?
KING MORPHEUS HAS SENT THEM TO WELCOME YOU TO THE PALACE OF SLUMBERLAND.
THIS IS ALL FOR ME?
TO BE SURE!
N
E
W
C
M
N
SLUMBERLAND BAND

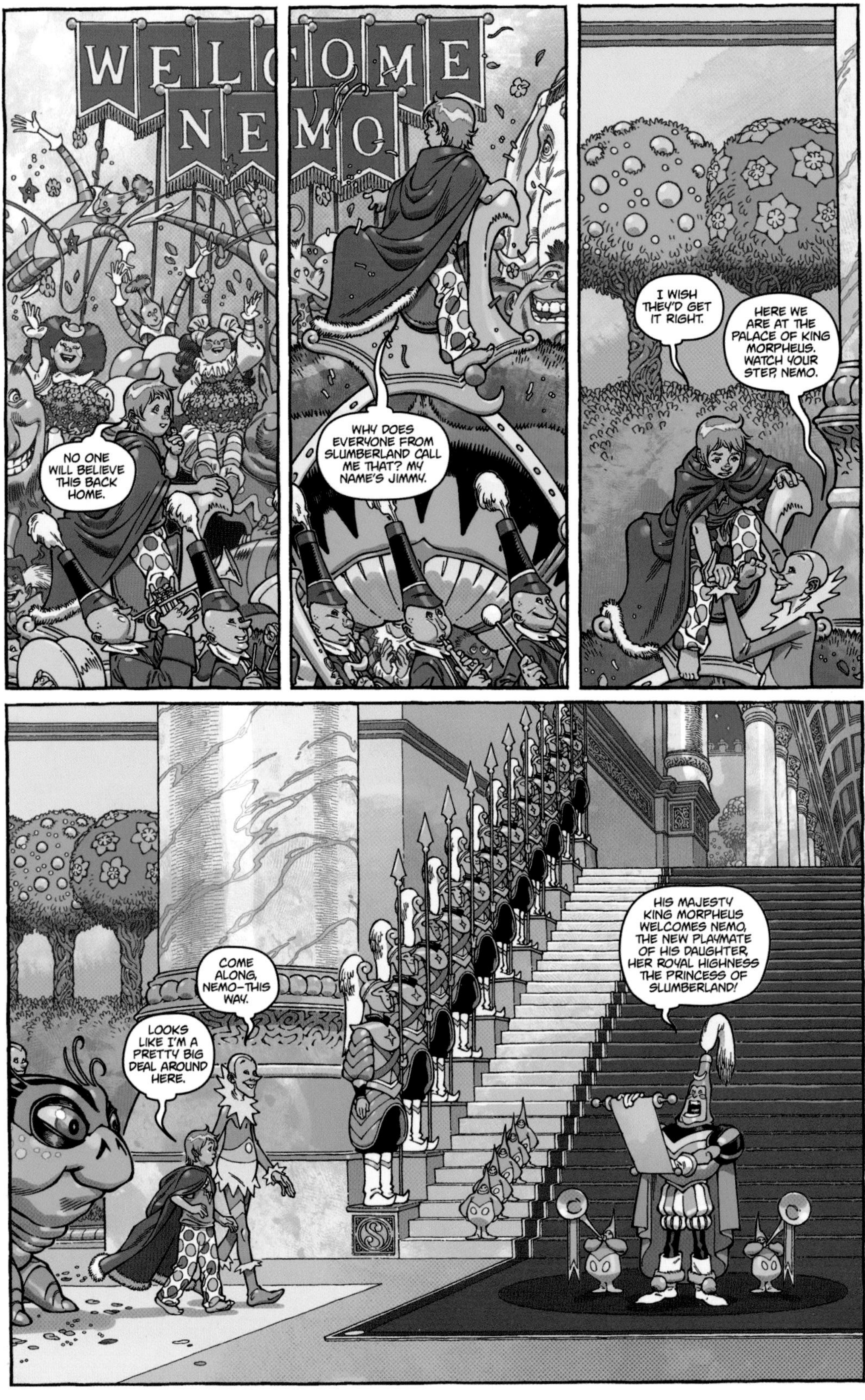
WELCOME
NEMO
NO ONE WILL BELIEVE THIS BACK HOME.
WHY DOES EVERYONE FROM SLUMBERLAND CALL ME THAT? MY NAME'S JIMMY.
I WISH THEY'D GET IT RIGHT.
HERE WE ARE AT THE PALACE OF KING MORPHEUS. WATCH YOUR STEP, NEMO.
COME ALONG, NEMO--THIS WAY.
LOOKS LIKE I'M A PRETTY BIG DEAL AROUND HERE.
HIS MAJESTY KING MORPHEUS WELCOMES NEMO, THE NEW PLAYMATE OF HIS DAUGHTER, HER ROYAL HIGHNESS THE PRINCESS OF SLUMBERLAND!

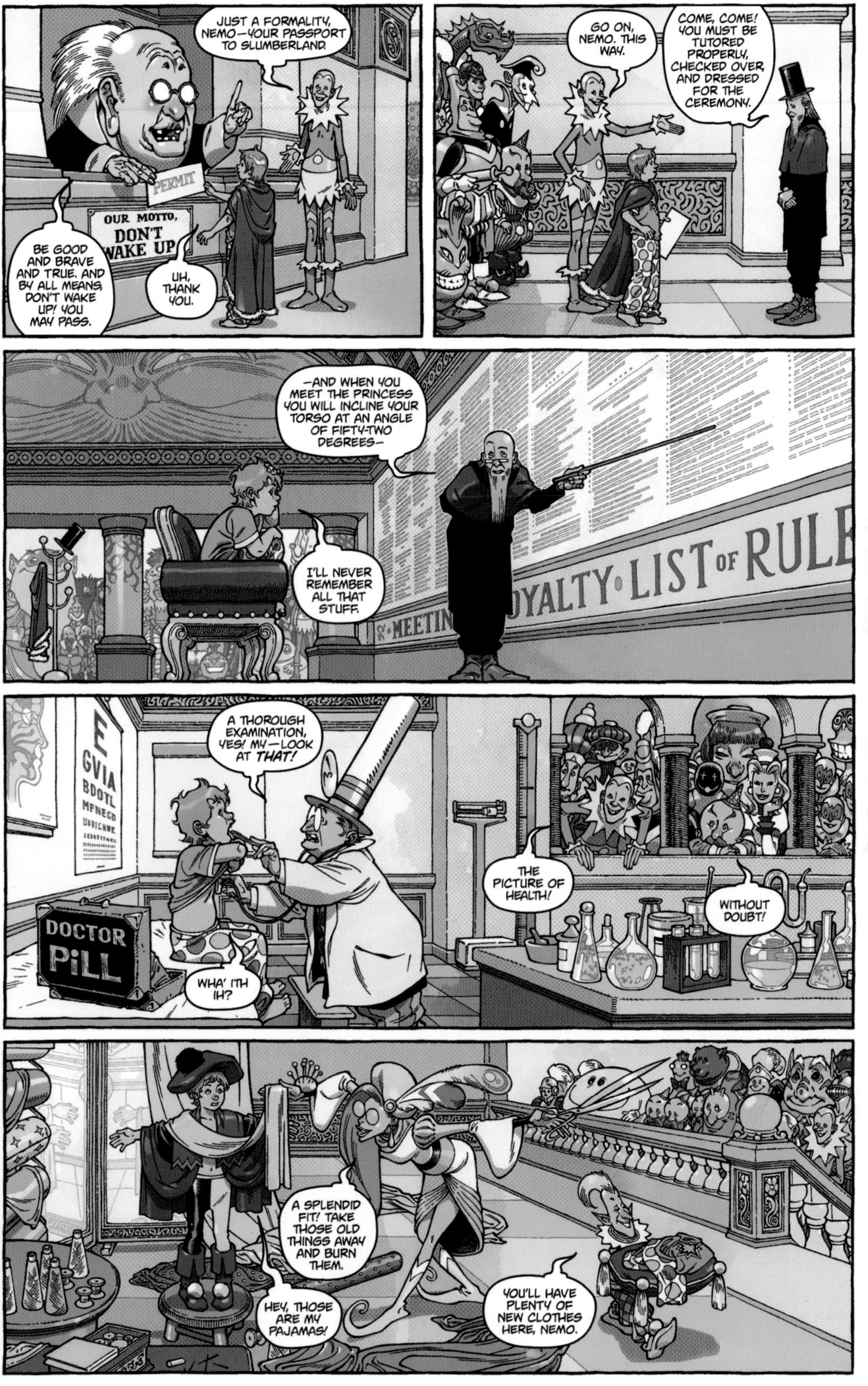
JUST A FORMALITY, NEMO—YOUR PASSPORT TO SLUMBERLAND.
PERMIT
OUR MOTTO, DON'T WAKE UP
BE GOOD AND BRAVE AND TRUE. AND BY ALL MEANS, DON'T WAKE UP! YOU MAY PASS.
UH, THANK YOU.
GO ON, NEMO. THIS WAY.
COME, COME! YOU MUST BE TUTORED PROPERLY, CHECKED OVER, AND DRESSED FOR THE CEREMONY.
—AND WHEN YOU MEET THE PRINCESS YOU WILL INCLINE YOUR TORSO AT AN ANGLE OF FIFTY-TWO DEGREES—
I'LL NEVER REMEMBER ALL THAT STUFF.
MEETIN... OYALTY · LIST OF RULE
A THOROUGH EXAMINATION, YES! MY—LOOK AT *THAT!*
DOCTOR PiLL
WHA' ITH IH?
THE PICTURE OF HEALTH!
WITHOUT DOUBT!
A SPLENDID FIT! TAKE THOSE OLD THINGS AWAY AND BURN THEM.
HEY, THOSE ARE MY PAJAMAS!
YOU'LL HAVE PLENTY OF NEW CLOTHES HERE, NEMO.

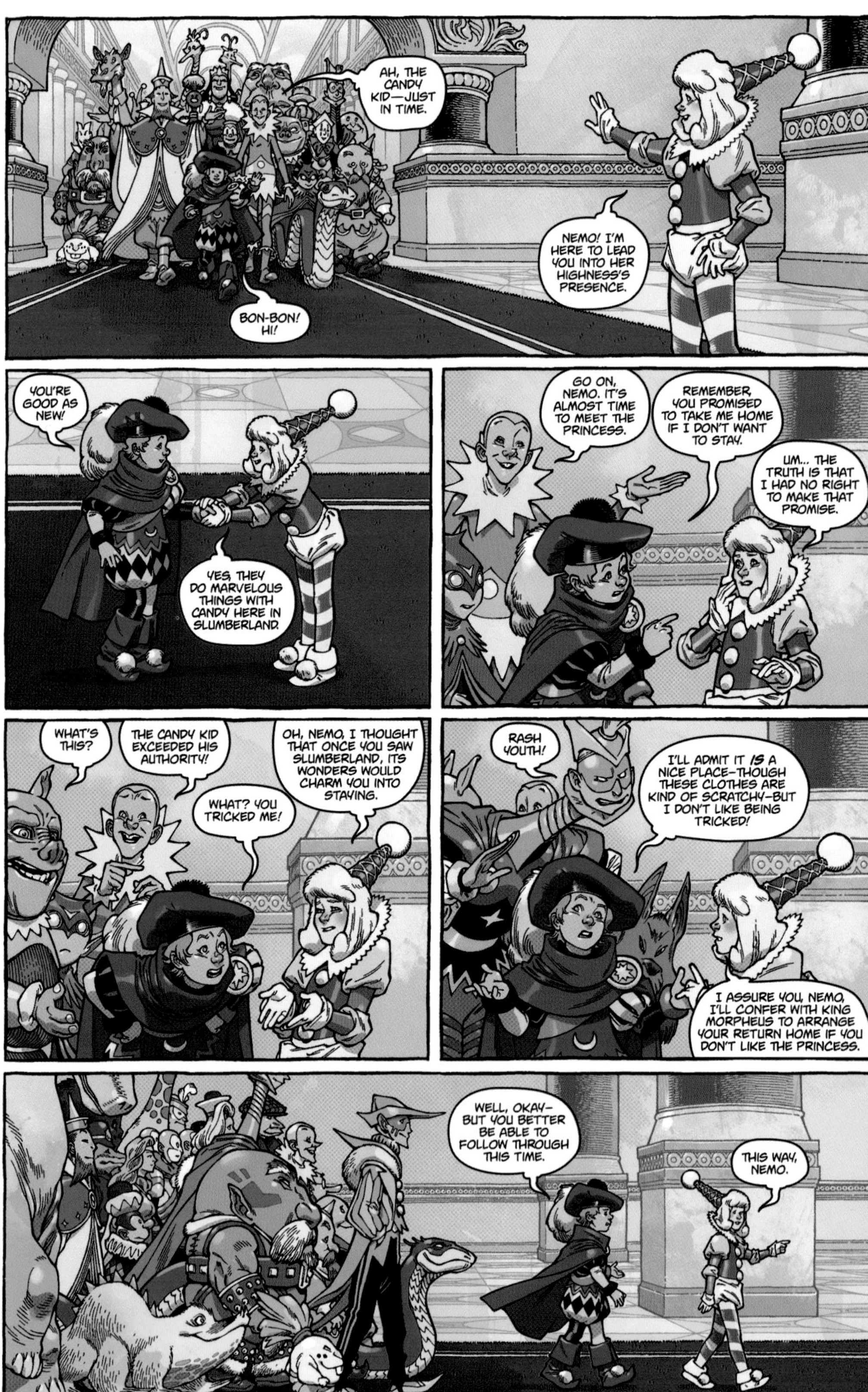
AH, THE CANDY KID—JUST IN TIME.
NEMO! I'M HERE TO LEAD YOU INTO HER HIGHNESS'S PRESENCE.
BON-BON! HI!
YOU'RE GOOD AS NEW!
YES, THEY DO MARVELOUS THINGS WITH CANDY HERE IN SLUMBERLAND.
GO ON, NEMO. IT'S ALMOST TIME TO MEET THE PRINCESS.
REMEMBER, YOU PROMISED TO TAKE ME HOME IF I DON'T WANT TO STAY.
UM... THE TRUTH IS THAT I HAD NO RIGHT TO MAKE THAT PROMISE.
WHAT'S THIS?
THE CANDY KID EXCEEDED HIS AUTHORITY!
OH, NEMO, I THOUGHT THAT ONCE YOU SAW SLUMBERLAND, ITS WONDERS WOULD CHARM YOU INTO STAYING.
WHAT? YOU TRICKED ME!
RASH YOUTH!
I'LL ADMIT IT *IS* A NICE PLACE—THOUGH THESE CLOTHES ARE KIND OF SCRATCHY—BUT I DON'T LIKE BEING TRICKED!
I ASSURE YOU, NEMO, I'LL CONFER WITH KING MORPHEUS TO ARRANGE YOUR RETURN HOME IF YOU DON'T LIKE THE PRINCESS.
WELL, OKAY—BUT YOU BETTER BE ABLE TO FOLLOW THROUGH THIS TIME.
THIS WAY, NEMO.

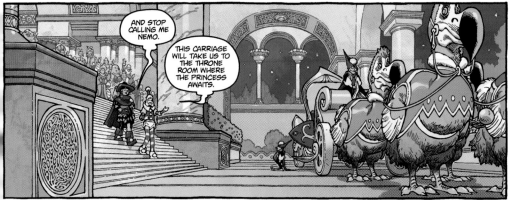

AND STOP CALLING ME NEMO.

THIS CARRIAGE WILL TAKE US TO THE THRONE ROOM WHERE THE PRINCESS AWAITS.

WHY ARE YOU LOOKING AT THE SKY? IS SOMETHING UP THERE?

OH-ER-I WAS SEARCHING FOR FLIP, THE NEPHEW OF THE DAWN GUARD.

FLIP FLAP'S A ROUGH-AND-TUMBLE LITTLE BRAT WHO LIKES TO WAKE UP THE PRINCESS'S PLAYMATES.

I FEAR HE'LL CALL HIS UNCLE TO BRING THE SUN AND WAKE YOU UP IN THE MIDDLE OF THE CEREMONY.

YOU EXPECT TO SEE HIM IN THE SKY?

HE'S GOTTEN INTO THE PALACE BEFORE BY RIDING ON A SKYROCKET AND BY SLIDING DOWN A RAY OF SUNLIGHT.

FINE THING, I DON'T THINK-FORCING ME TO GET IN THROUGH A DRAINAGE TUNNEL! ME, THE NEPHEW OF THE DAWN GUARD-PRACTICALLY ROYALTY MYSELF!

WAKE UP

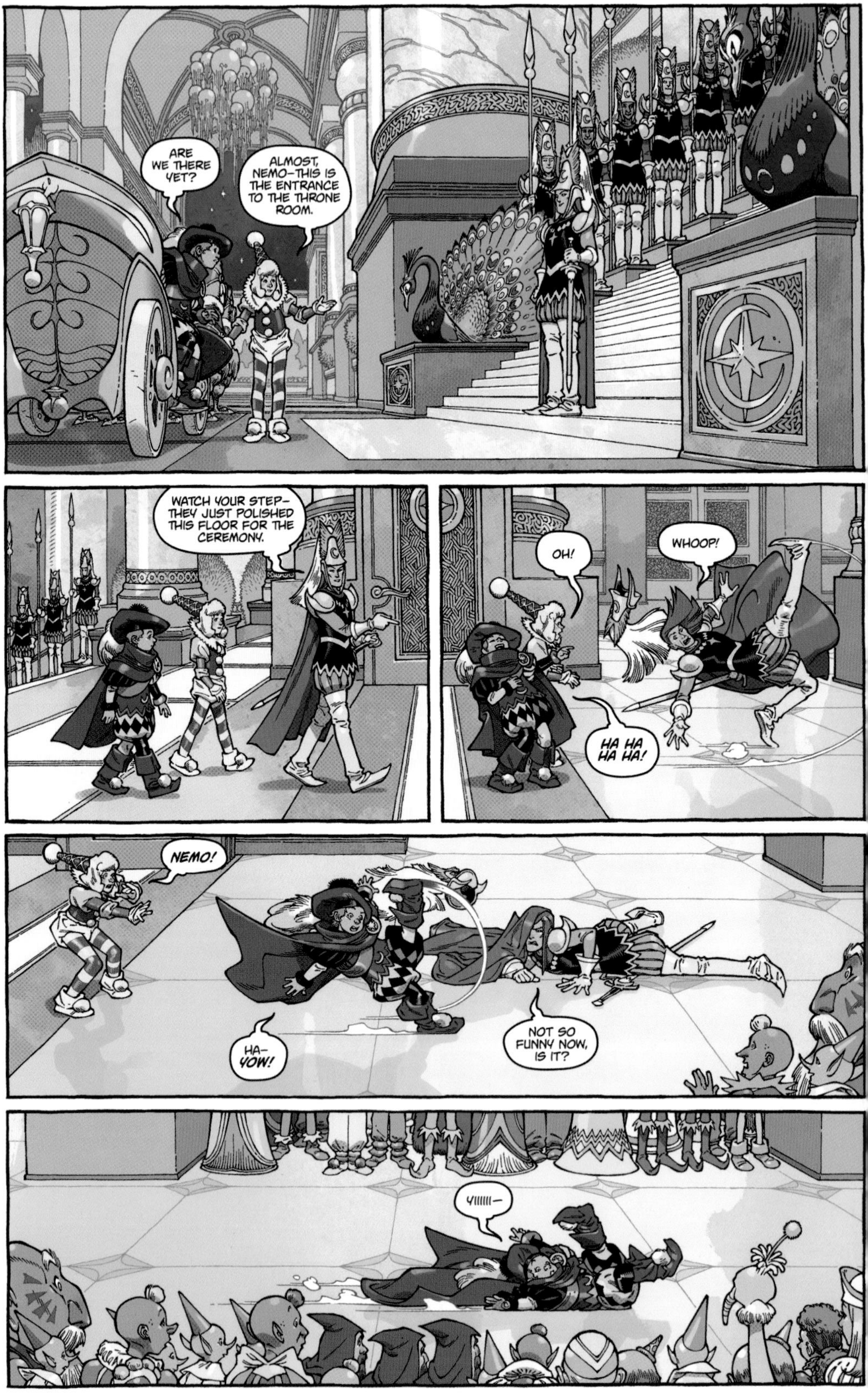
ARE WE THERE YET?
ALMOST, NEMO—THIS IS THE ENTRANCE TO THE THRONE ROOM.
WATCH YOUR STEP—THEY JUST POLISHED THIS FLOOR FOR THE CEREMONY.
OH!
WHOOP!
HA HA HA HA!
NEMO!
HA-YOW!
NOT SO FUNNY NOW, IS IT?
YIIIII—

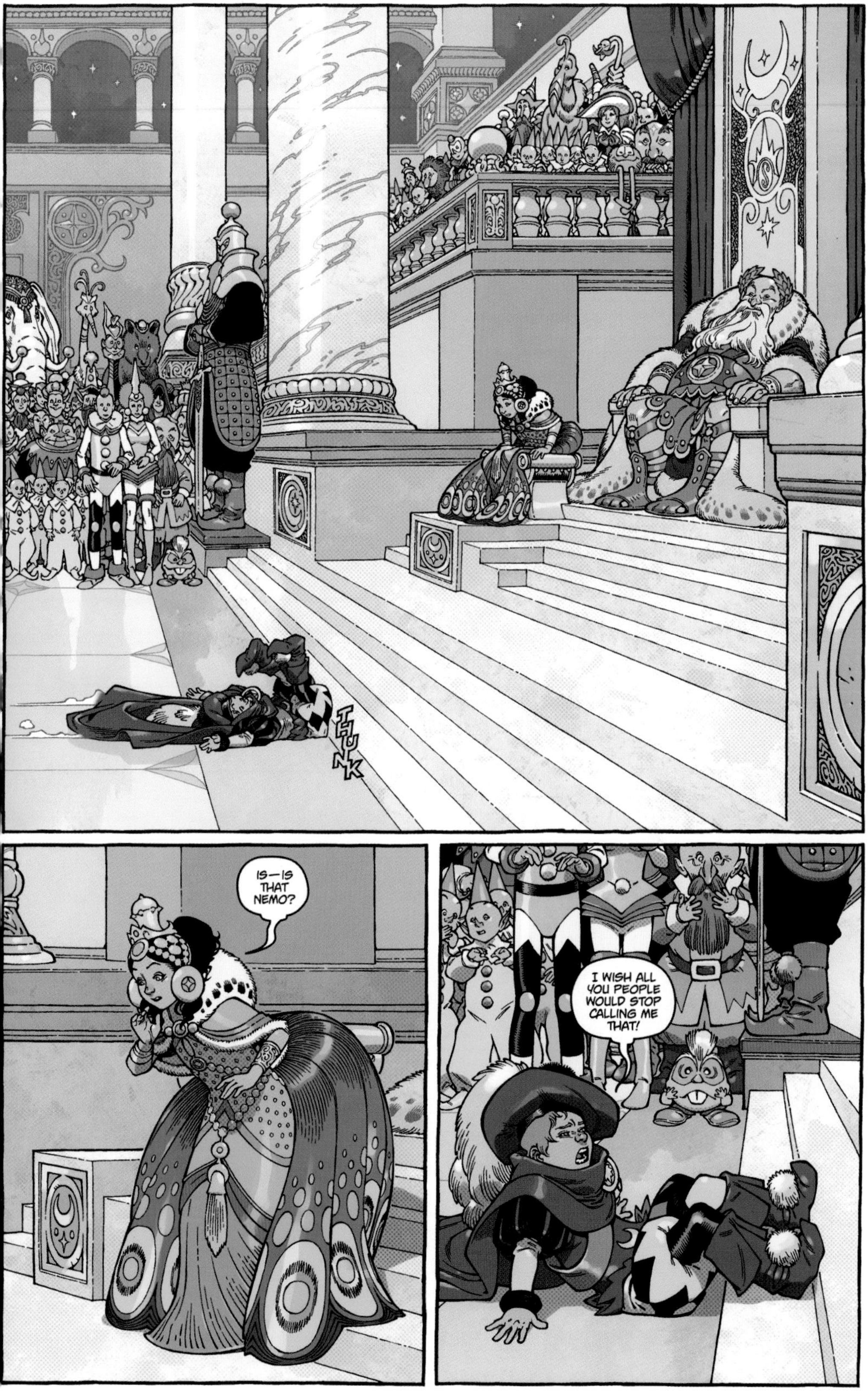
THUNK
IS—IS THAT NEMO?
I WISH ALL YOU PEOPLE WOULD STOP CALLING ME THAT!

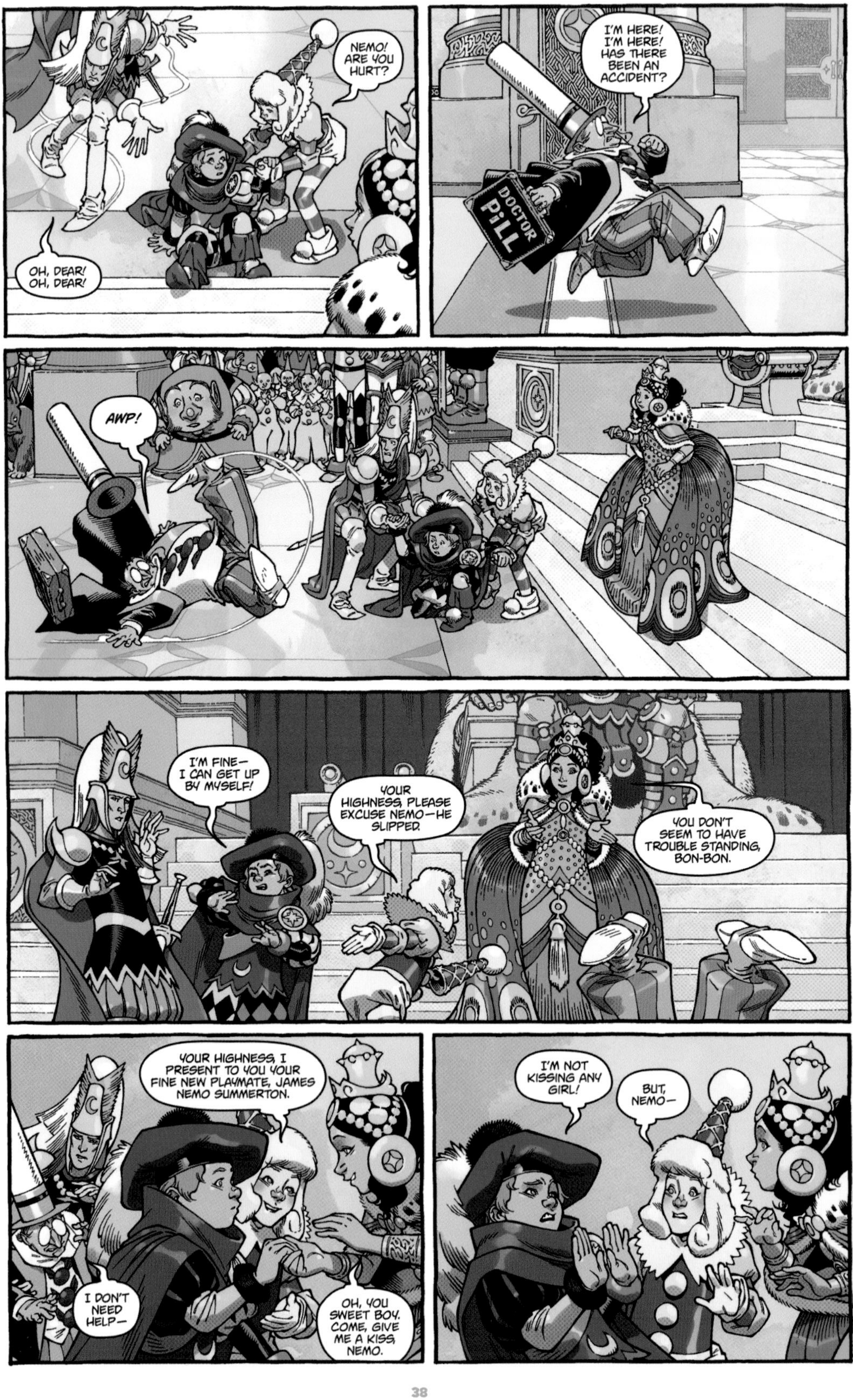
NEMO! ARE YOU HURT?
OH, DEAR! OH, DEAR!
I'M HERE! I'M HERE! HAS THERE BEEN AN ACCIDENT?
DOCTOR PILL
AWP!
I'M FINE— I CAN GET UP BY MYSELF!
YOUR HIGHNESS, PLEASE EXCUSE NEMO—HE SLIPPED.
YOU DON'T SEEM TO HAVE TROUBLE STANDING, BON-BON.
YOUR HIGHNESS, I PRESENT TO YOU YOUR FINE NEW PLAYMATE, JAMES NEMO SUMMERTON.
I DON'T NEED HELP—
OH, YOU SWEET BOY. COME, GIVE ME A KISS, NEMO.
I'M NOT KISSING ANY GIRL!
BUT, NEMO—

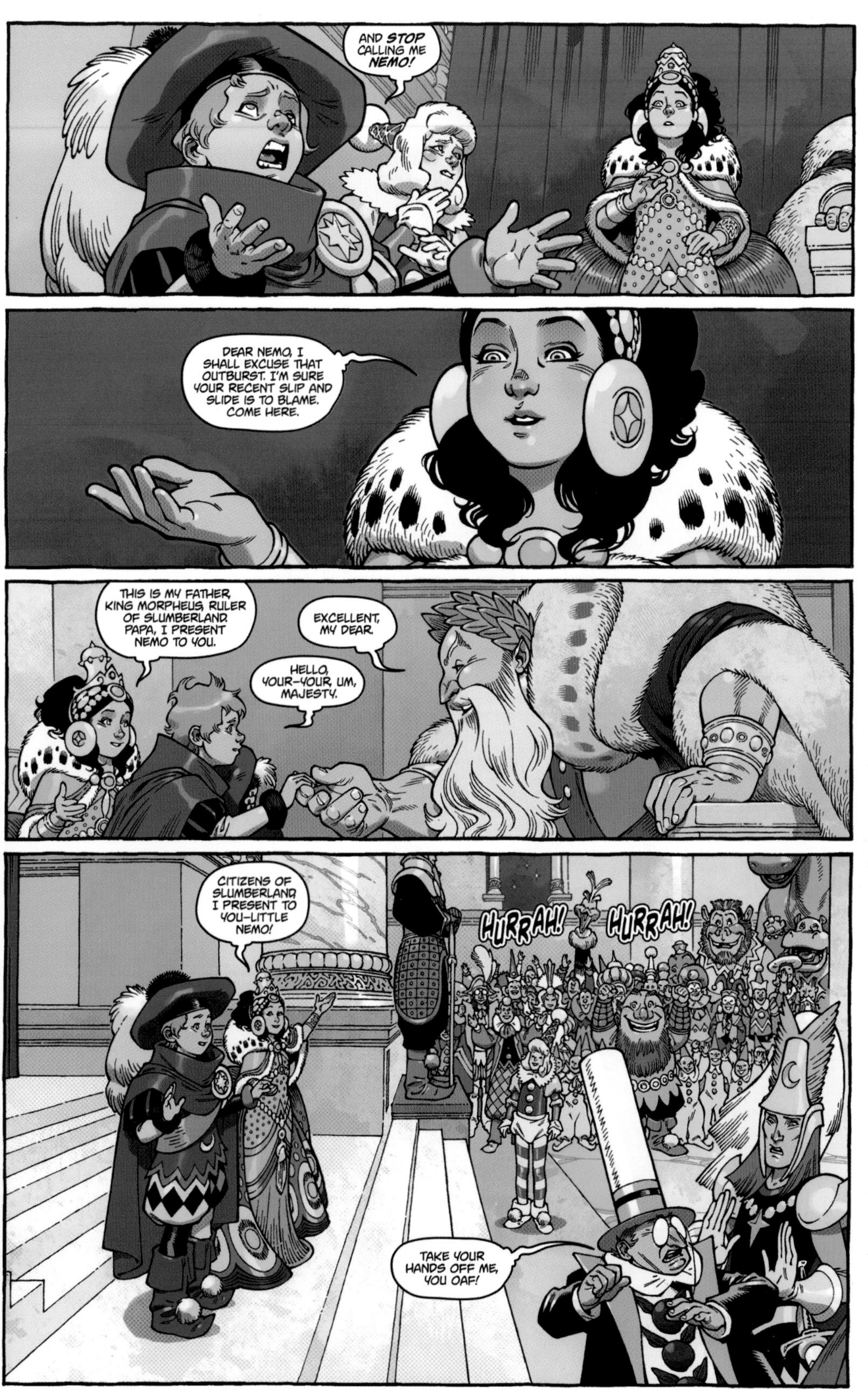
AND STOP CALLING ME NEMO!
DEAR NEMO, I SHALL EXCUSE THAT OUTBURST. I'M SURE YOUR RECENT SLIP AND SLIDE IS TO BLAME. COME HERE.
THIS IS MY FATHER, KING MORPHEUS, RULER OF SLUMBERLAND. PAPA, I PRESENT NEMO TO YOU.
EXCELLENT, MY DEAR.
HELLO, YOUR–YOUR, UM, MAJESTY.
CITIZENS OF SLUMBERLAND, I PRESENT TO YOU–LITTLE NEMO!
HURRAH! HURRAH!
TAKE YOUR HANDS OFF ME, YOU OAF!

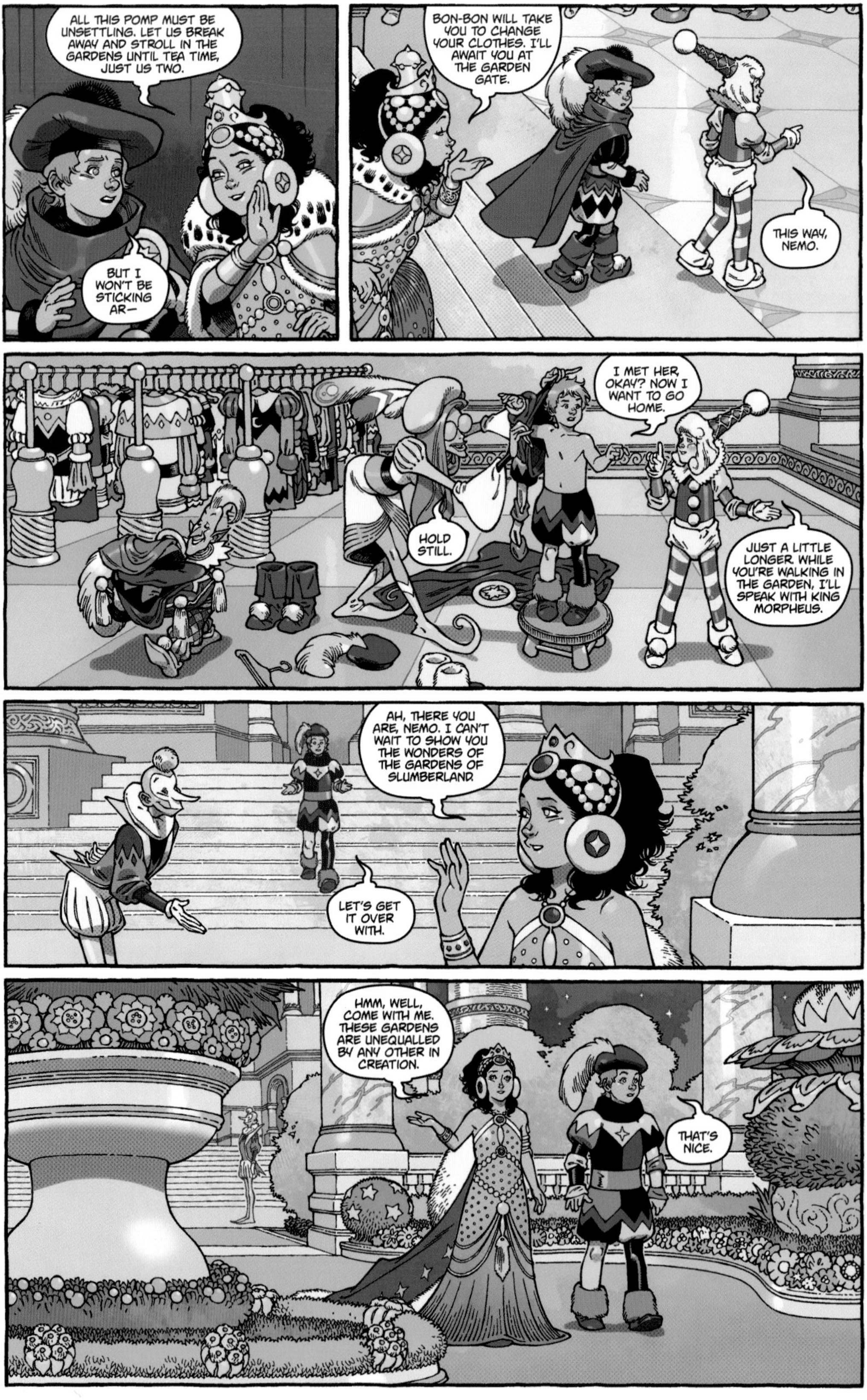
ALL THIS POMP MUST BE UNSETTLING. LET US BREAK AWAY AND STROLL IN THE GARDENS UNTIL TEA TIME, JUST US TWO.
BUT I WON'T BE STICKING AR—
BON-BON WILL TAKE YOU TO CHANGE YOUR CLOTHES. I'LL AWAIT YOU AT THE GARDEN GATE.
THIS WAY, NEMO.
I MET HER, OKAY? NOW I WANT TO GO HOME.
HOLD STILL.
JUST A LITTLE LONGER. WHILE YOU'RE WALKING IN THE GARDEN, I'LL SPEAK WITH KING MORPHEUS.
AH, THERE YOU ARE, NEMO. I CAN'T WAIT TO SHOW YOU THE WONDERS OF THE GARDENS OF SLUMBERLAND.
LET'S GET IT OVER WITH.
HMM, WELL, COME WITH ME. THESE GARDENS ARE UNEQUALLED BY ANY OTHER IN CREATION.
THAT'S NICE.

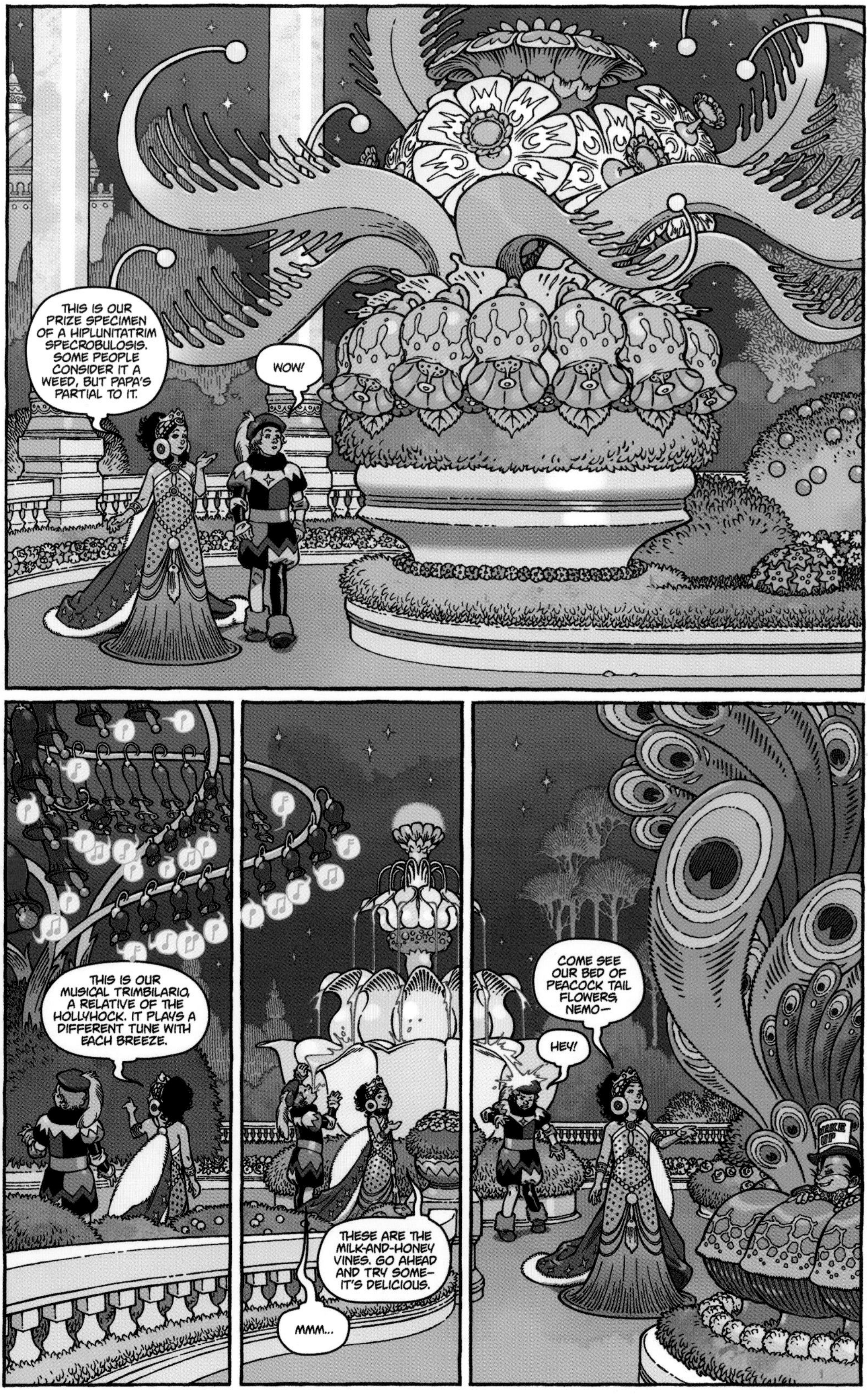
THIS IS OUR PRIZE SPECIMEN OF A HIPLUNITATRIM SPECROBULOSIS. SOME PEOPLE CONSIDER IT A WEED, BUT PAPA'S PARTIAL TO IT.
WOW!
THIS IS OUR MUSICAL TRIMBILARIO, A RELATIVE OF THE HOLLYHOCK. IT PLAYS A DIFFERENT TUNE WITH EACH BREEZE.
THESE ARE THE MILK-AND-HONEY VINES. GO AHEAD AND TRY SOME– IT'S DELICIOUS.
MMM...
COME SEE OUR BED OF PEACOCK TAIL FLOWERS, NEMO–
HEY!
WAKE UP

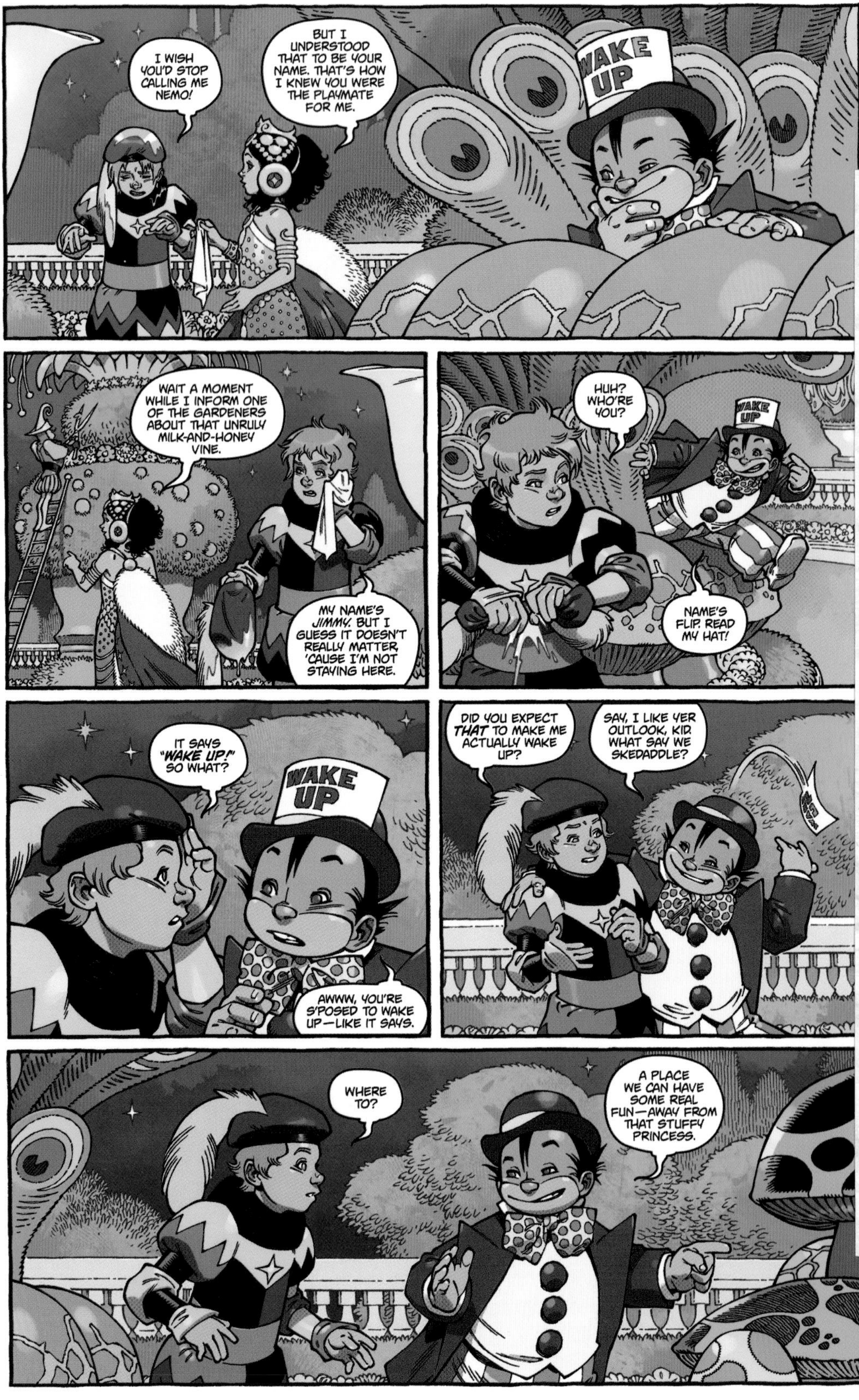
I WISH YOU'D STOP CALLING ME NEMO!
BUT I UNDERSTOOD THAT TO BE YOUR NAME. THAT'S HOW I KNEW YOU WERE THE PLAYMATE FOR ME.
WAKE UP
WAIT A MOMENT WHILE I INFORM ONE OF THE GARDENERS ABOUT THAT UNRULY MILK-AND-HONEY VINE.
MY NAME'S JIMMY. BUT I GUESS IT DOESN'T REALLY MATTER, 'CAUSE I'M NOT STAYING HERE.
HUH? WHO'RE YOU?
WAKE UP
NAME'S FLIP. READ MY HAT!
IT SAYS "WAKE UP!" SO WHAT?
WAKE UP
AWWW, YOU'RE S'POSED TO WAKE UP—LIKE IT SAYS.
DID YOU EXPECT THAT TO MAKE ME ACTUALLY WAKE UP?
SAY, I LIKE YER OUTLOOK, KID. WHAT SAY WE SKEDADDLE?
WHERE TO?
A PLACE WE CAN HAVE SOME REAL FUN—AWAY FROM THAT STUFFY PRINCESS.

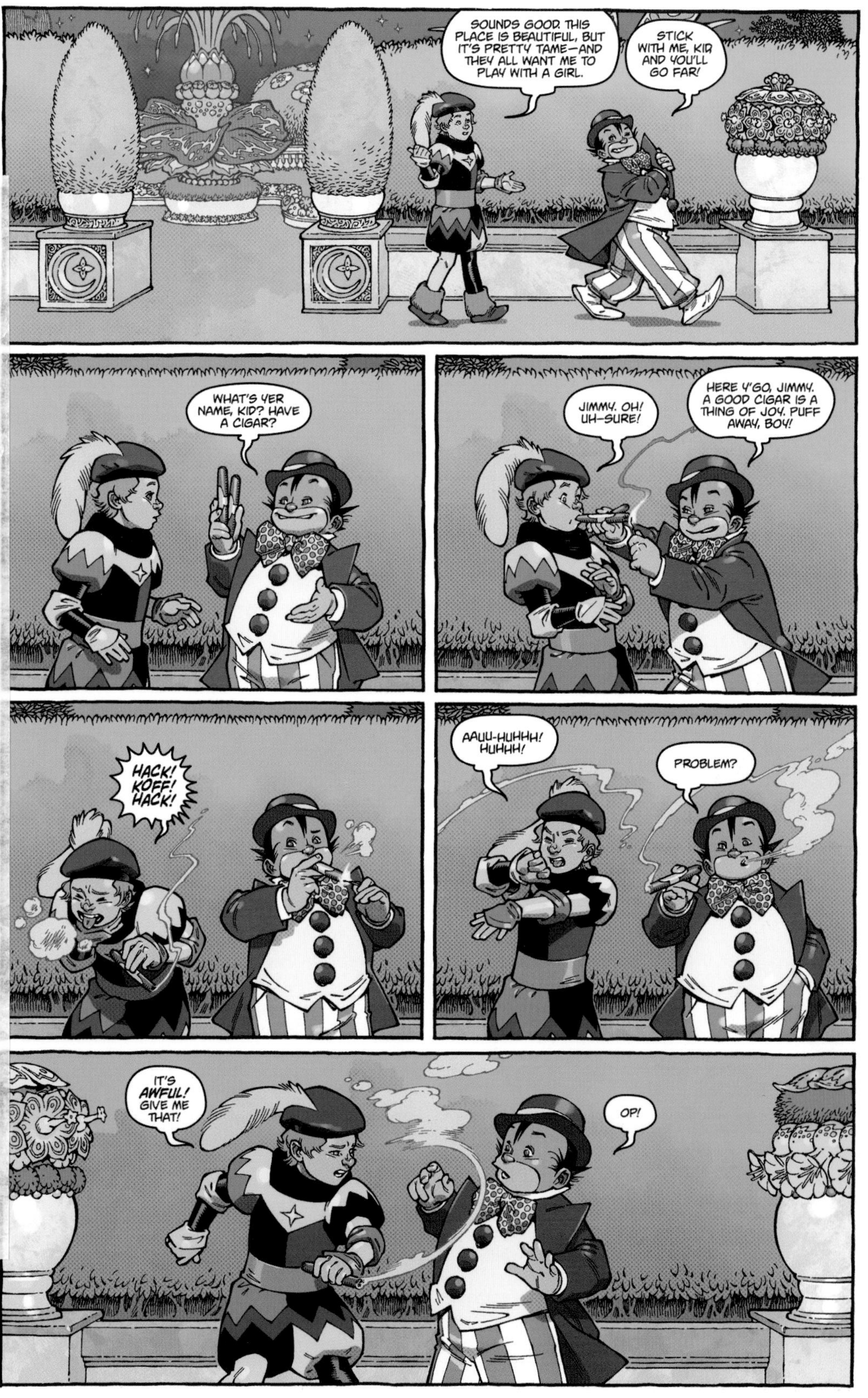
SOUNDS GOOD. THIS PLACE IS BEAUTIFUL, BUT IT'S PRETTY TAME—AND THEY ALL WANT ME TO PLAY WITH A GIRL.
STICK WITH ME, KID AND YOU'LL GO FAR!
WHAT'S YER NAME, KID? HAVE A CIGAR?
JIMMY. OH! UH–SURE!
HERE Y'GO, JIMMY. A GOOD CIGAR IS A THING OF JOY. PUFF AWAY, BOY!
HACK! KOFF! HACK!
AAUU-HUHHH! HUHHH!
PROBLEM?
IT'S AWFUL! GIVE ME THAT!
OP!

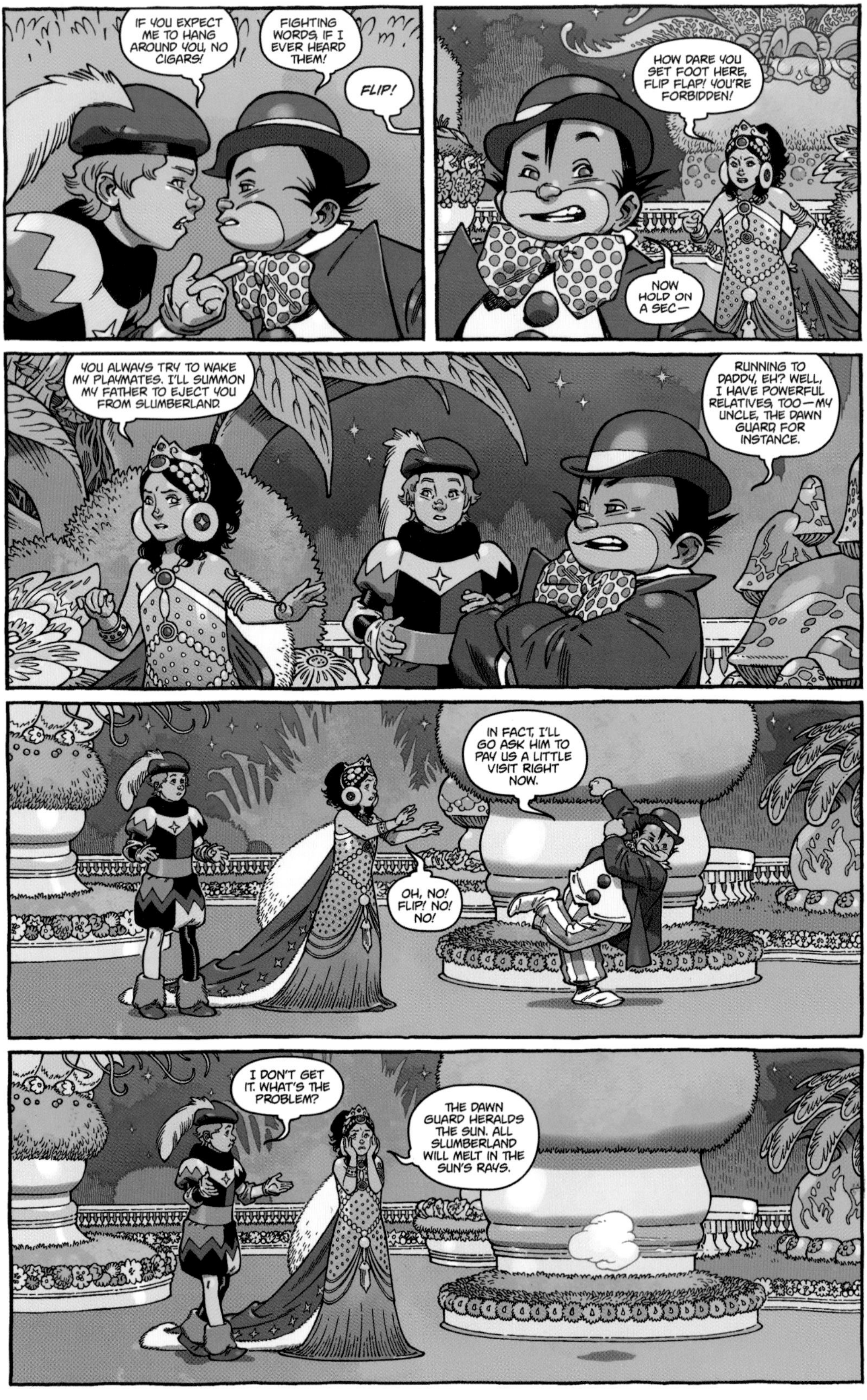
IF YOU EXPECT ME TO HANG AROUND YOU, NO CIGARS!
FIGHTING WORDS, IF I EVER HEARD THEM!
FLIP!
HOW DARE YOU SET FOOT HERE, FLIP FLAP! YOU'RE FORBIDDEN!
NOW HOLD ON A SEC—
YOU ALWAYS TRY TO WAKE MY PLAYMATES. I'LL SUMMON MY FATHER TO EJECT YOU FROM SLUMBERLAND.
RUNNING TO DADDY, EH? WELL, I HAVE POWERFUL RELATIVES, TOO—MY UNCLE, THE DAWN GUARD, FOR INSTANCE.
IN FACT, I'LL GO ASK HIM TO PAY US A LITTLE VISIT RIGHT NOW.
OH, NO! FLIP! NO! NO!
I DON'T GET IT. WHAT'S THE PROBLEM?
THE DAWN GUARD HERALDS THE SUN. ALL SLUMBERLAND WILL MELT IN THE SUN'S RAYS.

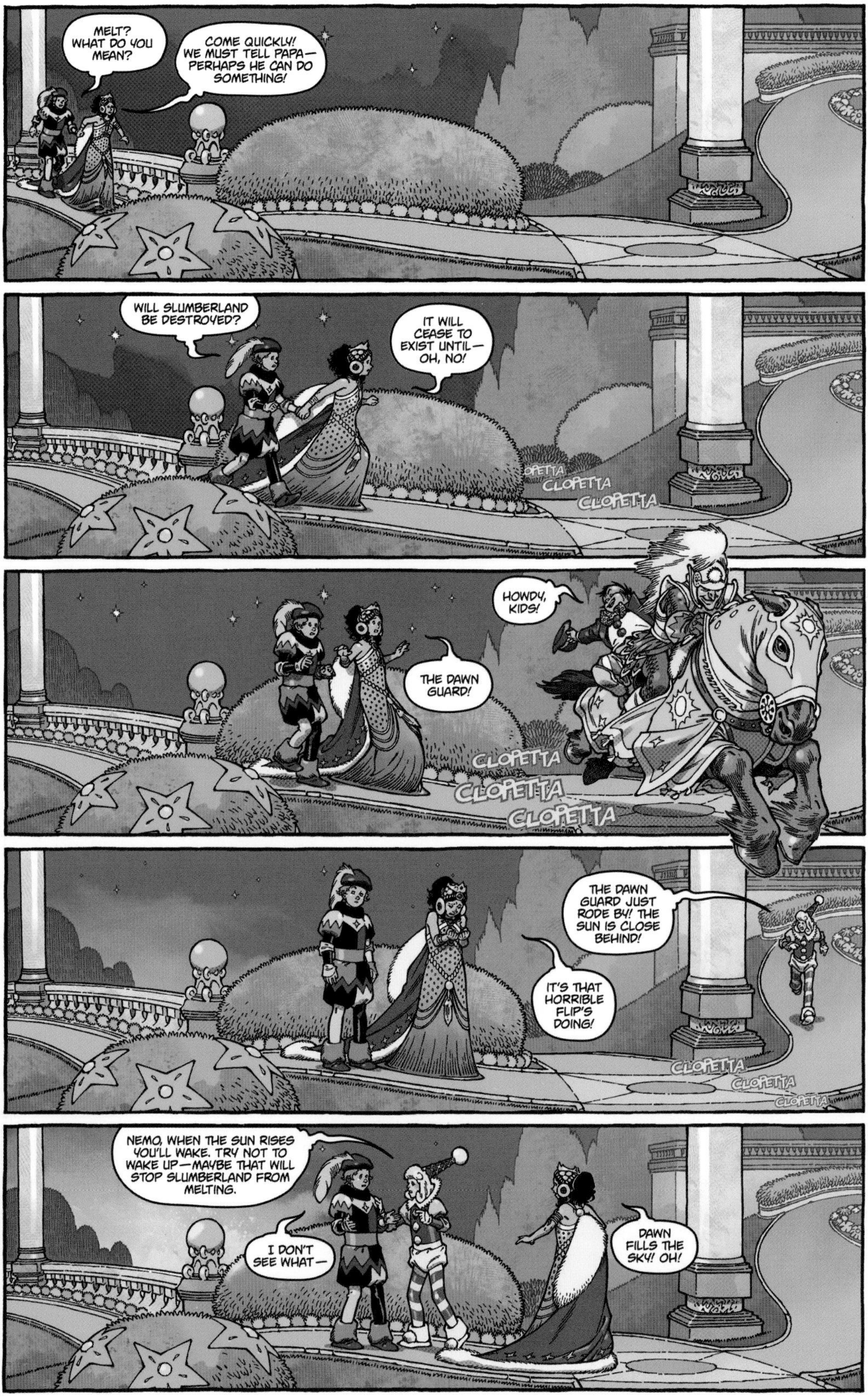
MELT? WHAT DO YOU MEAN?
COME QUICKLY! WE MUST TELL PAPA— PERHAPS HE CAN DO SOMETHING!
WILL SLUMBERLAND BE DESTROYED?
IT WILL CEASE TO EXIST UNTIL— OH, NO!
CLOPETTA CLOPETTA CLOPETTA
HOWDY, KIDS!
THE DAWN GUARD!
CLOPETTA CLOPETTA CLOPETTA
THE DAWN GUARD JUST RODE BY! THE SUN IS CLOSE BEHIND!
IT'S THAT HORRIBLE FLIP'S DOING!
CLOPETTA CLOPETTA CLOPETTA
NEMO, WHEN THE SUN RISES YOU'LL WAKE. TRY NOT TO WAKE UP—MAYBE THAT WILL STOP SLUMBERLAND FROM MELTING.
I DON'T SEE WHAT—
DAWN FILLS THE SKY! OH!

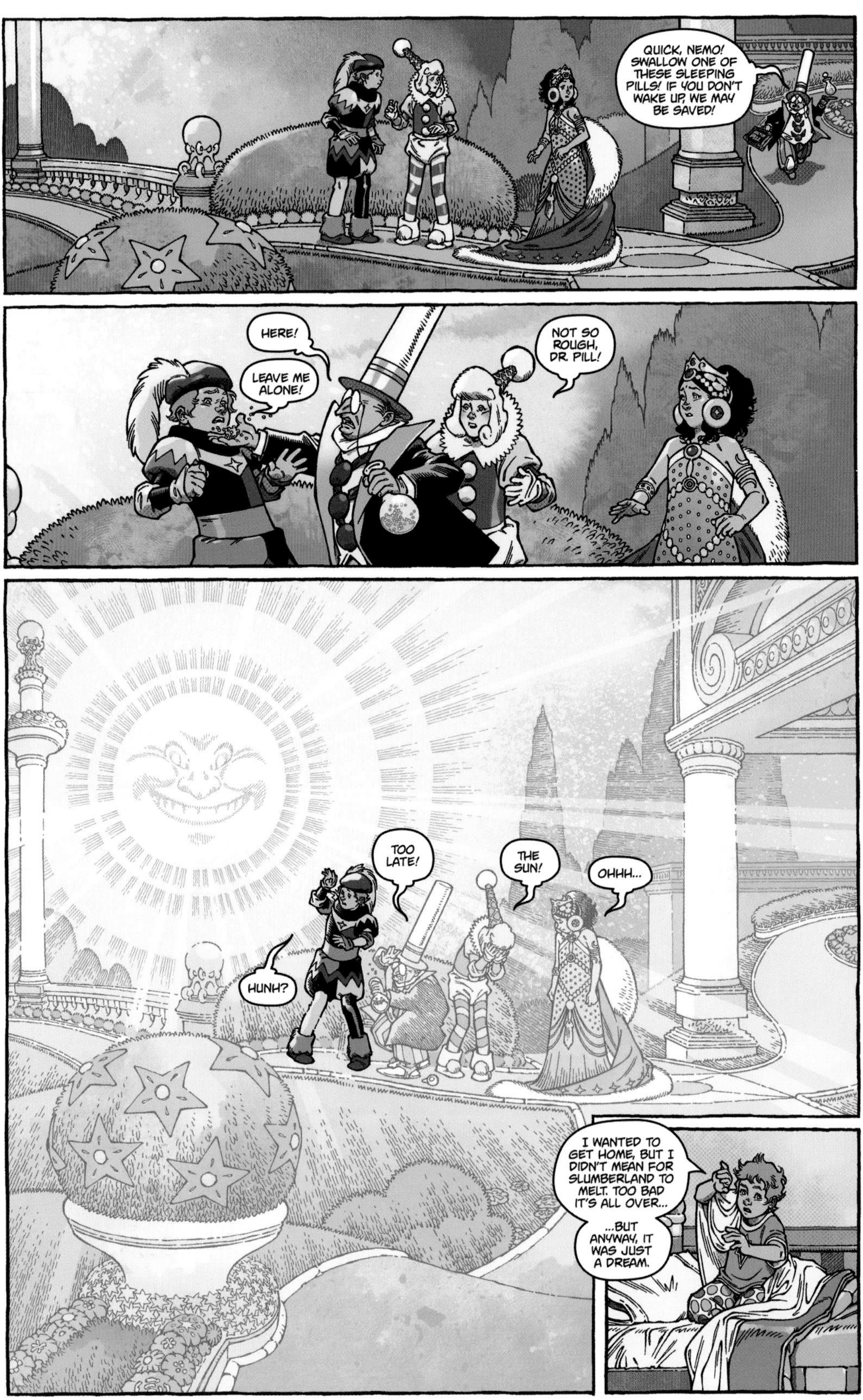
QUICK, NEMO! SWALLOW ONE OF THESE SLEEPING PILLS! IF YOU DON'T WAKE UP, WE MAY BE SAVED!
HERE!
LEAVE ME ALONE!
NOT SO ROUGH, DR. PILL!
TOO LATE!
THE SUN!
OHHH...
HUNH?
I WANTED TO GET HOME, BUT I DIDN'T MEAN FOR SLUMBERLAND TO MELT. TOO BAD IT'S ALL OVER...
...BUT ANYWAY, IT WAS JUST A DREAM.

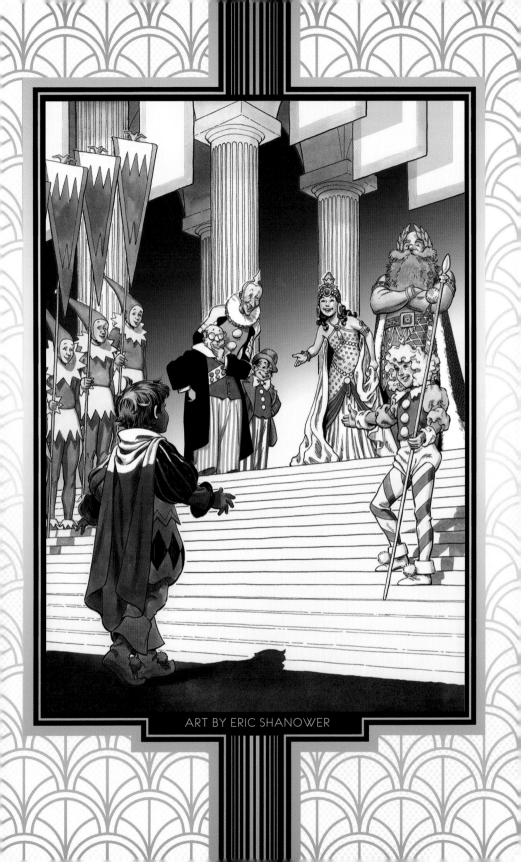

ART BY ERIC SHANOWER

CHAPTER THREE

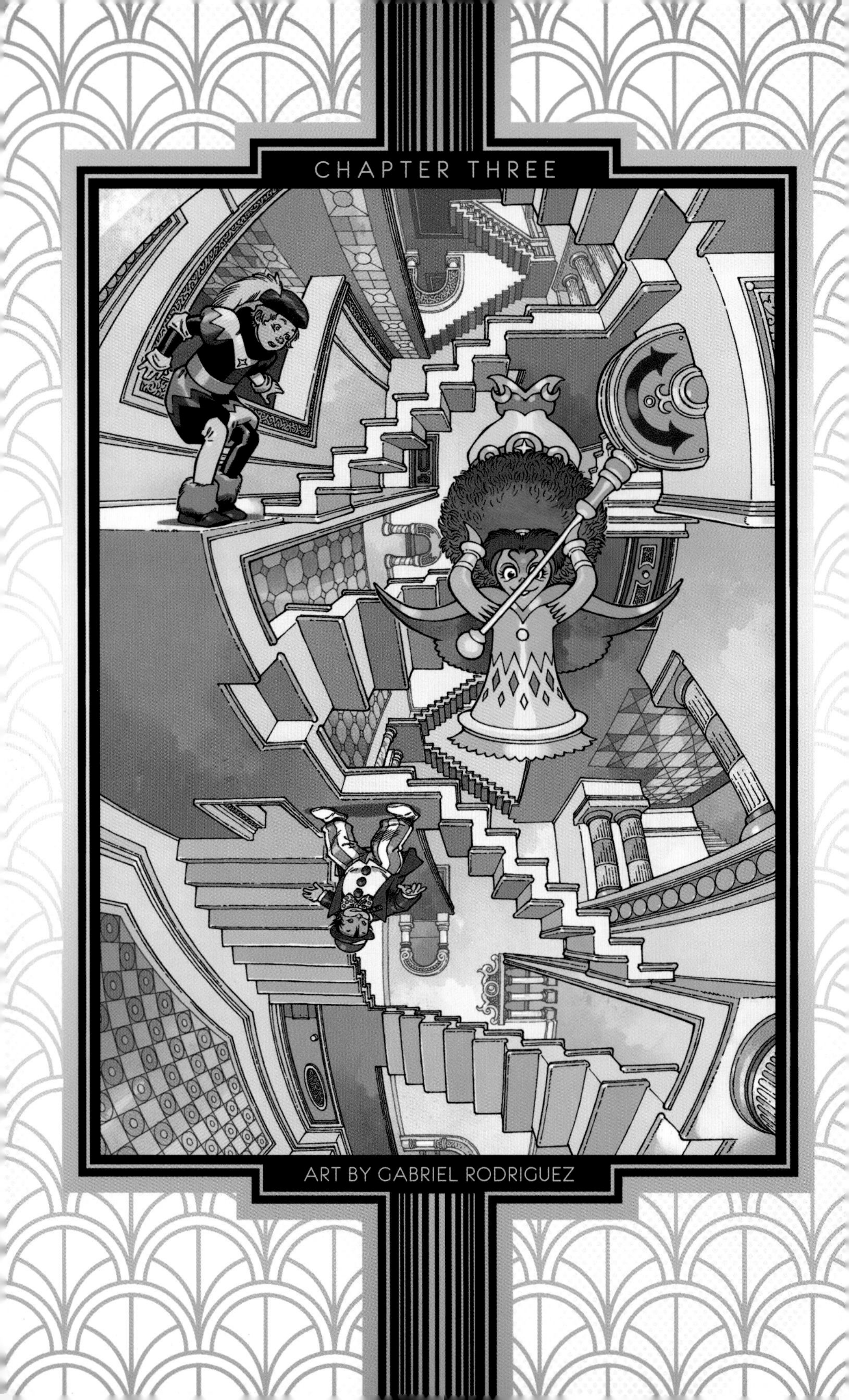

ART BY GABRIEL RODRIGUEZ

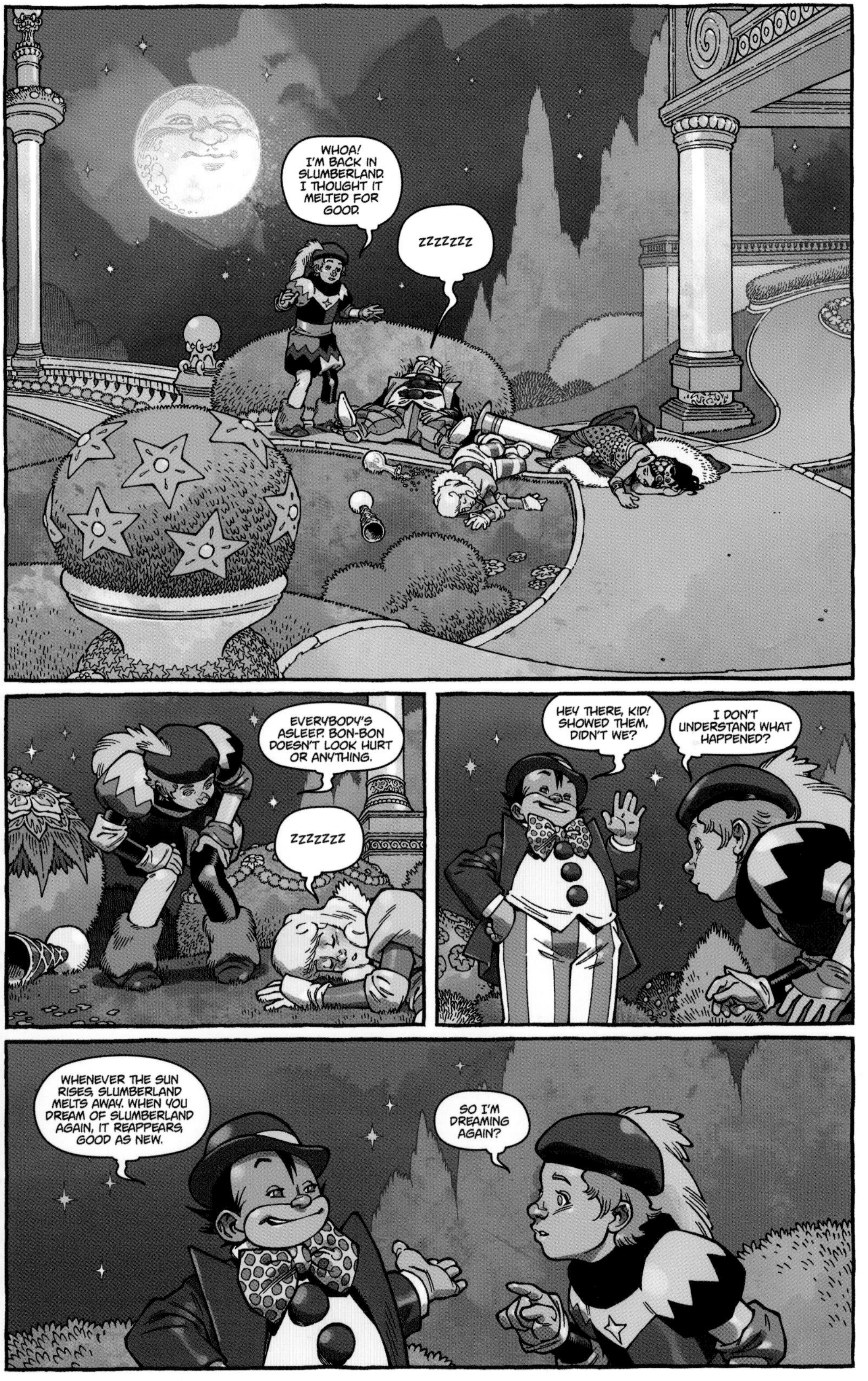
WHOA! I'M BACK IN SLUMBERLAND. I THOUGHT IT MELTED FOR GOOD.
ZZZZZZZ
EVERYBODY'S ASLEEP. BON-BON DOESN'T LOOK HURT OR ANYTHING.
ZZZZZZ
HEY THERE, KID! SHOWED THEM, DIDN'T WE?
I DON'T UNDERSTAND. WHAT HAPPENED?
WHENEVER THE SUN RISES, SLUMBERLAND MELTS AWAY. WHEN YOU DREAM OF SLUMBERLAND AGAIN, IT REAPPEARS, GOOD AS NEW.
SO I'M DREAMING AGAIN?

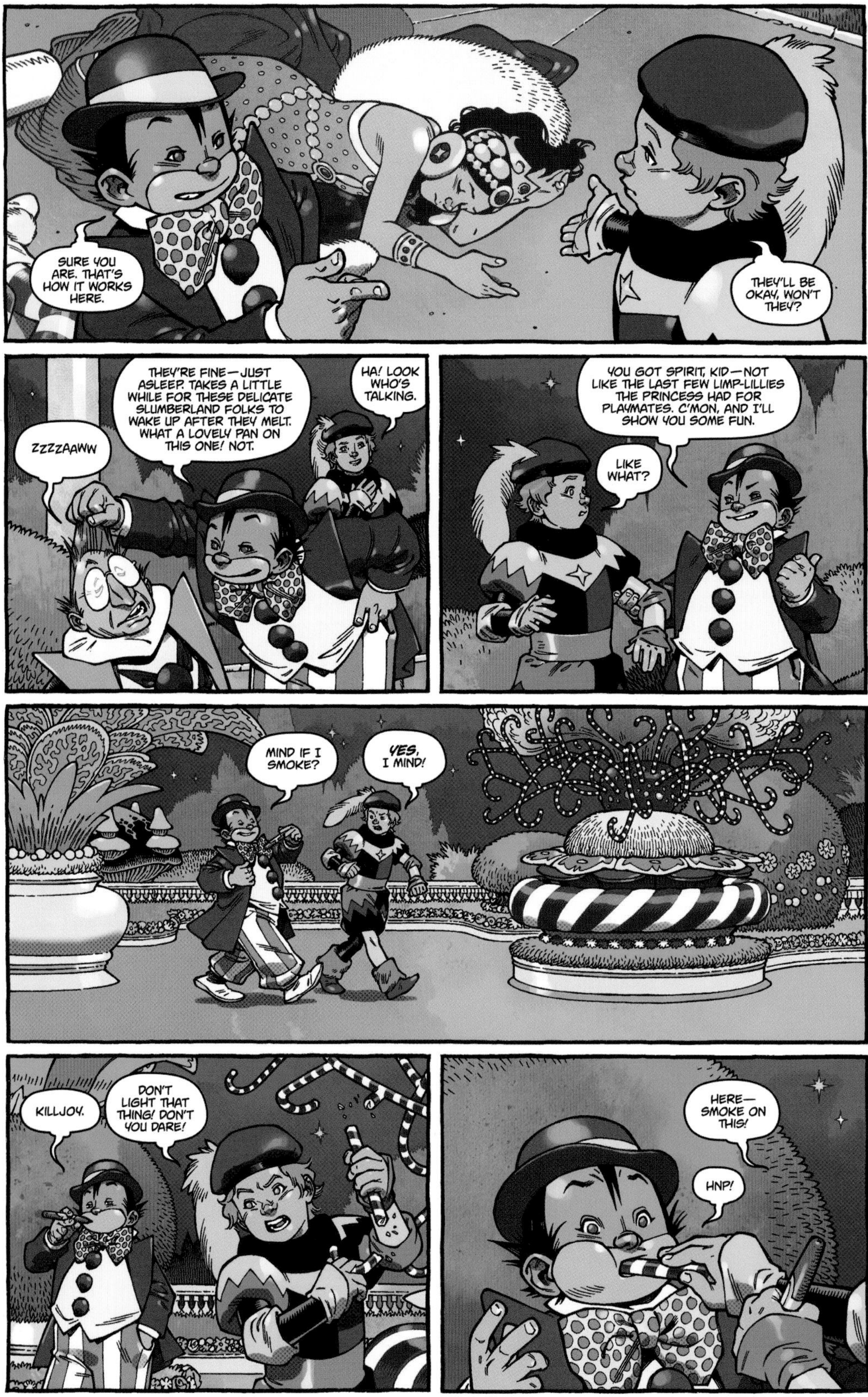
THEY'LL BE OKAY, WON'T THEY?
SURE YOU ARE. THAT'S HOW IT WORKS HERE.
ZZZZAAWW
THEY'RE FINE—JUST ASLEEP. TAKES A LITTLE WHILE FOR THESE DELICATE SLUMBERLAND FOLKS TO WAKE UP AFTER THEY MELT. WHAT A LOVELY PAN ON THIS ONE! NOT.
HA! LOOK WHO'S TALKING.
YOU GOT SPIRIT, KID—NOT LIKE THE LAST FEW LIMP-LILLIES THE PRINCESS HAD FOR PLAYMATES. C'MON, AND I'LL SHOW YOU SOME FUN.
LIKE WHAT?
MIND IF I SMOKE?
YES, I MIND!
KILLJOY.
DON'T LIGHT THAT THING! DON'T YOU DARE!
HERE—SMOKE ON THIS!
HNP!

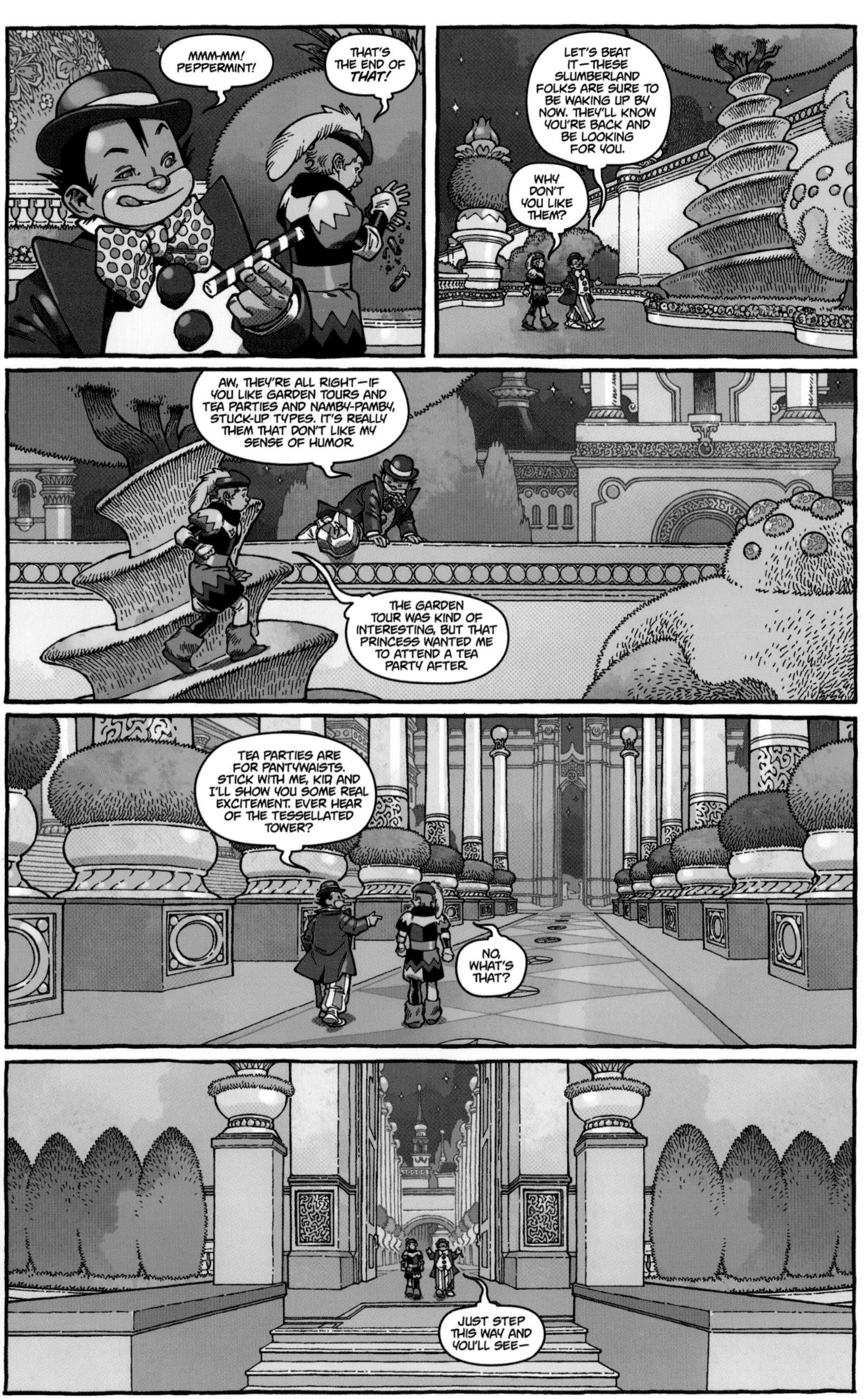
MMM-MM! PEPPERMINT!
THAT'S THE END OF *THAT!*
LET'S BEAT IT—THESE SLUMBERLAND FOLKS ARE SURE TO BE WAKING UP BY NOW. THEY'LL KNOW YOU'RE BACK AND BE LOOKING FOR YOU.
WHY DON'T YOU LIKE THEM?
AW, THEY'RE ALL RIGHT—IF YOU LIKE GARDEN TOURS AND TEA PARTIES AND NAMBY-PAMBY, STUCK-UP TYPES. IT'S REALLY THEM THAT DON'T LIKE MY SENSE OF HUMOR.
THE GARDEN TOUR WAS KIND OF INTERESTING, BUT THAT PRINCESS WANTED ME TO ATTEND A TEA PARTY AFTER.
TEA PARTIES ARE FOR PANTYWAISTS. STICK WITH ME, KID AND I'LL SHOW YOU SOME REAL EXCITEMENT. EVER HEAR OF THE TESSELLATED TOWER?
NO, WHAT'S THAT?
JUST STEP THIS WAY AND YOU'LL SEE—

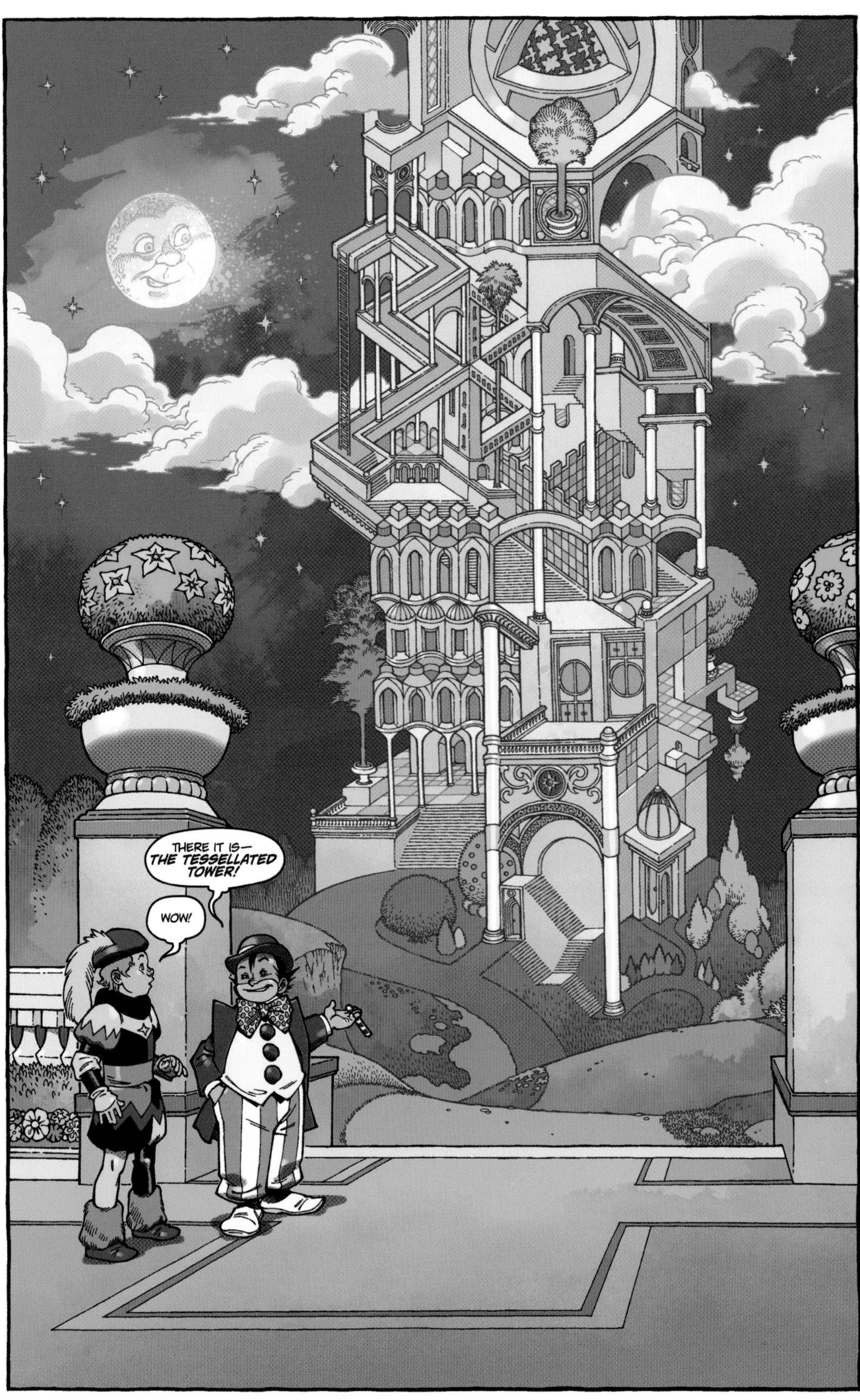
THERE IT IS—
THE TESSELLATED TOWER!
WOW!

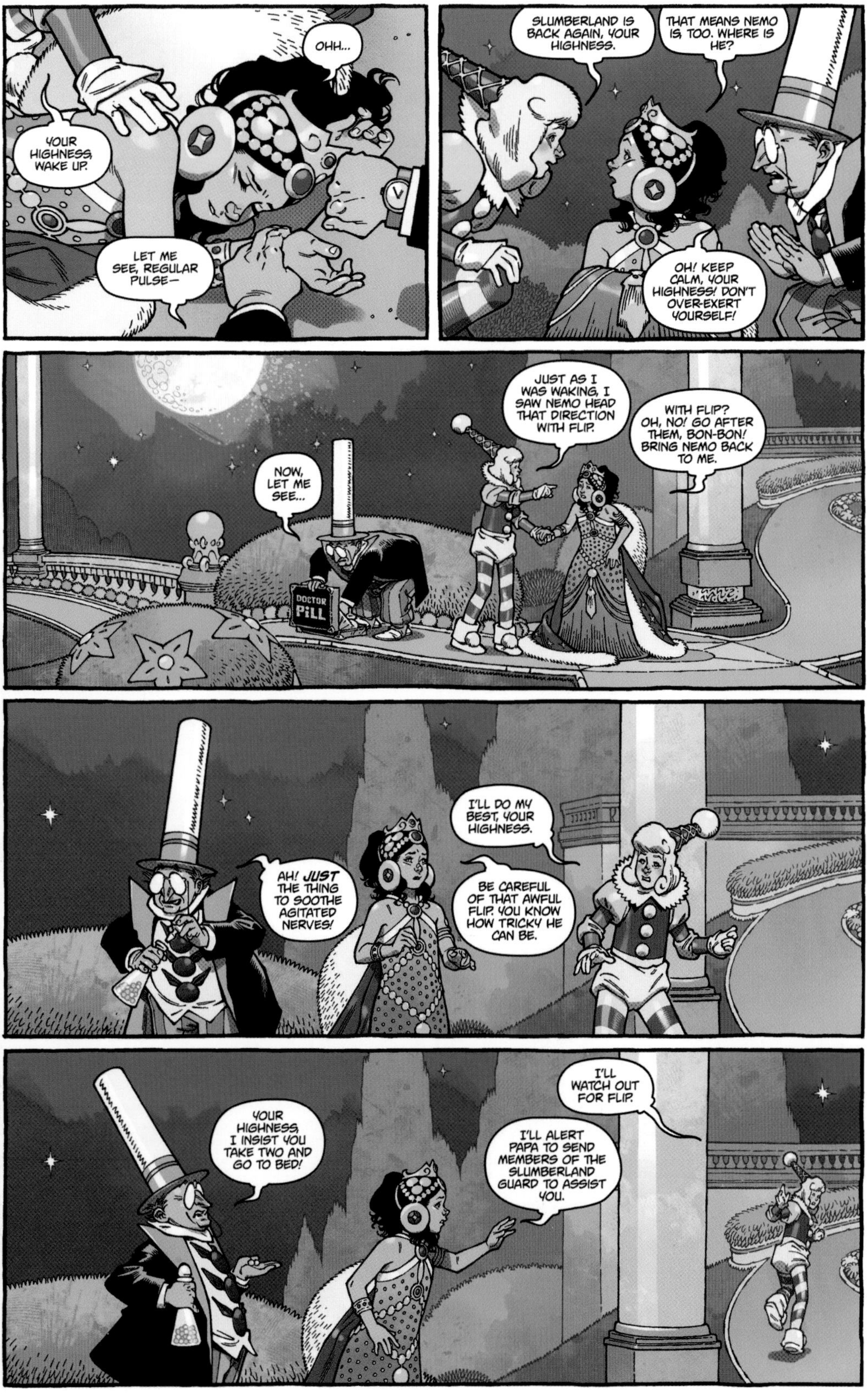
OHH...
YOUR HIGHNESS, WAKE UP.
LET ME SEE, REGULAR PULSE—
SLUMBERLAND IS BACK AGAIN, YOUR HIGHNESS.
THAT MEANS NEMO IS, TOO. WHERE IS HE?
OH! KEEP CALM, YOUR HIGHNESS! DON'T OVER-EXERT YOURSELF!
NOW, LET ME SEE...
JUST AS I WAS WAKING, I SAW NEMO HEAD THAT DIRECTION WITH FLIP.
WITH FLIP? OH, NO! GO AFTER THEM, BON-BON! BRING NEMO BACK TO ME.
DOCTOR PILL
AH! JUST THE THING TO SOOTHE AGITATED NERVES!
I'LL DO MY BEST, YOUR HIGHNESS.
BE CAREFUL OF THAT AWFUL FLIP. YOU KNOW HOW TRICKY HE CAN BE.
YOUR HIGHNESS, I INSIST YOU TAKE TWO AND GO TO BED!
I'LL WATCH OUT FOR FLIP.
I'LL ALERT PAPA TO SEND MEMBERS OF THE SLUMBERLAND GUARD TO ASSIST YOU.

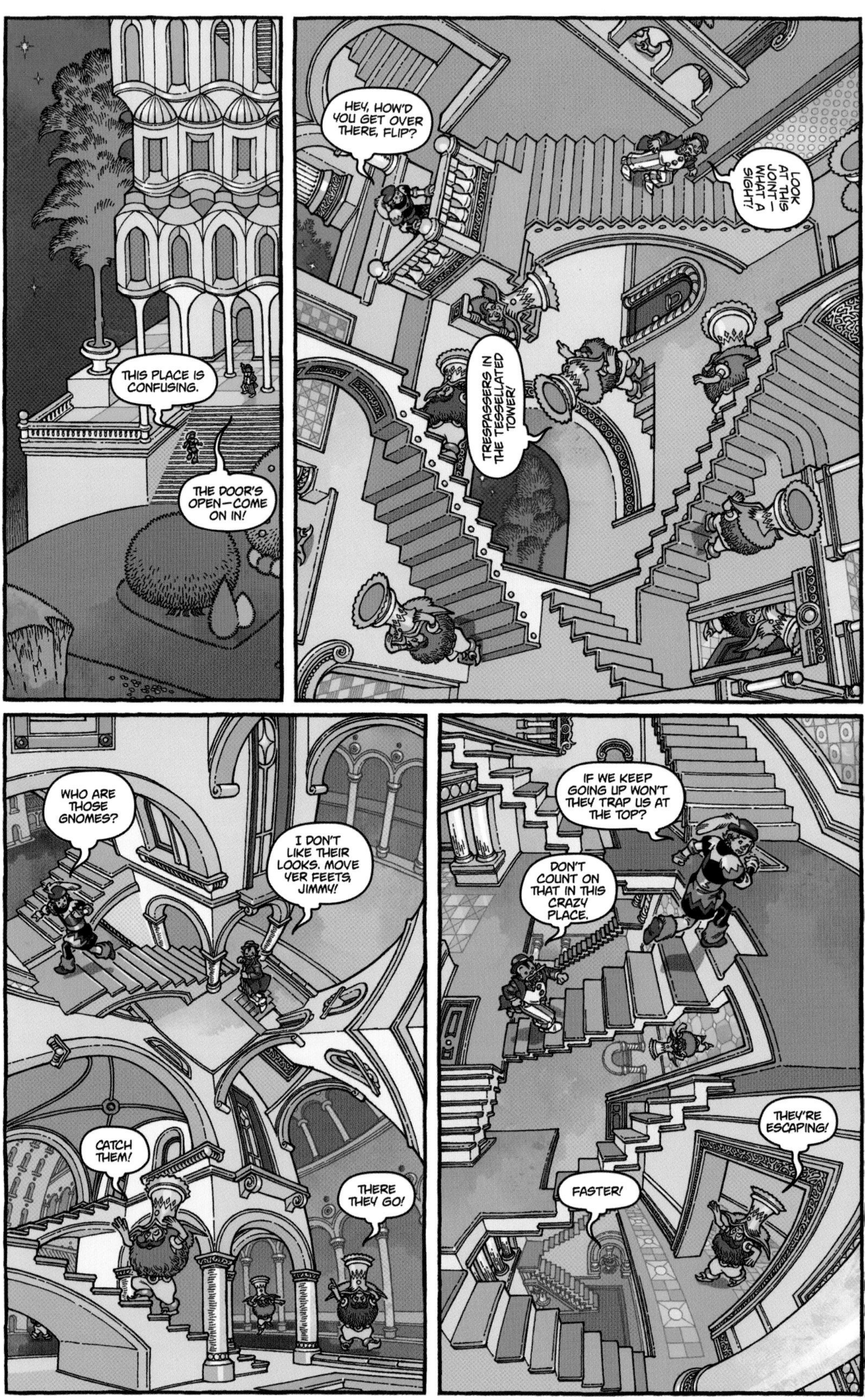
THIS PLACE IS CONFUSING.
THE DOOR'S OPEN—COME ON IN!
HEY, HOW'D YOU GET OVER THERE, FLIP?
LOOK AT THIS JOINT—WHAT A SIGHT!
TRESPASSERS IN THE TESSELLATED TOWER!
WHO ARE THOSE GNOMES?
I DON'T LIKE THEIR LOOKS. MOVE YER FEETS, JIMMY!
CATCH THEM!
THERE THEY GO!
IF WE KEEP GOING UP WON'T THEY TRAP US AT THE TOP?
DON'T COUNT ON THAT IN THIS CRAZY PLACE.
THEY'RE ESCAPING!
FASTER!

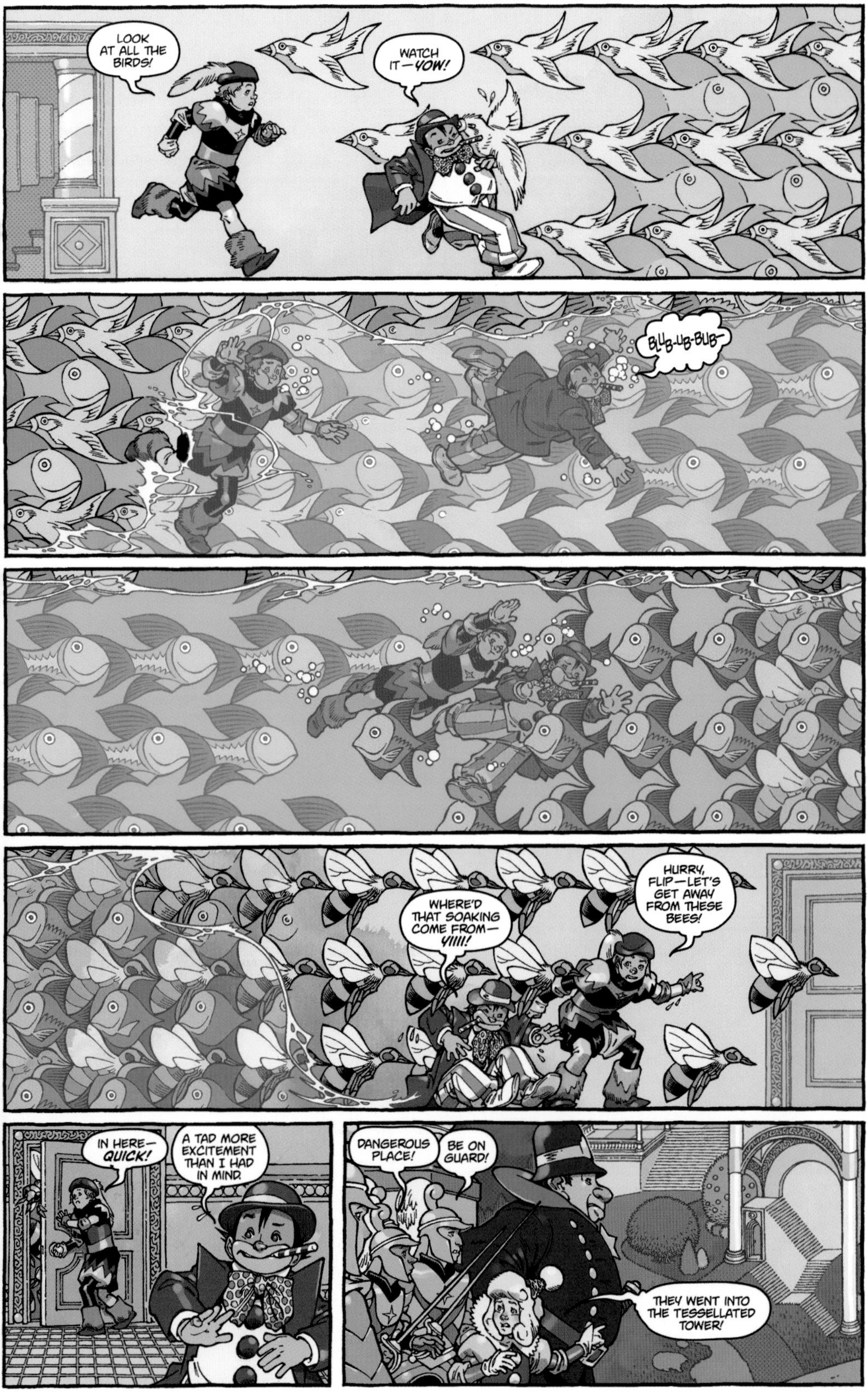
LOOK AT ALL THE BIRDS!
WATCH IT—YOW!
BLUB-UB-BUB—
WHERE'D THAT SOAKING COME FROM—YIIII!
HURRY, FLIP—LET'S GET AWAY FROM THESE BEES!
IN HERE—QUICK!
A TAD MORE EXCITEMENT THAN I HAD IN MIND.
DANGEROUS PLACE!
BE ON GUARD!
THEY WENT INTO THE TESSELLATED TOWER!

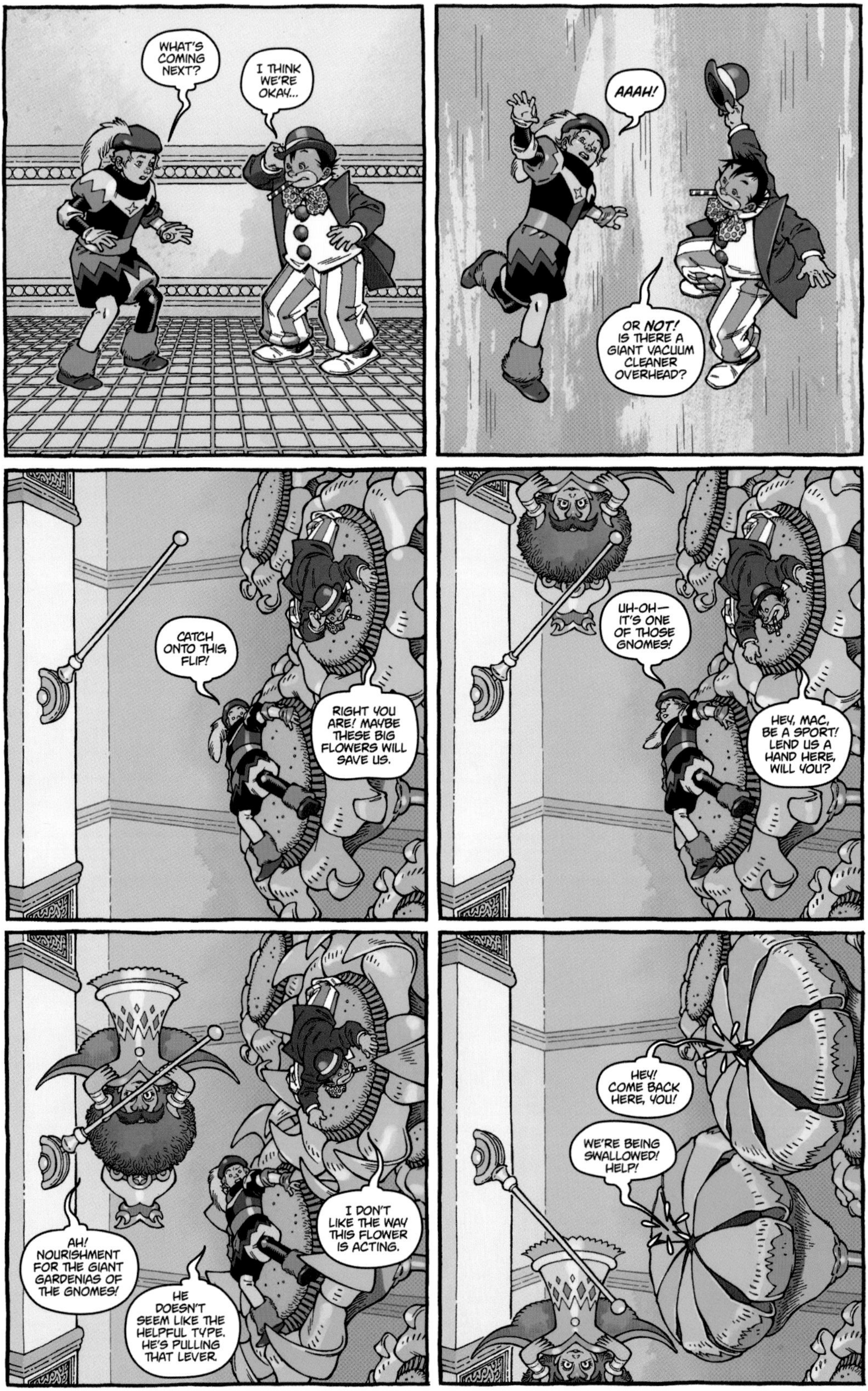
WHAT'S COMING NEXT?
I THINK WE'RE OKAY...
AAAH!
OR NOT! IS THERE A GIANT VACUUM CLEANER OVERHEAD?
CATCH ONTO THIS, FLIP!
RIGHT YOU ARE! MAYBE THESE BIG FLOWERS WILL SAVE US.
UH-OH— IT'S ONE OF THOSE GNOMES!
HEY, MAC, BE A SPORT! LEND US A HAND HERE, WILL YOU?
AH! NOURISHMENT FOR THE GIANT GARDENIAS OF THE GNOMES!
I DON'T LIKE THE WAY THIS FLOWER IS ACTING.
HE DOESN'T SEEM LIKE THE HELPFUL TYPE. HE'S PULLING THAT LEVER.
HEY! COME BACK HERE, YOU!
WE'RE BEING SWALLOWED! HELP!

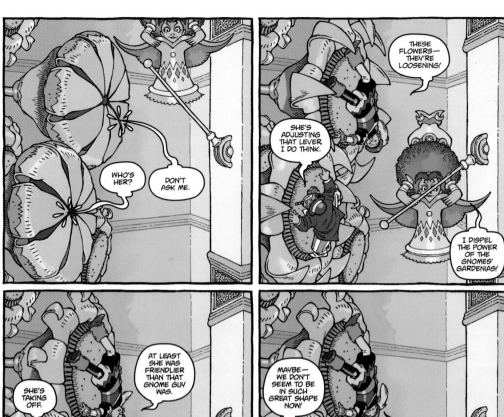

WHO'S HER?

DON'T ASK ME.

THESE FLOWERS— THEY'RE LOOSENING!

SHE'S ADJUSTING THAT LEVER I DO THINK.

I DISPEL THE POWER OF THE GNOMES' GARDENIAS!

SHE'S TAKING OFF.

AT LEAST SHE WAS FRIENDLIER THAN THAT GNOME GUY WAS.

MAYBE— WE DON'T SEEM TO BE IN SUCH GREAT SHAPE NOW!

WE'RE BEING SUCKED UPWARD AGAIN!

AAAAAH!

WAKE ME WHEN WE LAND!

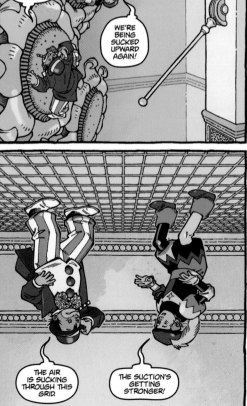

THE AIR IS SUCKING THROUGH THIS GRID.

THE SUCTION'S GETTING STRONGER!

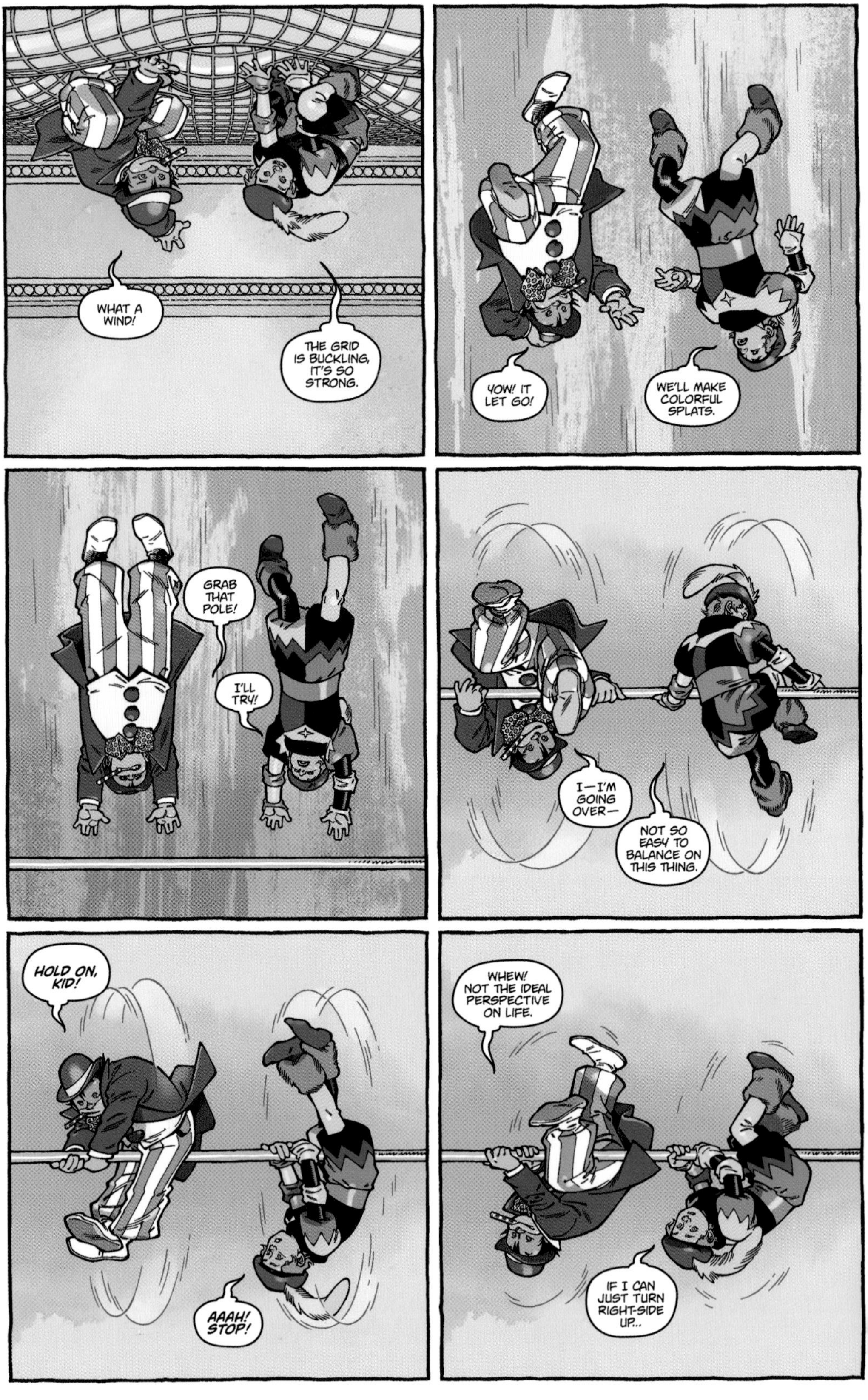
WHAT A WIND!
THE GRID IS BUCKLING, IT'S SO STRONG.
YOW! IT LET GO!
WE'LL MAKE COLORFUL SPLATS.
GRAB THAT POLE!
I'LL TRY!
I—I'M GOING OVER—
NOT SO EASY TO BALANCE ON THIS THING.
HOLD ON, KID!
AAAH! STOP!
WHEW! NOT THE IDEAL PERSPECTIVE ON LIFE.
IF I CAN JUST TURN RIGHT-SIDE UP...

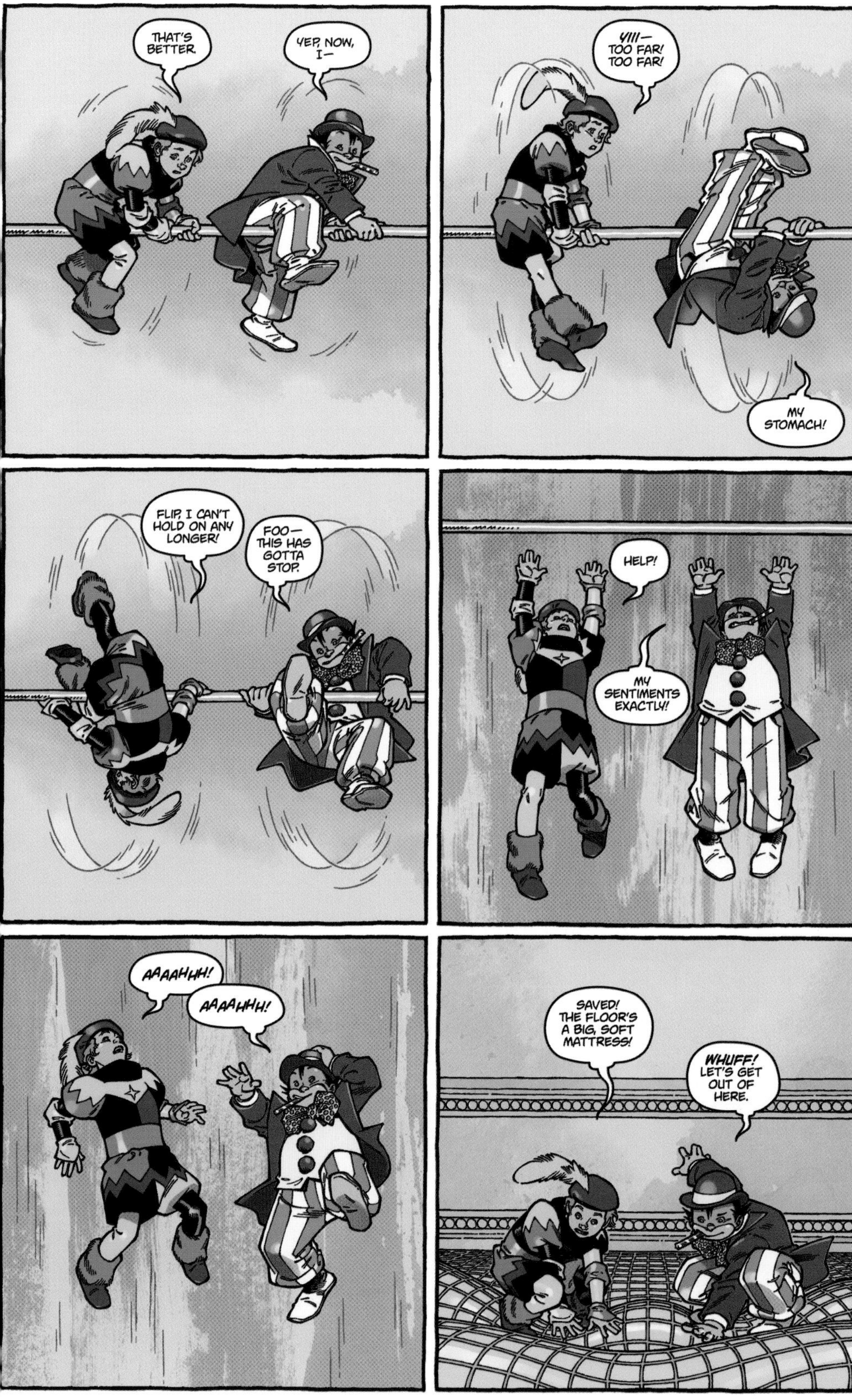
THAT'S BETTER.
YEP, NOW, I—
YIII— TOO FAR! TOO FAR!
MY STOMACH!
FLIP, I CAN'T HOLD ON ANY LONGER!
FOO— THIS HAS GOTTA STOP.
HELP!
MY SENTIMENTS EXACTLY!
AAAAHHH!
AAAAHHH!
SAVED! THE FLOOR'S A BIG, SOFT MATTRESS!
WHUFF! LET'S GET OUT OF HERE.

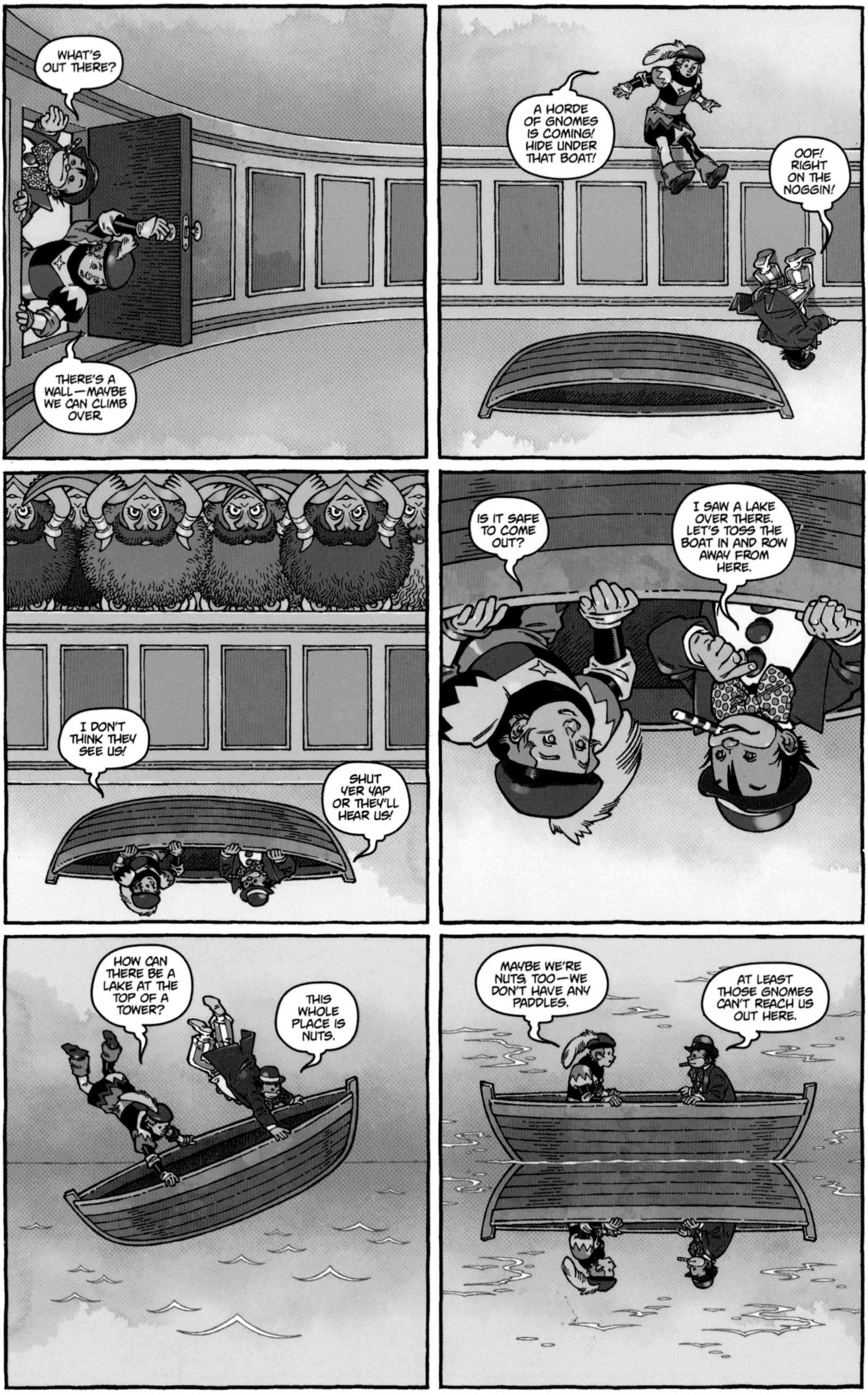
WHAT'S OUT THERE?
THERE'S A WALL—MAYBE WE CAN CLIMB OVER.
A HORDE OF GNOMES IS COMING! HIDE UNDER THAT BOAT!
OOF! RIGHT ON THE NOGGIN!
I DON'T THINK THEY SEE US!
SHUT YER YAP OR THEY'LL HEAR US!
IS IT SAFE TO COME OUT?
I SAW A LAKE OVER THERE. LET'S TOSS THE BOAT IN AND ROW AWAY FROM HERE.
HOW CAN THERE BE A LAKE AT THE TOP OF A TOWER?
THIS WHOLE PLACE IS NUTS.
MAYBE WE'RE NUTS, TOO—WE DON'T HAVE ANY PADDLES.
AT LEAST THOSE GNOMES CAN'T REACH US OUT HERE.

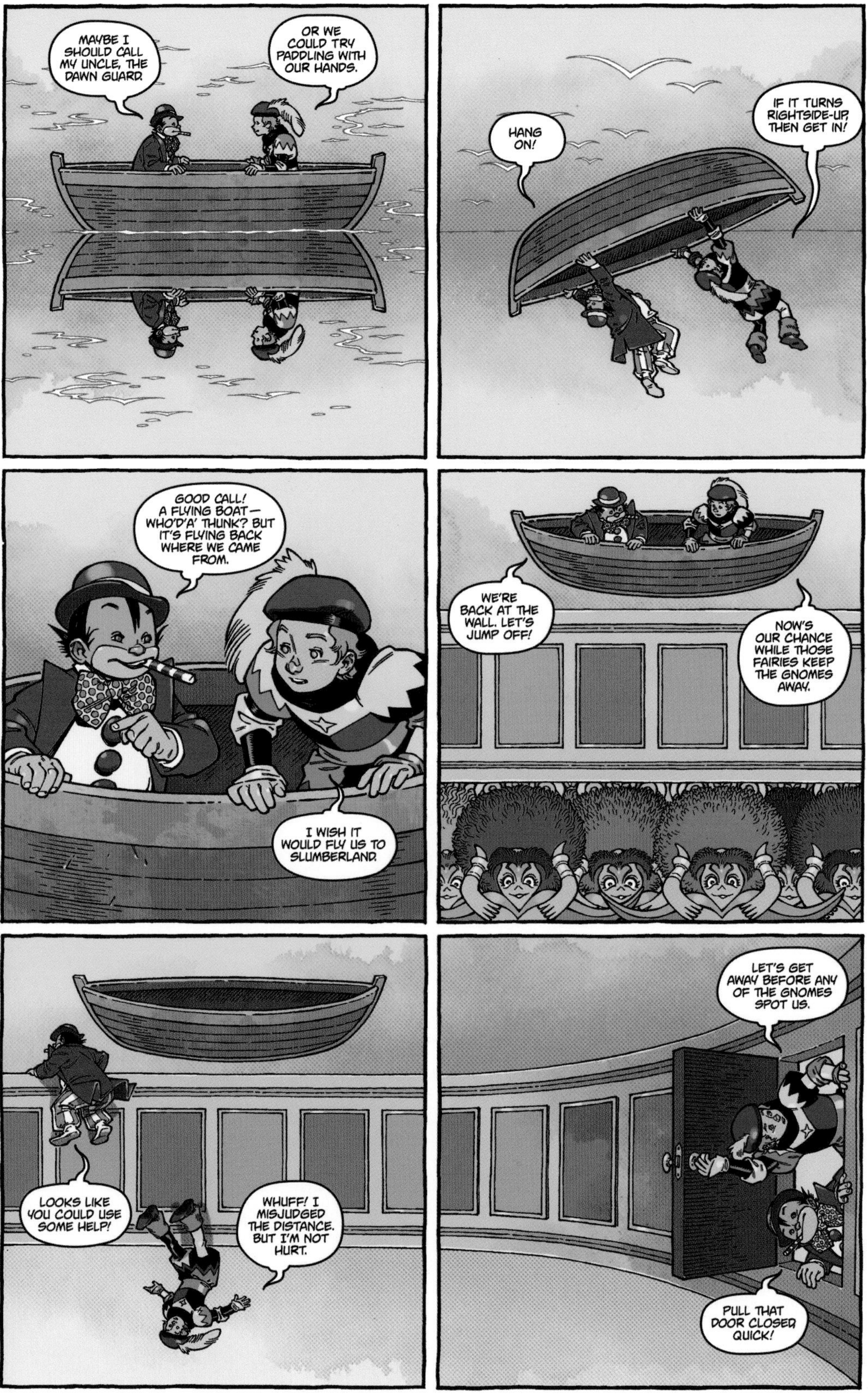
MAYBE I SHOULD CALL MY UNCLE, THE DAWN GUARD.
OR WE COULD TRY PADDLING WITH OUR HANDS.
HANG ON!
IF IT TURNS RIGHTSIDE-UP, THEN GET IN!
GOOD CALL! A FLYING BOAT—WHO'D'A' THUNK? BUT IT'S FLYING BACK WHERE WE CAME FROM.
I WISH IT WOULD FLY US TO SLUMBERLAND.
WE'RE BACK AT THE WALL. LET'S JUMP OFF!
NOW'S OUR CHANCE WHILE THOSE FAIRIES KEEP THE GNOMES AWAY.
LOOKS LIKE YOU COULD USE SOME HELP!
WHUFF! I MISJUDGED THE DISTANCE. BUT I'M NOT HURT.
LET'S GET AWAY BEFORE ANY OF THE GNOMES SPOT US.
PULL THAT DOOR CLOSED QUICK!

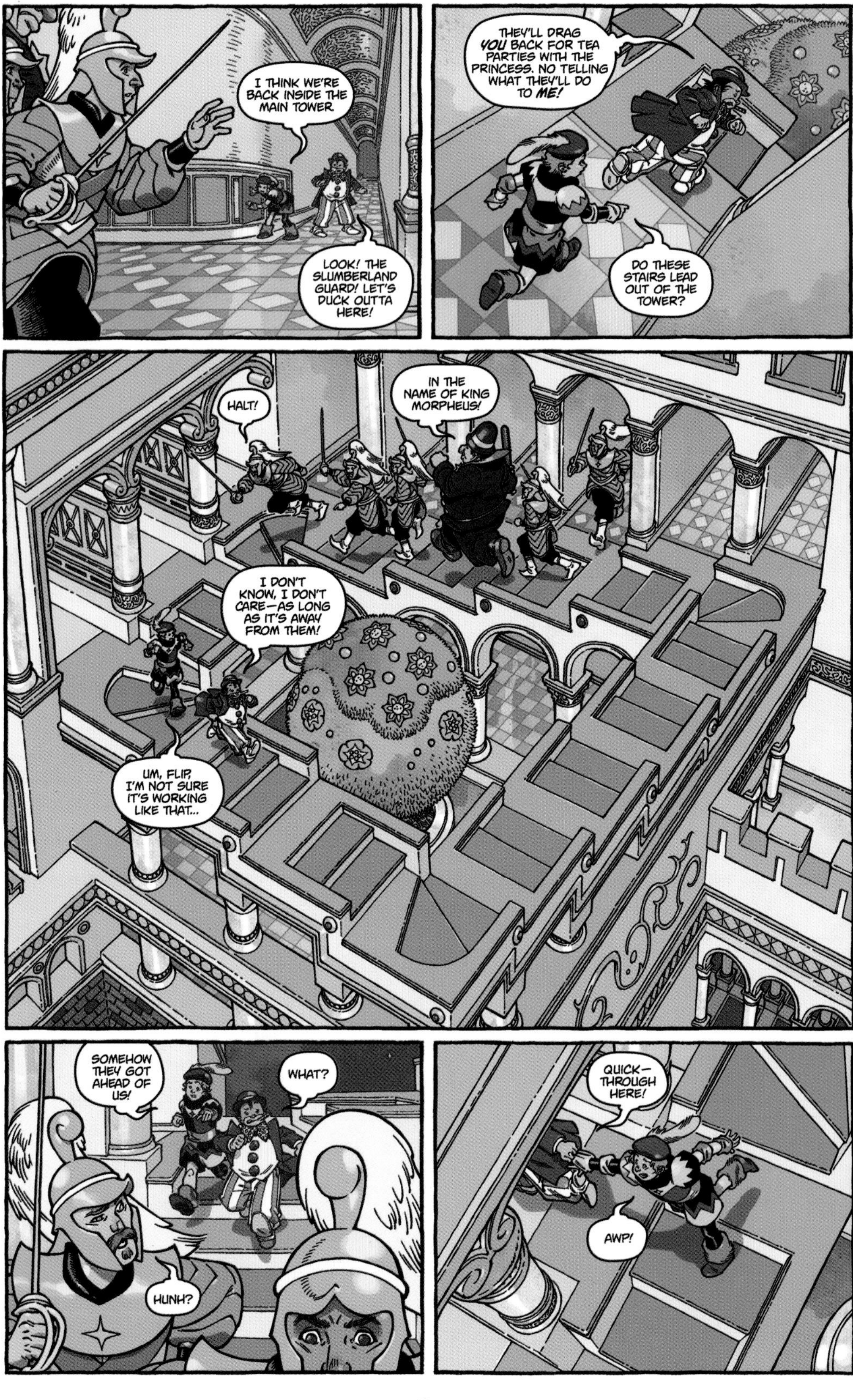
I THINK WE'RE BACK INSIDE THE MAIN TOWER.
LOOK! THE SLUMBERLAND GUARD! LET'S DUCK OUTTA HERE!
THEY'LL DRAG YOU BACK FOR TEA PARTIES WITH THE PRINCESS. NO TELLING WHAT THEY'LL DO TO ME!
DO THESE STAIRS LEAD OUT OF THE TOWER?
HALT!
IN THE NAME OF KING MORPHEUS!
I DON'T KNOW, I DON'T CARE—AS LONG AS IT'S AWAY FROM THEM!
UM, FLIP, I'M NOT SURE IT'S WORKING LIKE THAT...
SOMEHOW THEY GOT AHEAD OF US!
WHAT?
HUNH?
QUICK—THROUGH HERE!
AWP!

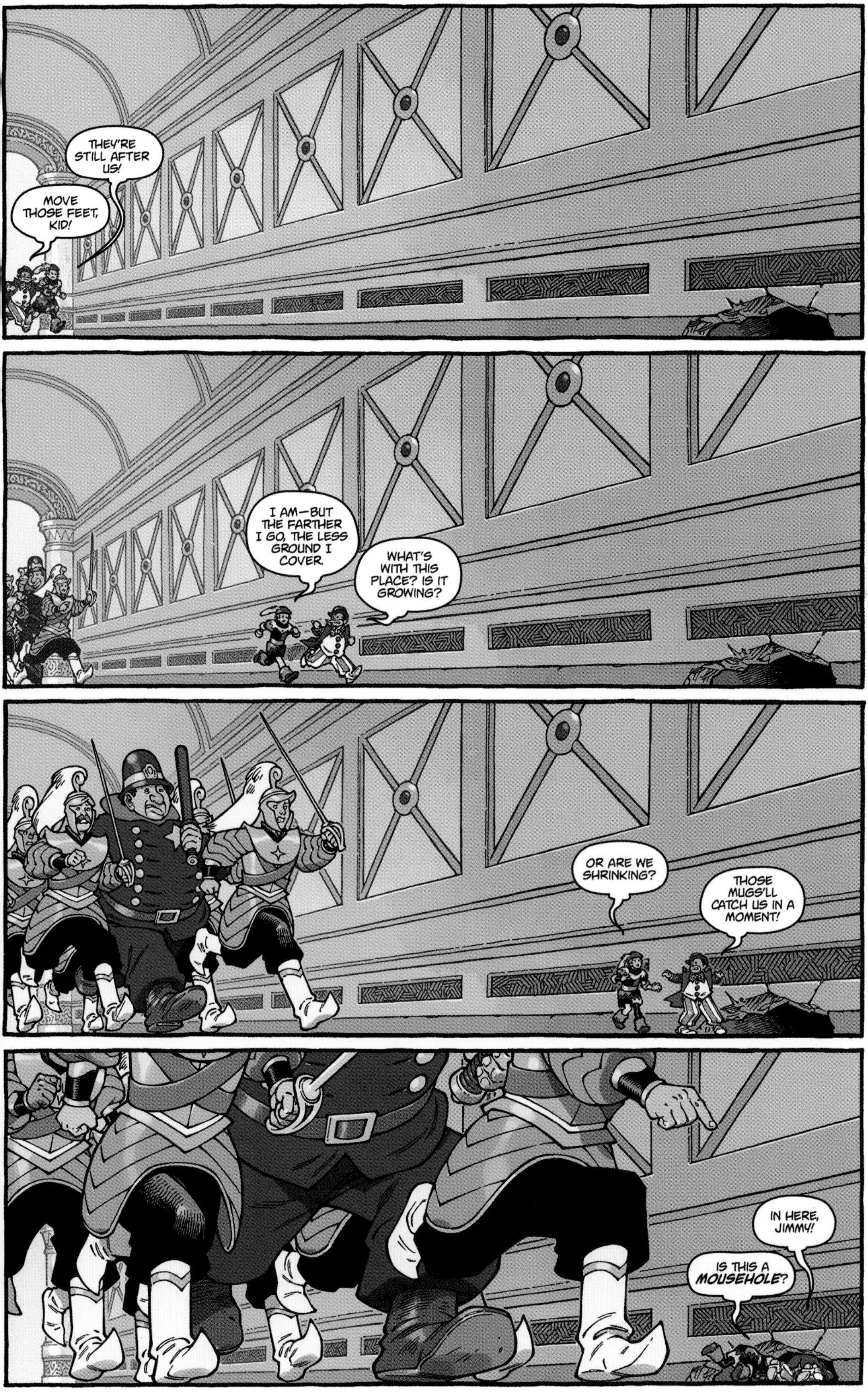
THEY'RE STILL AFTER US!
MOVE THOSE FEET, KID!
I AM—BUT THE FARTHER I GO, THE LESS GROUND I COVER.
WHAT'S WITH THIS PLACE? IS IT GROWING?
OR ARE WE SHRINKING?
THOSE MUGS'LL CATCH US IN A MOMENT!
IN HERE, JIMMY!
IS THIS A MOUSEHOLE?

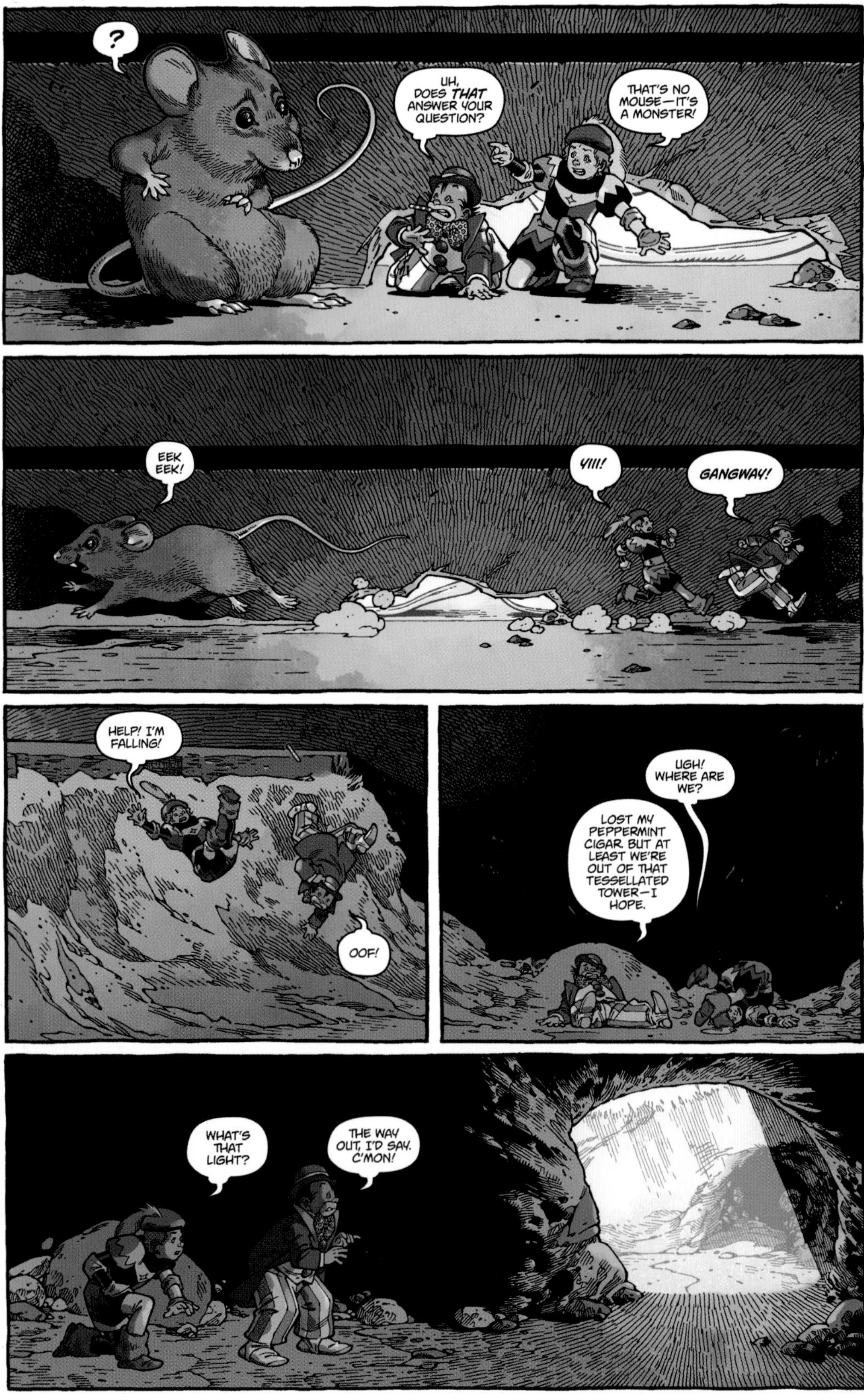
?
UH, DOES THAT ANSWER YOUR QUESTION?
THAT'S NO MOUSE—IT'S A MONSTER!
EEK EEK!
YIII!
GANGWAY!
HELP! I'M FALLING!
OOF!
UGH! WHERE ARE WE?
LOST MY PEPPERMINT CIGAR BUT AT LEAST WE'RE OUT OF THAT TESSELLATED TOWER—I HOPE.
WHAT'S THAT LIGHT?
THE WAY OUT, I'D SAY. C'MON!

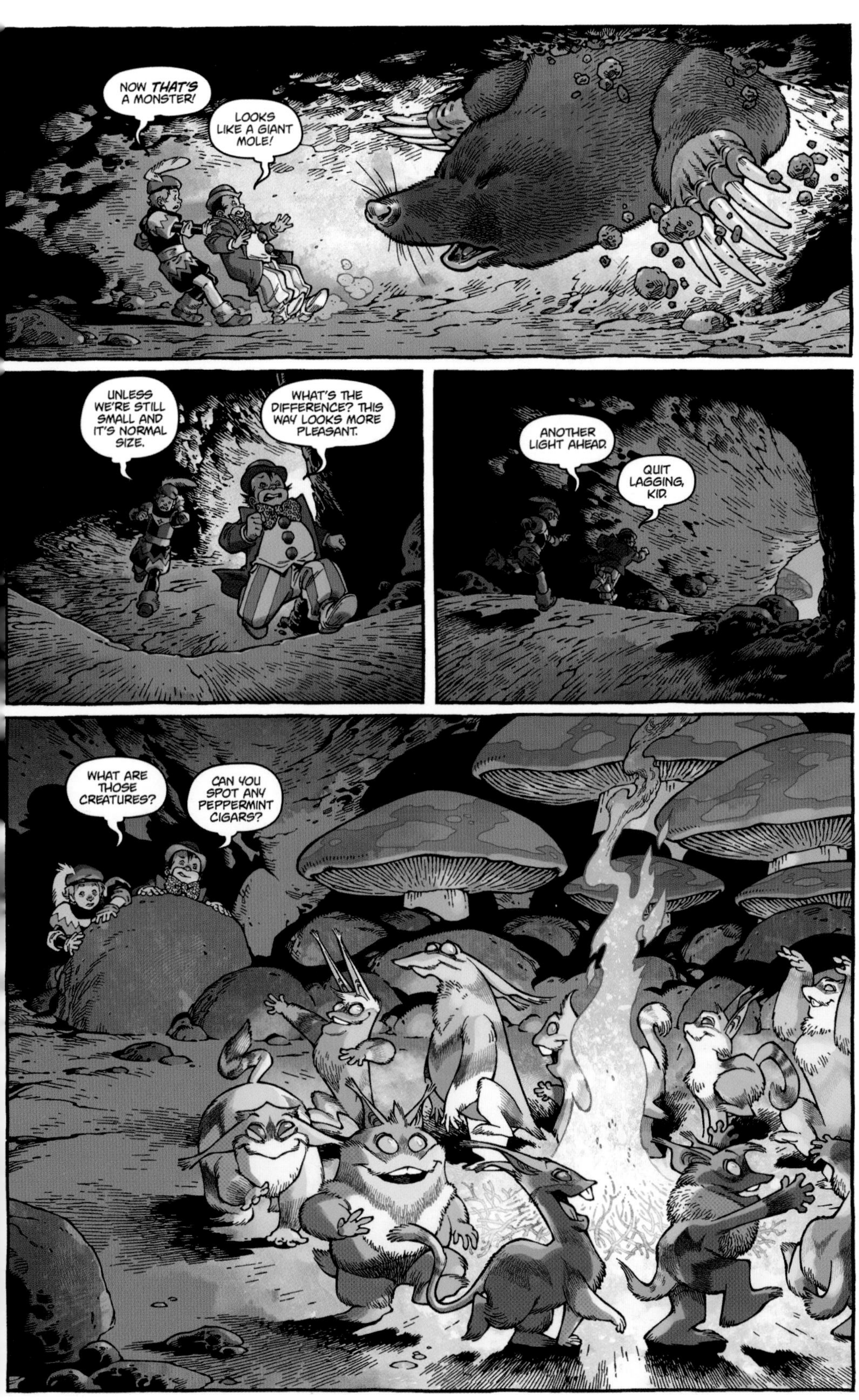
NOW THAT'S A MONSTER!
LOOKS LIKE A GIANT MOLE!
UNLESS WE'RE STILL SMALL AND IT'S NORMAL SIZE.
WHAT'S THE DIFFERENCE? THIS WAY LOOKS MORE PLEASANT.
ANOTHER LIGHT AHEAD.
QUIT LAGGING, KID.
WHAT ARE THOSE CREATURES?
CAN YOU SPOT ANY PEPPERMINT CIGARS?

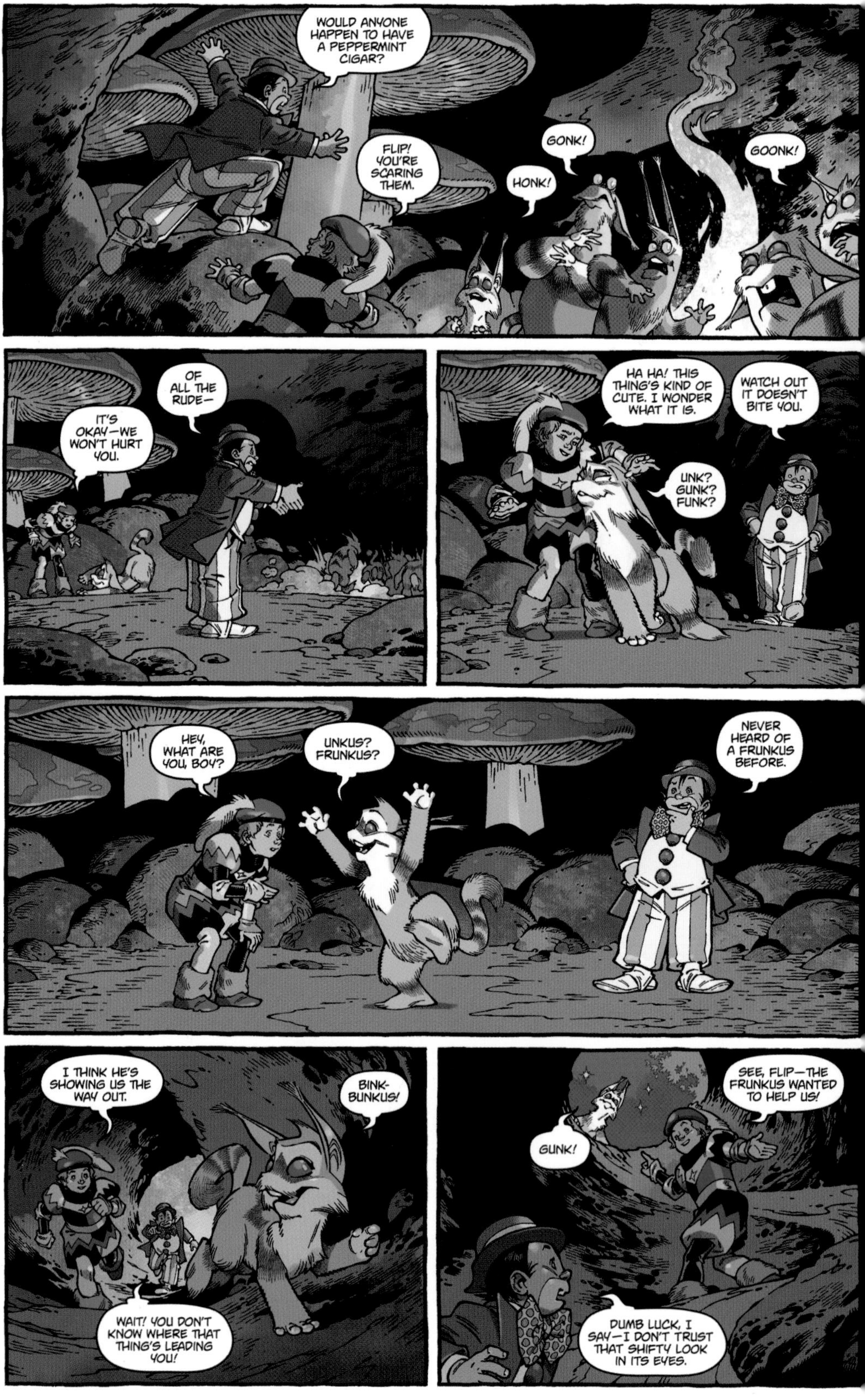
WOULD ANYONE HAPPEN TO HAVE A PEPPERMINT CIGAR?
FLIP! YOU'RE SCARING THEM.
GONK!
HONK!
GOONK!
OF ALL THE RUDE—
IT'S OKAY—WE WON'T HURT YOU.
HA HA! THIS THING'S KIND OF CUTE. I WONDER WHAT IT IS.
WATCH OUT IT DOESN'T BITE YOU.
UNK? GUNK? FUNK?
HEY, WHAT ARE YOU, BOY?
UNKUS? FRUNKUS?
NEVER HEARD OF A FRUNKUS BEFORE.
I THINK HE'S SHOWING US THE WAY OUT.
BINK-BUNKUS!
WAIT! YOU DON'T KNOW WHERE THAT THING'S LEADING YOU!
SEE, FLIP—THE FRUNKUS WANTED TO HELP US!
GUNK!
DUMB LUCK, I SAY—I DON'T TRUST THAT SHIFTY LOOK IN ITS EYES.

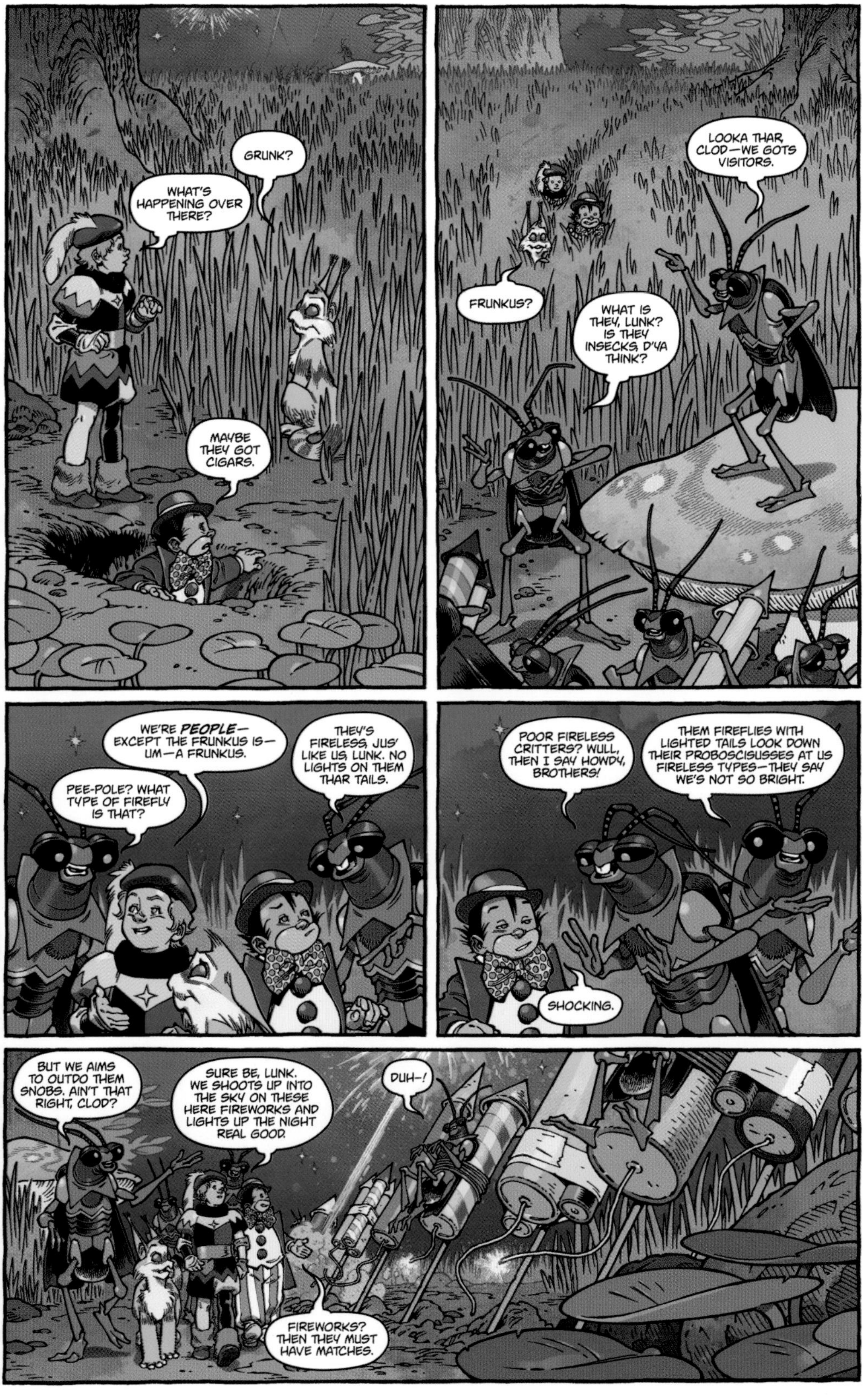
GRUNK?
WHAT'S HAPPENING OVER THERE?
MAYBE THEY GOT CIGARS.
LOOKA THAR, CLOD—WE GOTS VISITORS.
FRUNKUS?
WHAT IS THEY, LUNK? IS THEY INSECKS, D'YA THINK?
WE'RE *PEOPLE*— EXCEPT THE FRUNKUS IS— UM—A FRUNKUS.
PEE-POLE? WHAT TYPE OF FIREFLY IS THAT?
THEY'S FIRELESS, JUS' LIKE US, LUNK. NO LIGHTS ON THEM THAR TAILS.
POOR FIRELESS CRITTERS? WULL, THEN I SAY HOWDY, BROTHERS!
THEM FIREFLIES WITH LIGHTED TAILS LOOK DOWN THEIR PROBOSCISUSSES AT US FIRELESS TYPES—THEY SAY WE'S NOT SO BRIGHT.
SHOCKING.
BUT WE AIMS TO OUTDO THEM SNOBS. AIN'T THAT RIGHT, CLOD?
SURE BE, LUNK. WE SHOOTS UP INTO THE SKY ON THESE HERE FIREWORKS AND LIGHTS UP THE NIGHT REAL GOOD.
DUH-!
FIREWORKS? THEN THEY MUST HAVE MATCHES.

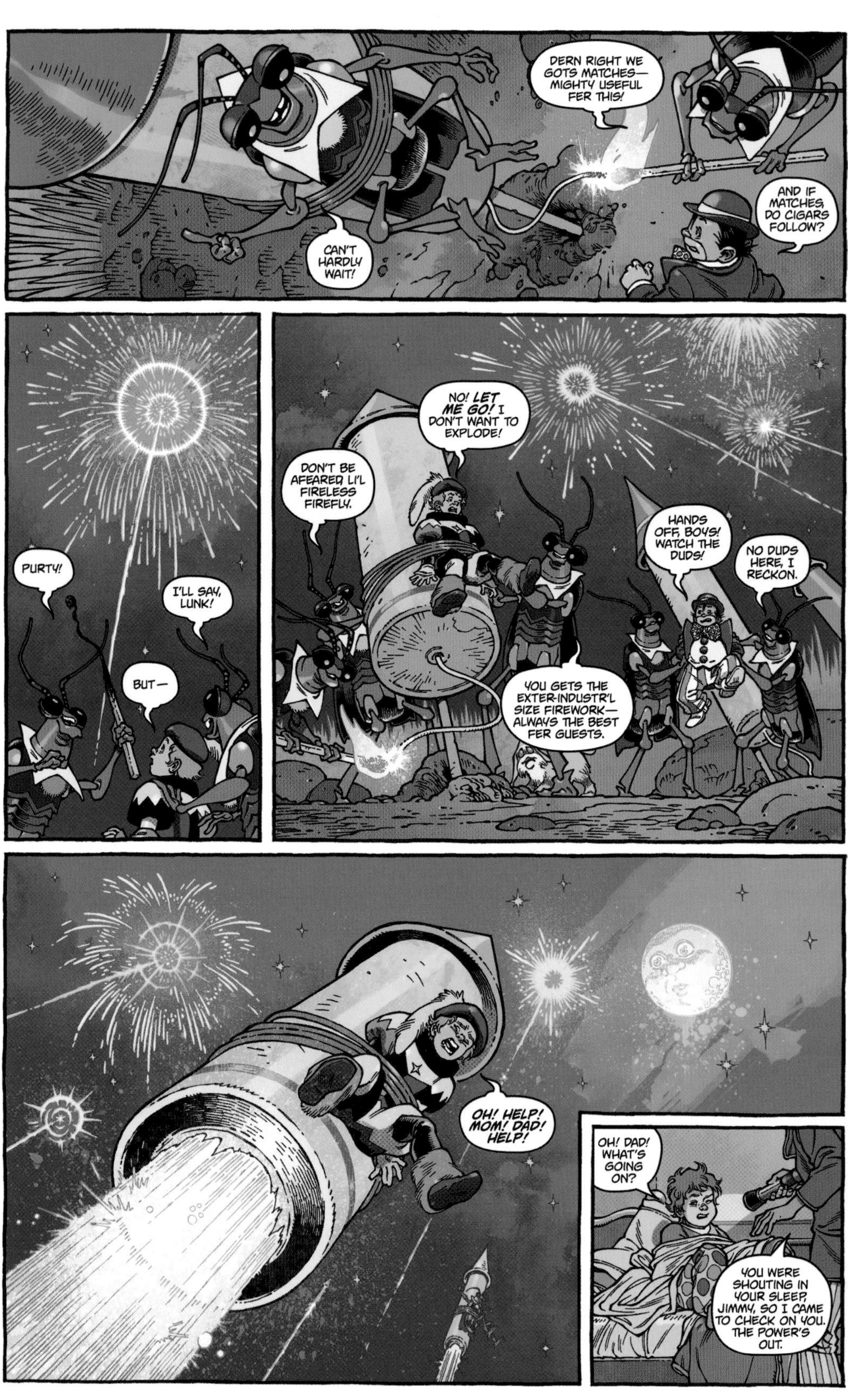

DERN RIGHT WE GOTS MATCHES— MIGHTY USEFUL FER THIS!
CAN'T HARDLY WAIT!
AND IF MATCHES, DO CIGARS FOLLOW?
PURTY!
I'LL SAY, LUNK!
BUT—
NO! LET ME GO! I DON'T WANT TO EXPLODE!
DON'T BE AFEARED, LI'L FIRELESS FIREFLY.
HANDS OFF, BOYS! WATCH THE DUDS!
NO DUDS HERE, I RECKON.
YOU GETS THE EXTER-INDUSTR'L SIZE FIREWORK— ALWAYS THE BEST FER GUESTS.
OH! HELP! MOM! DAD! HELP!
OH! DAD! WHAT'S GOING ON?
YOU WERE SHOUTING IN YOUR SLEEP, JIMMY, SO I CAME TO CHECK ON YOU. THE POWER'S OUT.

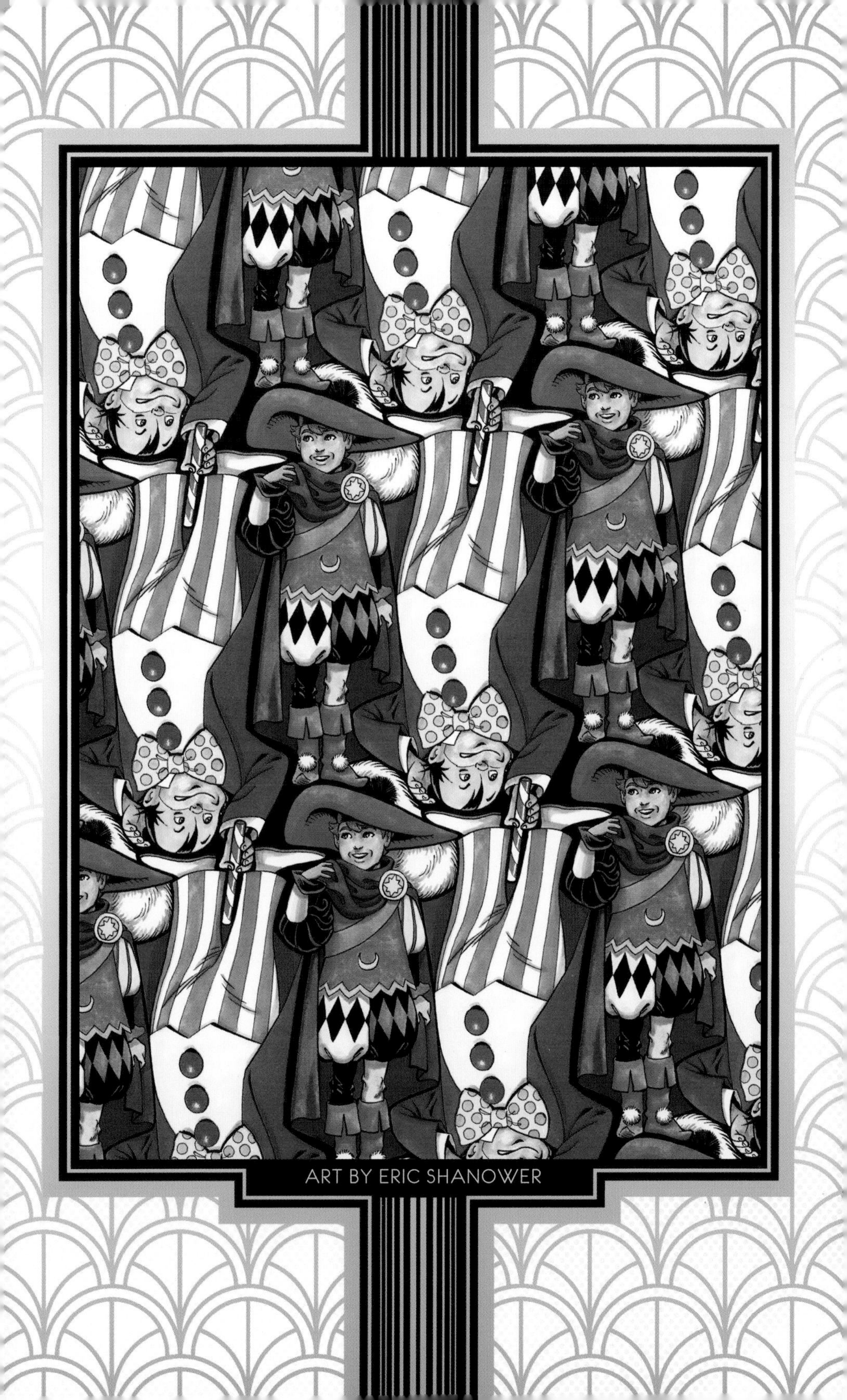

ART BY ERIC SHANOWER

CHAPTER FOUR

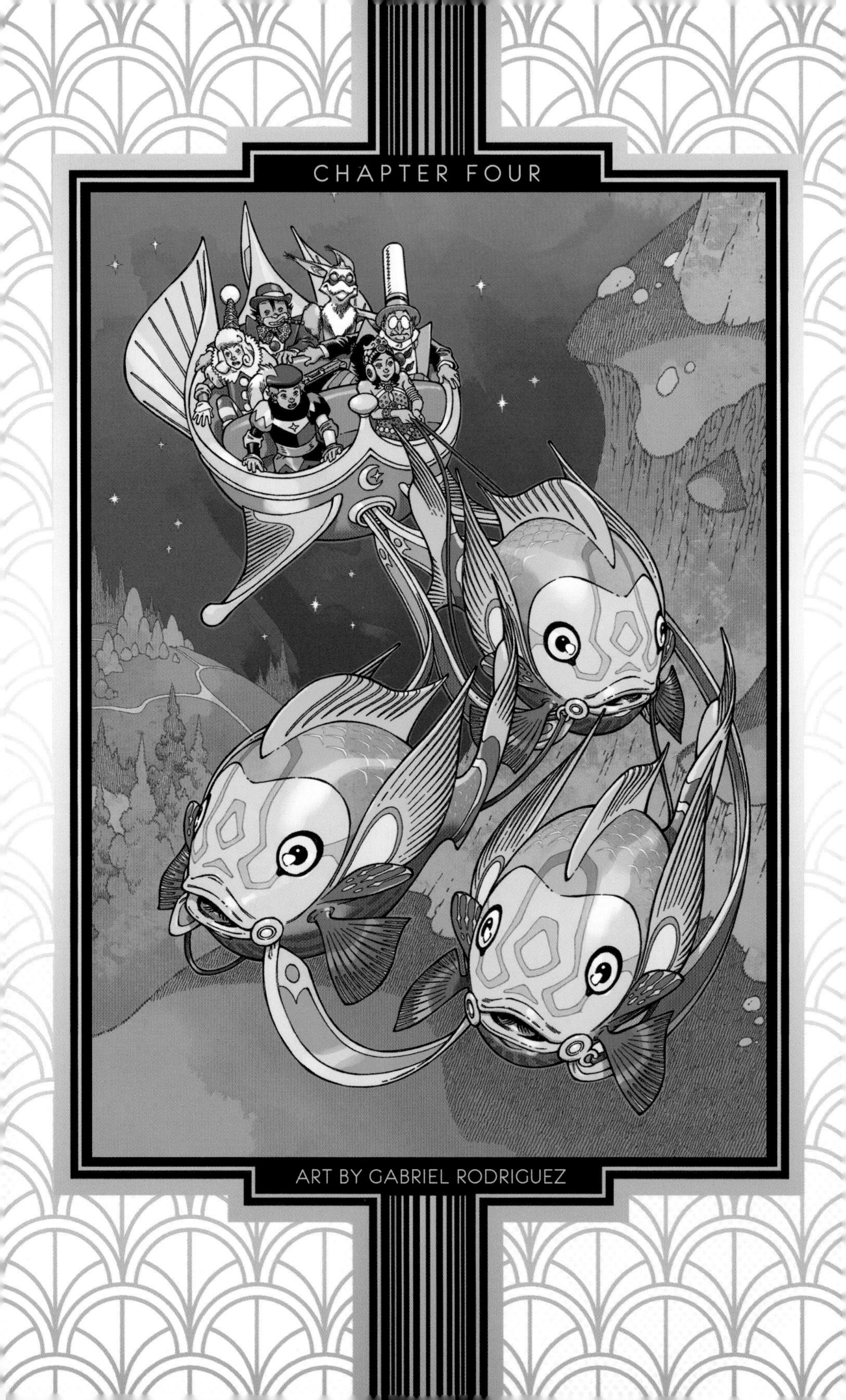

ART BY GABRIEL RODRIGUEZ

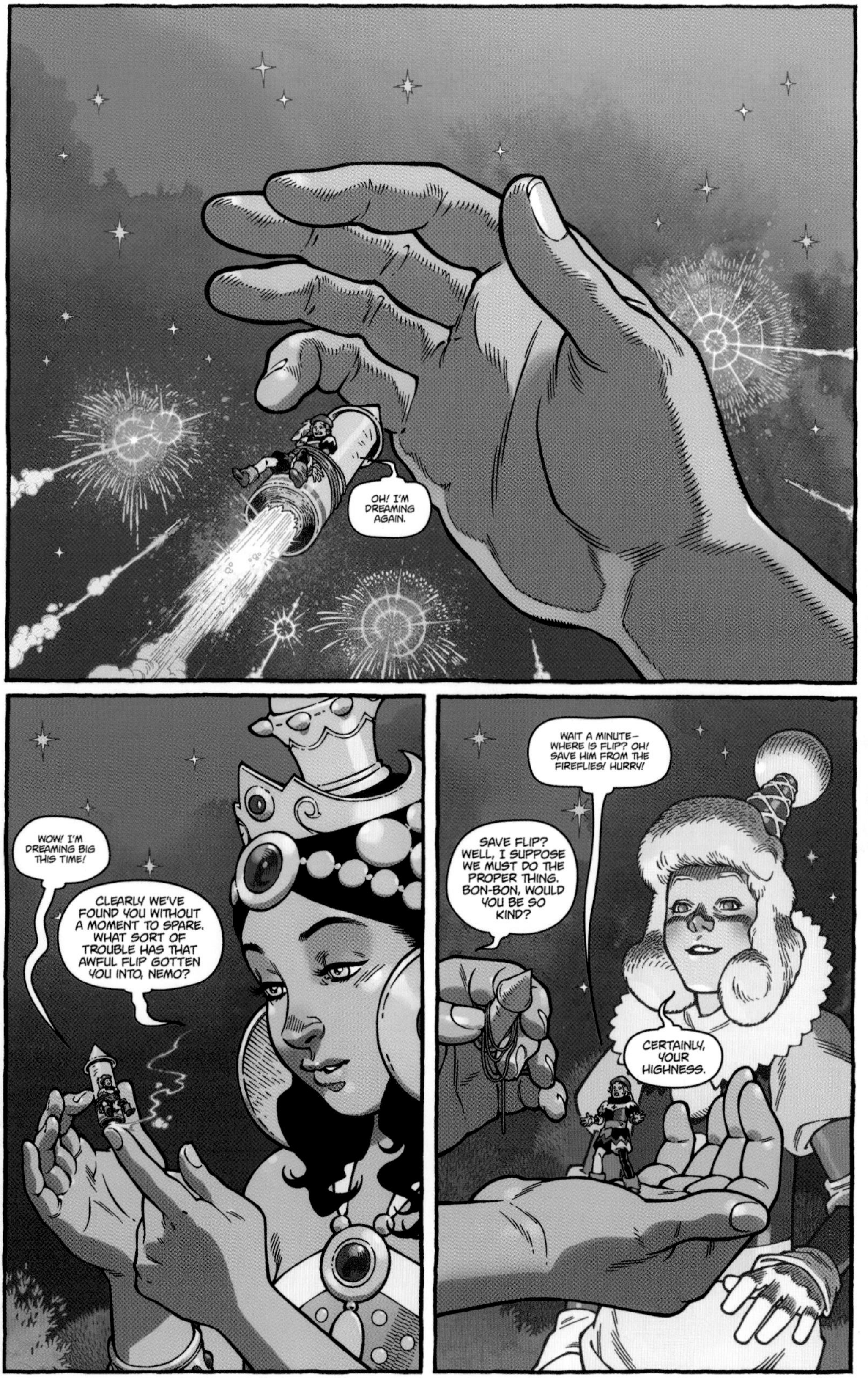
OH! I'M DREAMING AGAIN.
WOW! I'M DREAMING BIG THIS TIME!
CLEARLY WE'VE FOUND YOU WITHOUT A MOMENT TO SPARE. WHAT SORT OF TROUBLE HAS THAT AWFUL FLIP GOTTEN YOU INTO, NEMO?
WAIT A MINUTE— WHERE IS FLIP? OH! SAVE HIM FROM THE FIREFLIES! HURRY!
SAVE FLIP? WELL, I SUPPOSE WE MUST DO THE PROPER THING. BON-BON, WOULD YOU BE SO KIND?
CERTAINLY, YOUR HIGHNESS.

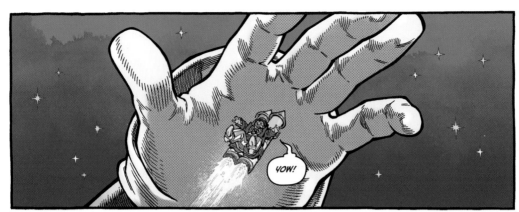

YOW!

SAVE THE FRUNKUS TOO! THERE HE GOES!

I'LL GET HIM, YOUR HIGHNESS.

QUIT SPOILIN' OUR FUN, YOU GIANTS!

GONK! BONK!

YOU TELL 'EM, LUNK!

HMF—CURIOUS SPECIMEN.

BUNK! KUNK!

DR. PILL, CAN YOU RETURN NEMO TO HIS ACCUSTOMED SIZE?

I'VE JUST THE THING, YOUR HIGHNESS!

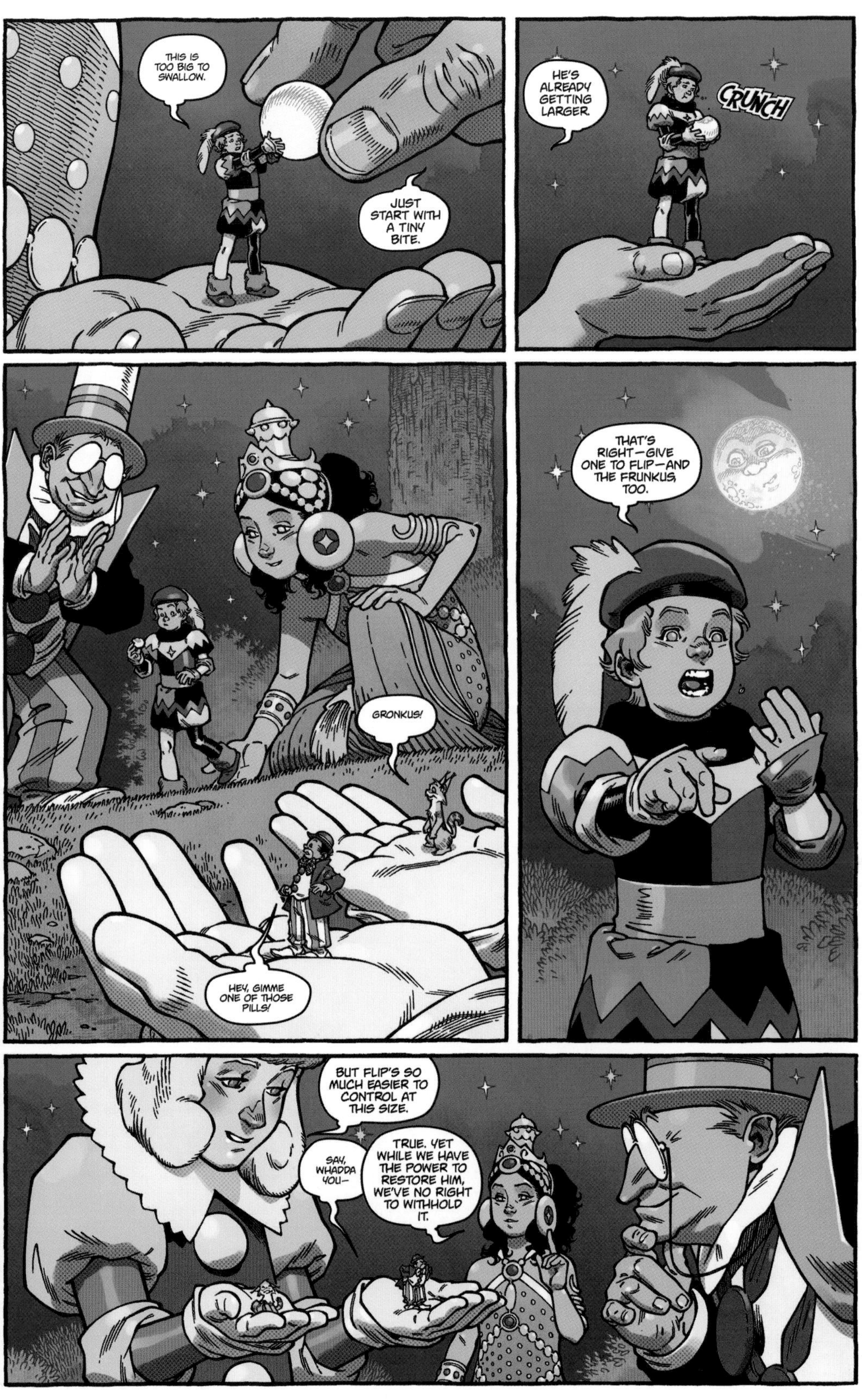
THIS IS TOO BIG TO SWALLOW.
JUST START WITH A TINY BITE.
HE'S ALREADY GETTING LARGER.
CRUNCH
GRONKUS!
HEY, GIMME ONE OF THOSE PILLS!
THAT'S RIGHT—GIVE ONE TO FLIP—AND THE FRUNKUS, TOO.
BUT FLIP'S SO MUCH EASIER TO CONTROL AT THIS SIZE.
SAY, WHADDA YOU—
TRUE. YET WHILE WE HAVE THE POWER TO RESTORE HIM, WE'VE NO RIGHT TO WITHHOLD IT.

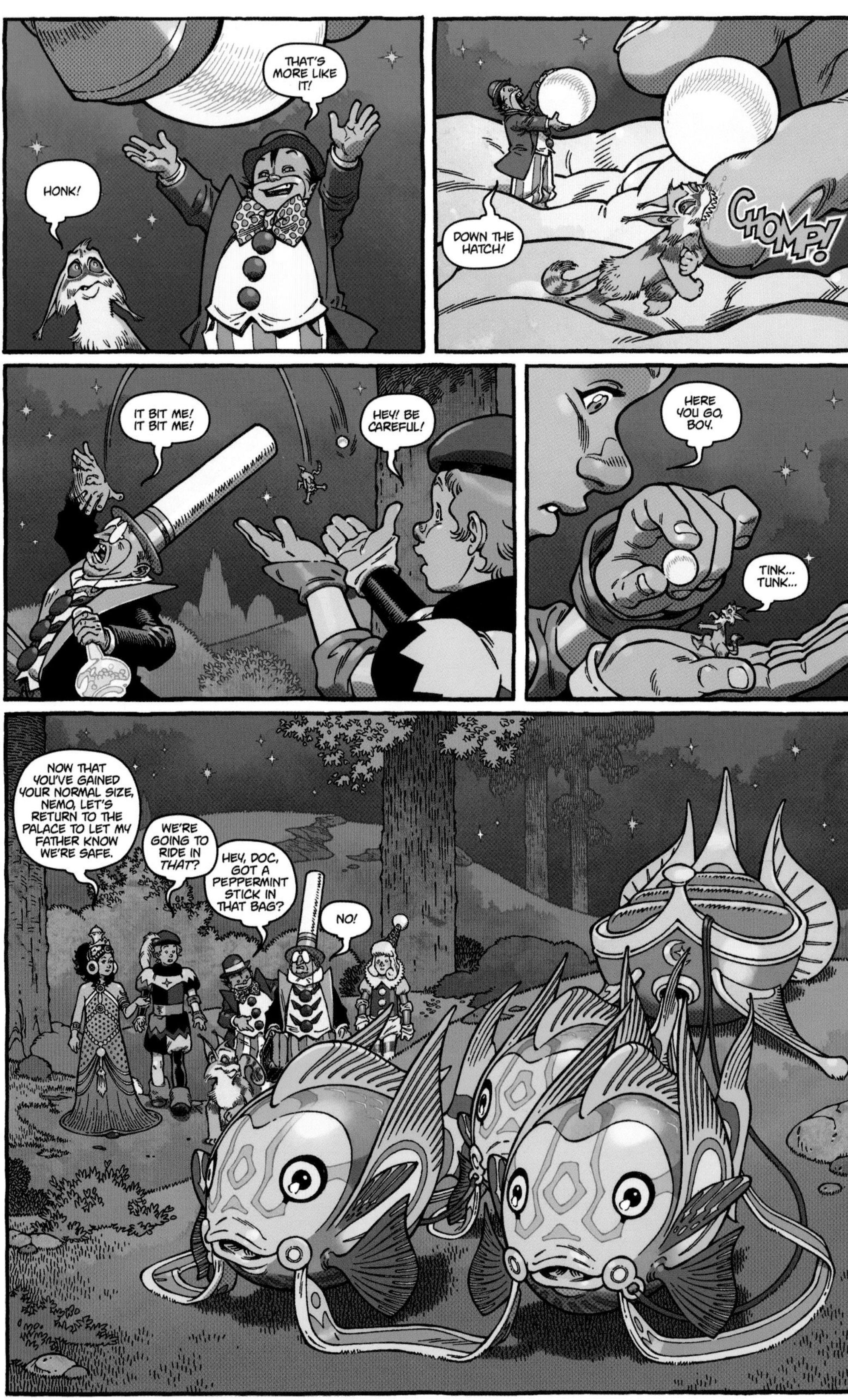
THAT'S MORE LIKE IT!
HONK!
DOWN THE HATCH!
CHOMP!
IT BIT ME! IT BIT ME!
HEY! BE CAREFUL!
HERE YOU GO, BOY.
TINK... TUNK...
NOW THAT YOU'VE GAINED YOUR NORMAL SIZE, NEMO, LET'S RETURN TO THE PALACE TO LET MY FATHER KNOW WE'RE SAFE.
WE'RE GOING TO RIDE IN *THAT*?
HEY, DOC, GOT A PEPPERMINT STICK IN THAT BAG?
NO!

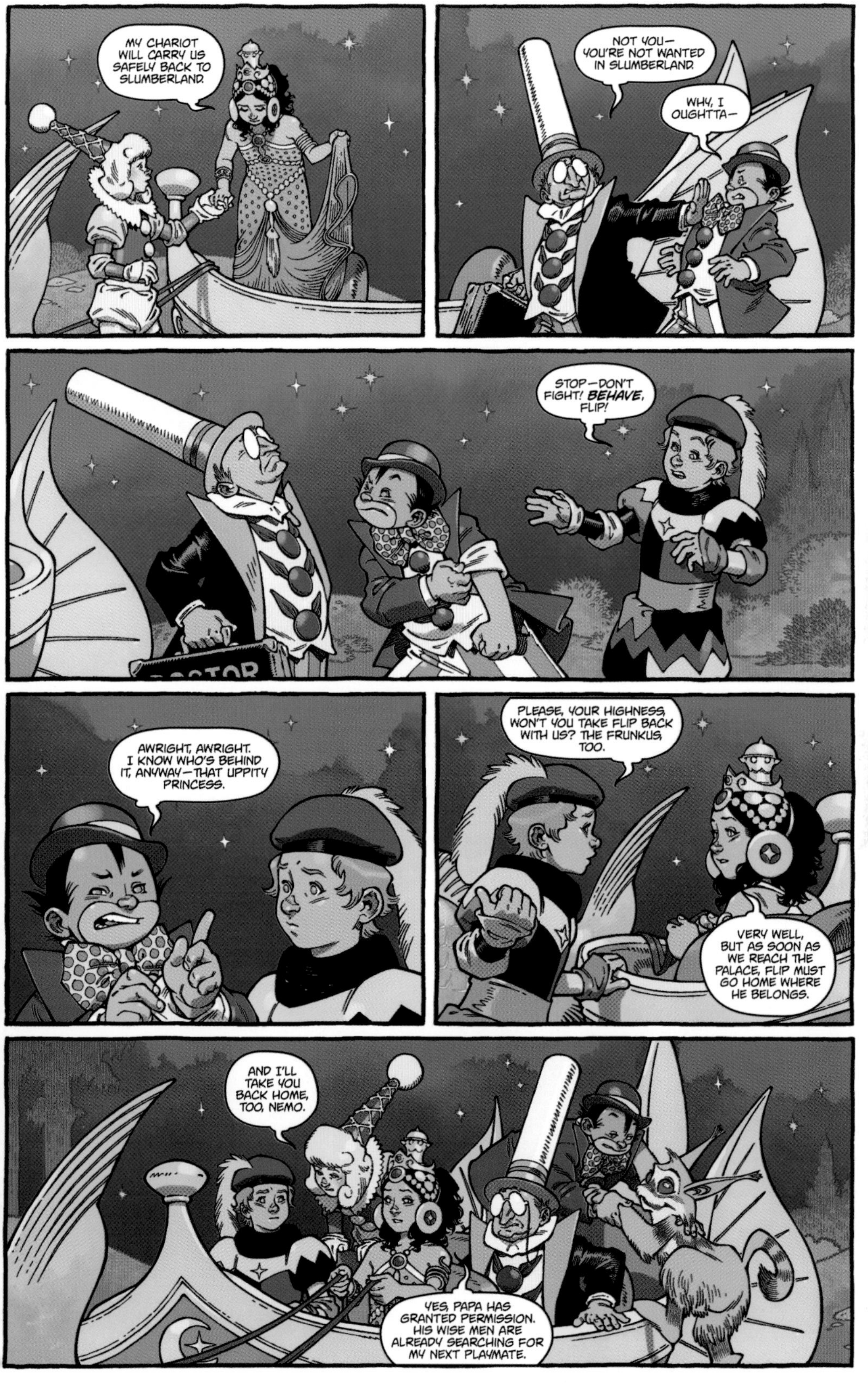
MY CHARIOT WILL CARRY US SAFELY BACK TO SLUMBERLAND.
NOT YOU— YOU'RE NOT WANTED IN SLUMBERLAND.
WHY, I OUGHTTA—
STOP—DON'T FIGHT! ***BEHAVE***, FLIP!
AWRIGHT, AWRIGHT. I KNOW WHO'S BEHIND IT, ANYWAY—THAT UPPITY PRINCESS.
PLEASE, YOUR HIGHNESS, WON'T YOU TAKE FLIP BACK WITH US? THE FRUNKUS, TOO.
VERY WELL, BUT AS SOON AS WE REACH THE PALACE, FLIP MUST GO HOME WHERE HE BELONGS.
AND I'LL TAKE YOU BACK HOME, TOO, NEMO.
YES, PAPA HAS GRANTED PERMISSION. HIS WISE MEN ARE ALREADY SEARCHING FOR MY NEXT PLAYMATE.

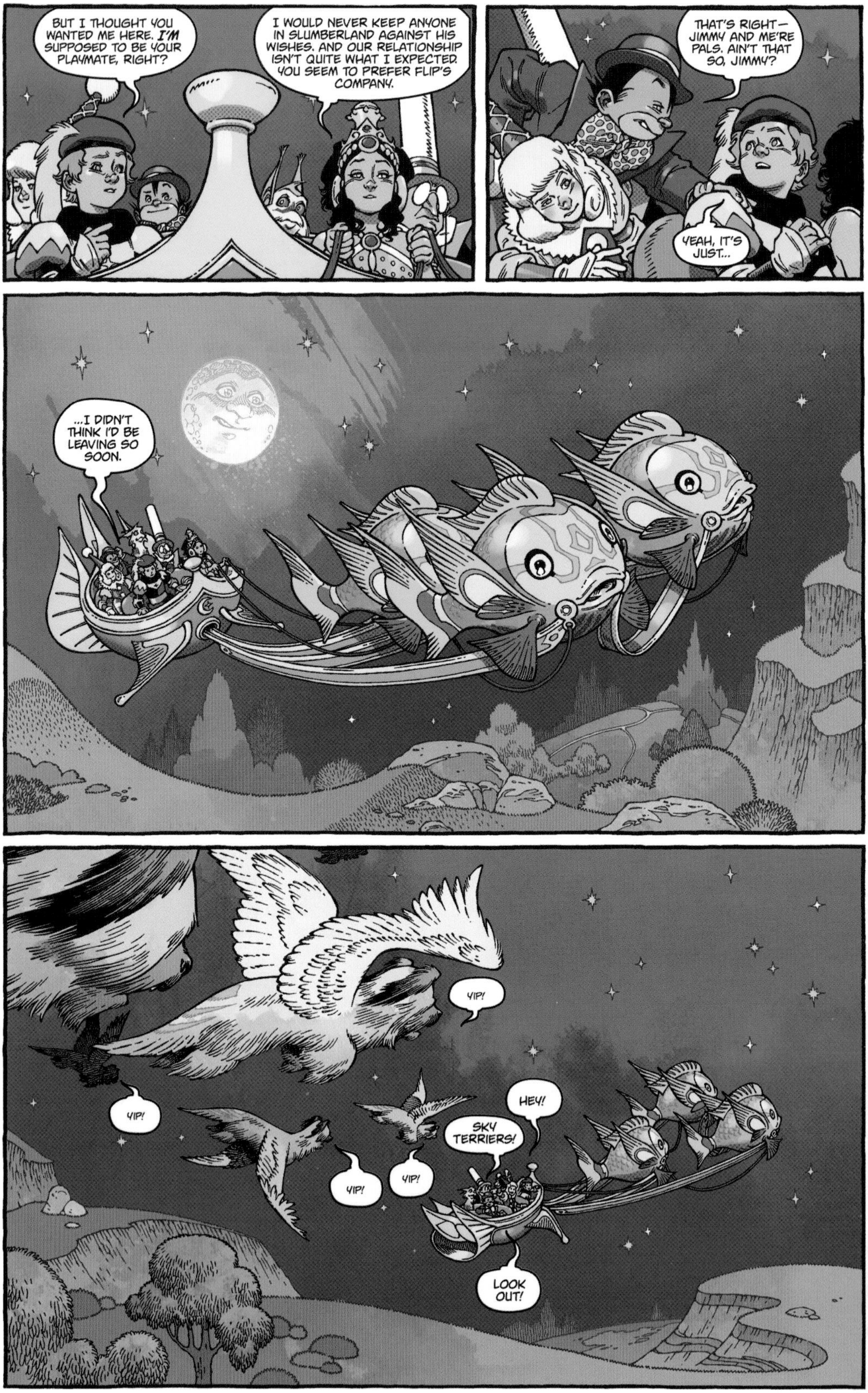
BUT I THOUGHT YOU WANTED ME HERE. *I'M* SUPPOSED TO BE YOUR PLAYMATE, RIGHT?
I WOULD NEVER KEEP ANYONE IN SLUMBERLAND AGAINST HIS WISHES. AND OUR RELATIONSHIP ISN'T QUITE WHAT I EXPECTED. YOU SEEM TO PREFER FLIP'S COMPANY.
THAT'S RIGHT— JIMMY AND ME'RE PALS. AIN'T THAT SO, JIMMY?
YEAH, IT'S JUST...
...I DIDN'T THINK I'D BE LEAVING SO SOON.
YIP!
YIP!
YIP!
YIP!
SKY TERRIERS!
HEY!
LOOK OUT!

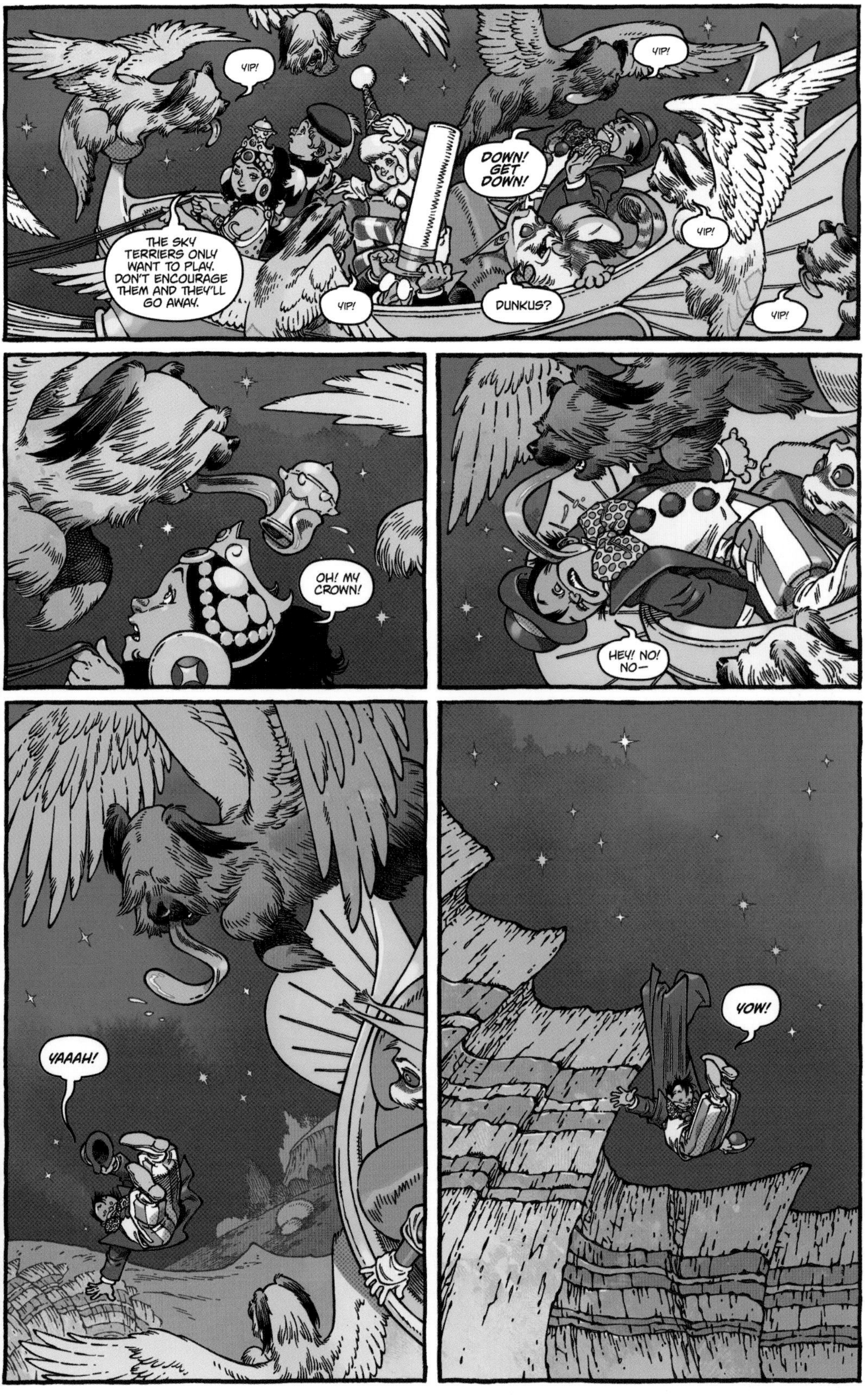
YIP!
THE SKY TERRIERS ONLY WANT TO PLAY. DON'T ENCOURAGE THEM AND THEY'LL GO AWAY.
YIP!
DOWN! GET DOWN!
YIP!
DUNKUS?
YIP!
YIP!
OH! MY CROWN!
HEY! NO! NO—
YAAAH!
YOW!

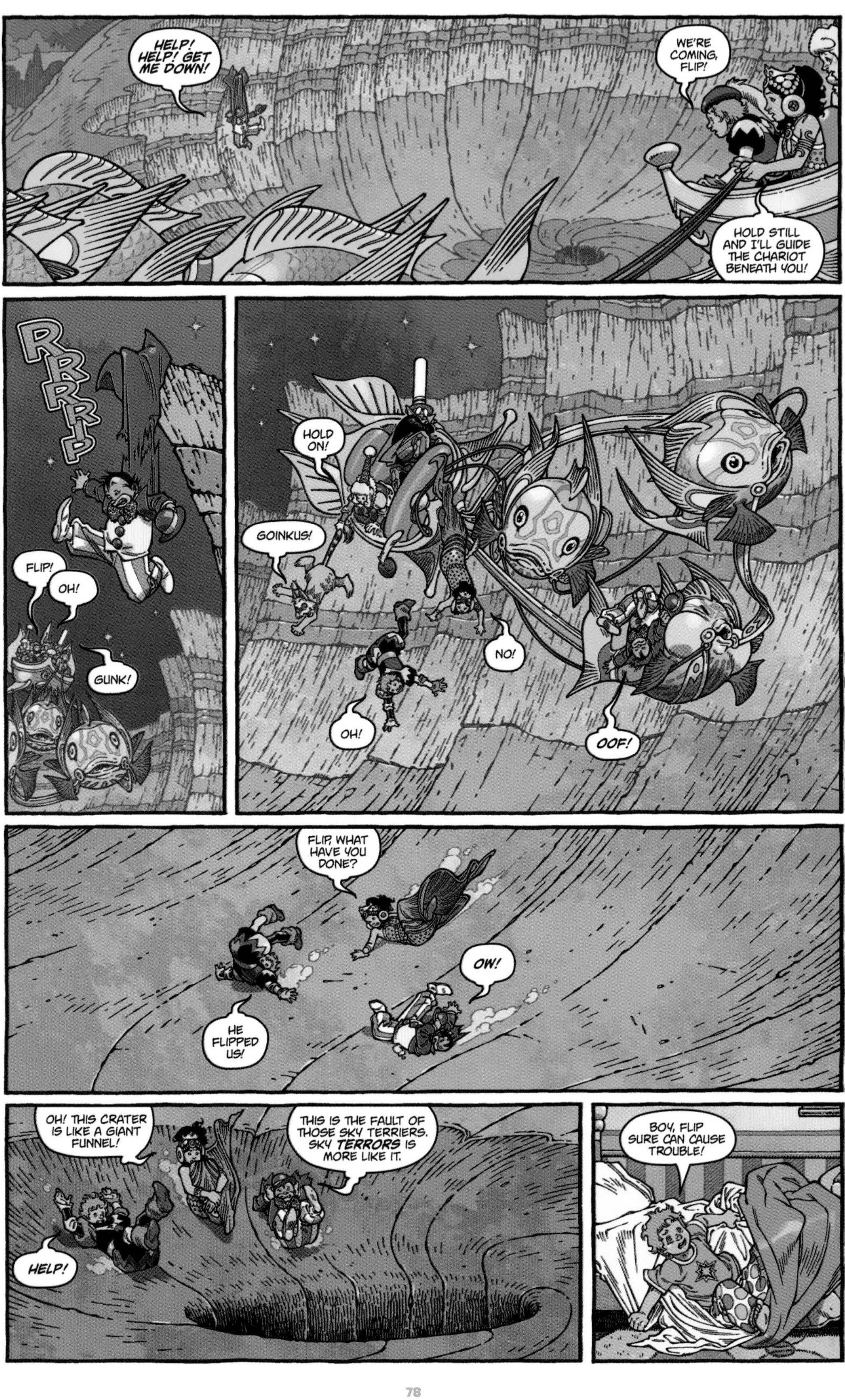

HELP! HELP! GET ME DOWN!
WE'RE COMING, FLIP!
HOLD STILL AND I'LL GUIDE THE CHARIOT BENEATH YOU!
RRRRIP
FLIP!
OH!
GUNK!
HOLD ON!
GOINKUS!
NO!
OH!
OOF!
FLIP, WHAT HAVE YOU DONE?
OW!
HE FLIPPED US!
OH! THIS CRATER IS LIKE A GIANT FUNNEL!
THIS IS THE FAULT OF THOSE SKY TERRIERS. SKY TERRORS IS MORE LIKE IT.
HELP!
BOY, FLIP SURE CAN CAUSE TROUBLE!

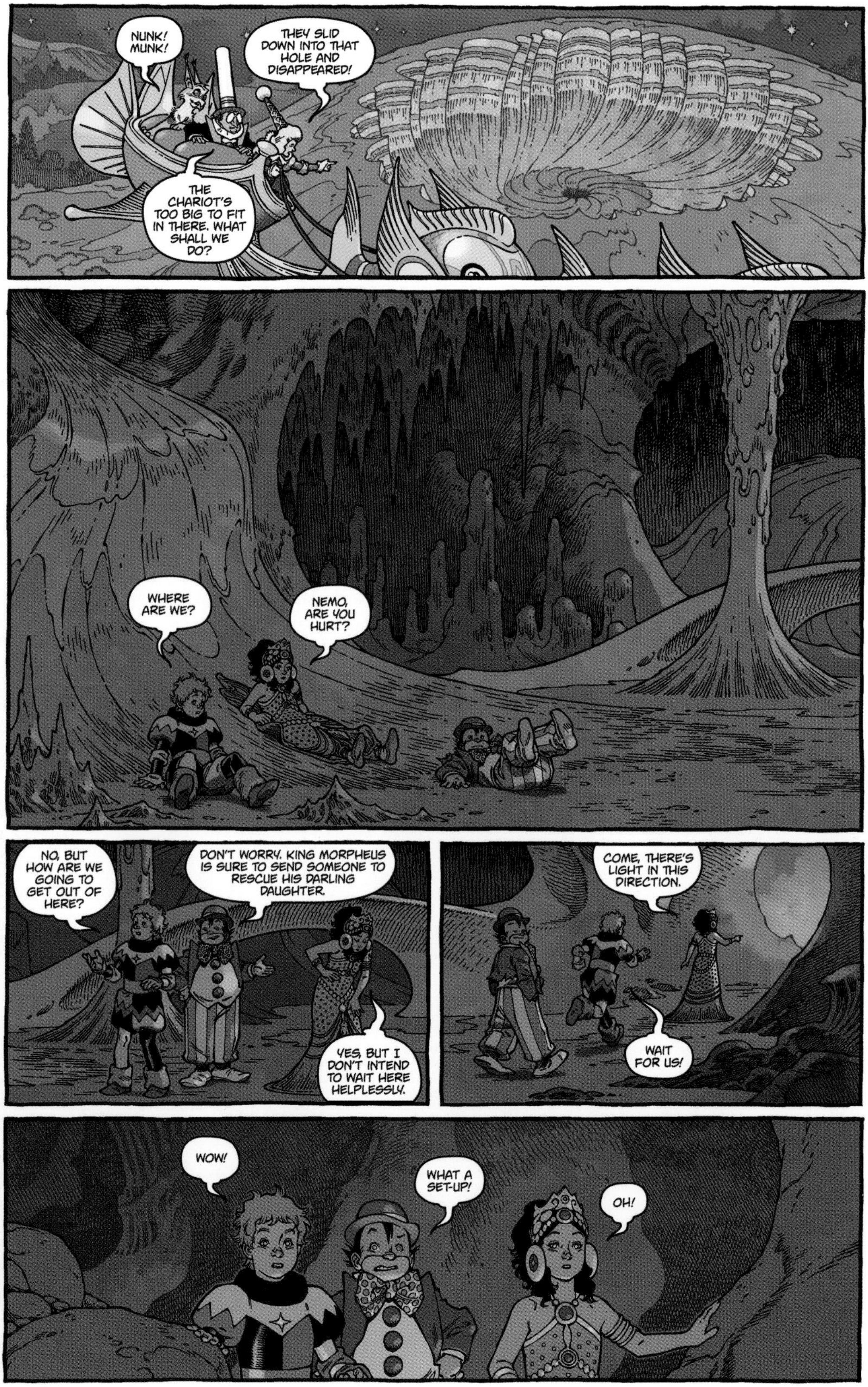
NUNK! MUNK!
THEY SLID DOWN INTO THAT HOLE AND DISAPPEARED!
THE CHARIOT'S TOO BIG TO FIT IN THERE. WHAT SHALL WE DO?
WHERE ARE WE?
NEMO, ARE YOU HURT?
NO, BUT HOW ARE WE GOING TO GET OUT OF HERE?
DON'T WORRY. KING MORPHEUS IS SURE TO SEND SOMEONE TO RESCUE HIS DARLING DAUGHTER.
YES, BUT I DON'T INTEND TO WAIT HERE HELPLESSLY.
COME, THERE'S LIGHT IN THIS DIRECTION.
WAIT FOR US!
WOW!
WHAT A SET-UP!
OH!

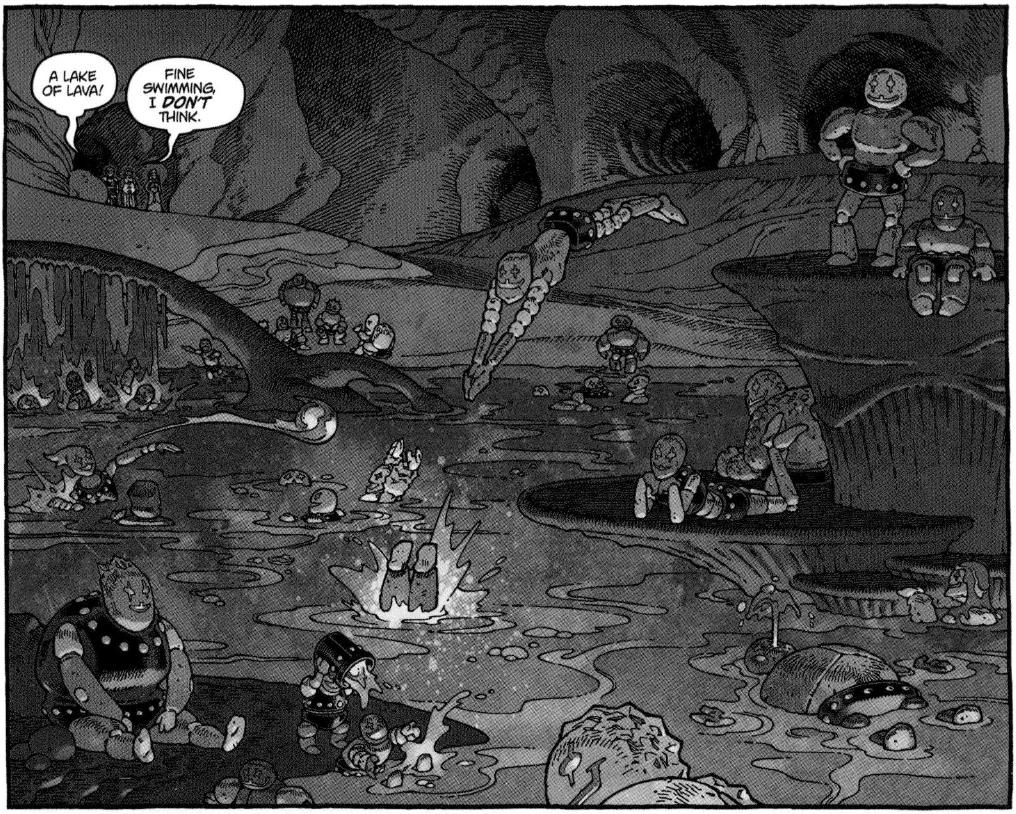
A LAKE OF LAVA!
FINE SWIMMING, I DON'T THINK.

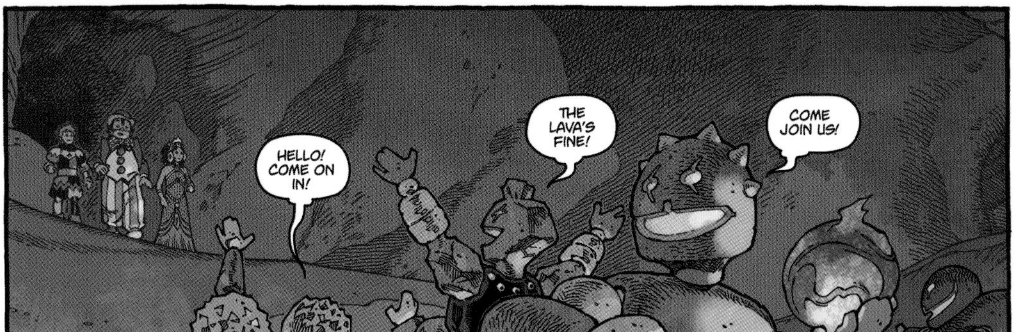
HELLO! COME ON IN!
THE LAVA'S FINE!
COME JOIN US!

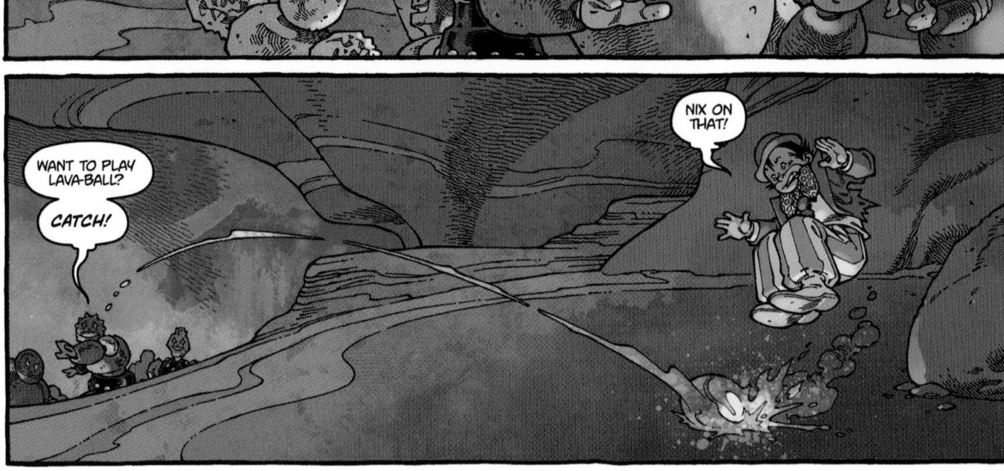
WANT TO PLAY LAVA-BALL?
CATCH!
NIX ON THAT!

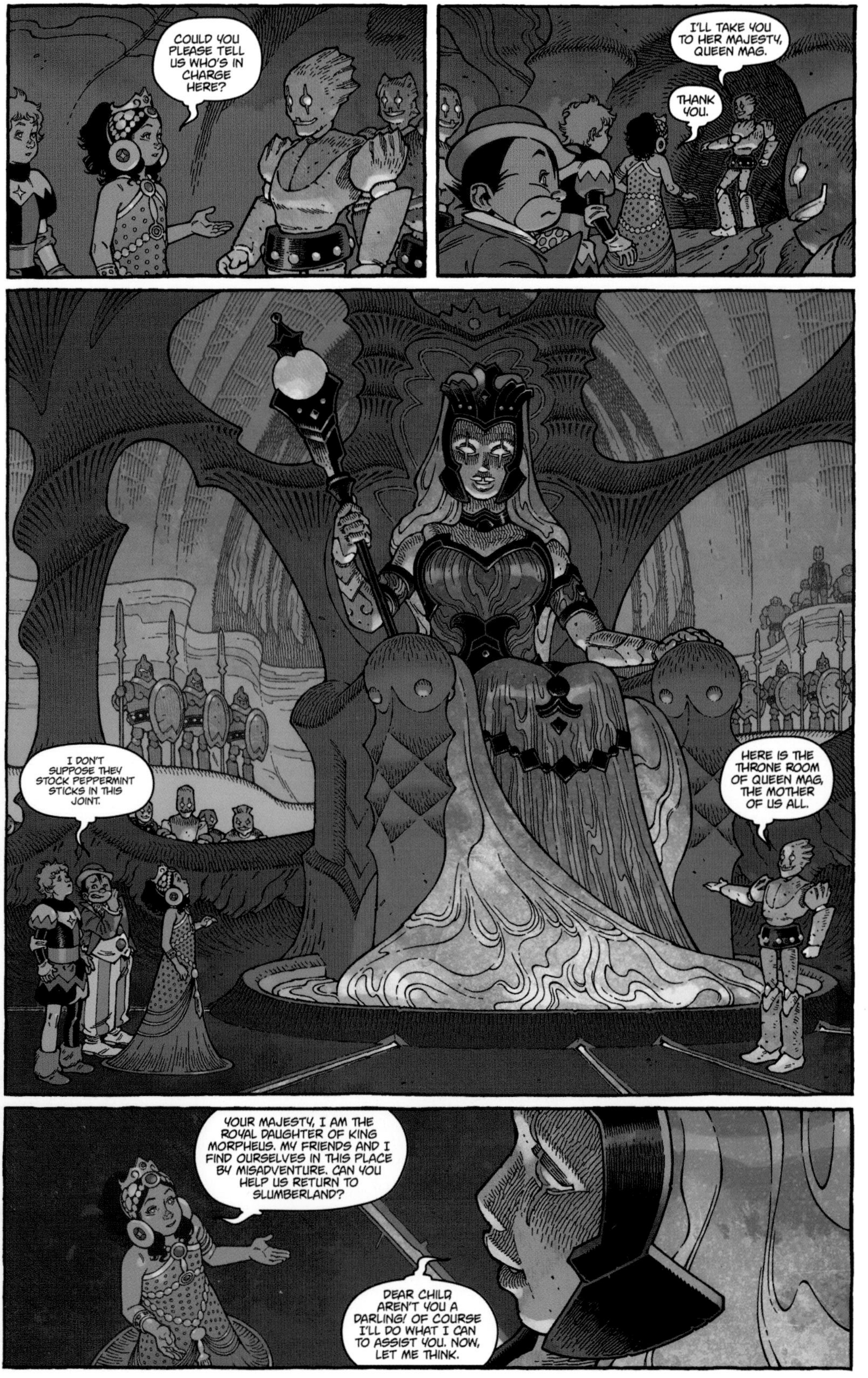
COULD YOU PLEASE TELL US WHO'S IN CHARGE HERE?
I'LL TAKE YOU TO HER MAJESTY, QUEEN MAG.
THANK YOU.
I DON'T SUPPOSE THEY STOCK PEPPERMINT STICKS IN THIS JOINT.
HERE IS THE THRONE ROOM OF QUEEN MAG, THE MOTHER OF US ALL.
YOUR MAJESTY, I AM THE ROYAL DAUGHTER OF KING MORPHEUS. MY FRIENDS AND I FIND OURSELVES IN THIS PLACE BY MISADVENTURE. CAN YOU HELP US RETURN TO SLUMBERLAND?
DEAR CHILD, AREN'T YOU A DARLING! OF COURSE I'LL DO WHAT I CAN TO ASSIST YOU. NOW, LET ME THINK.

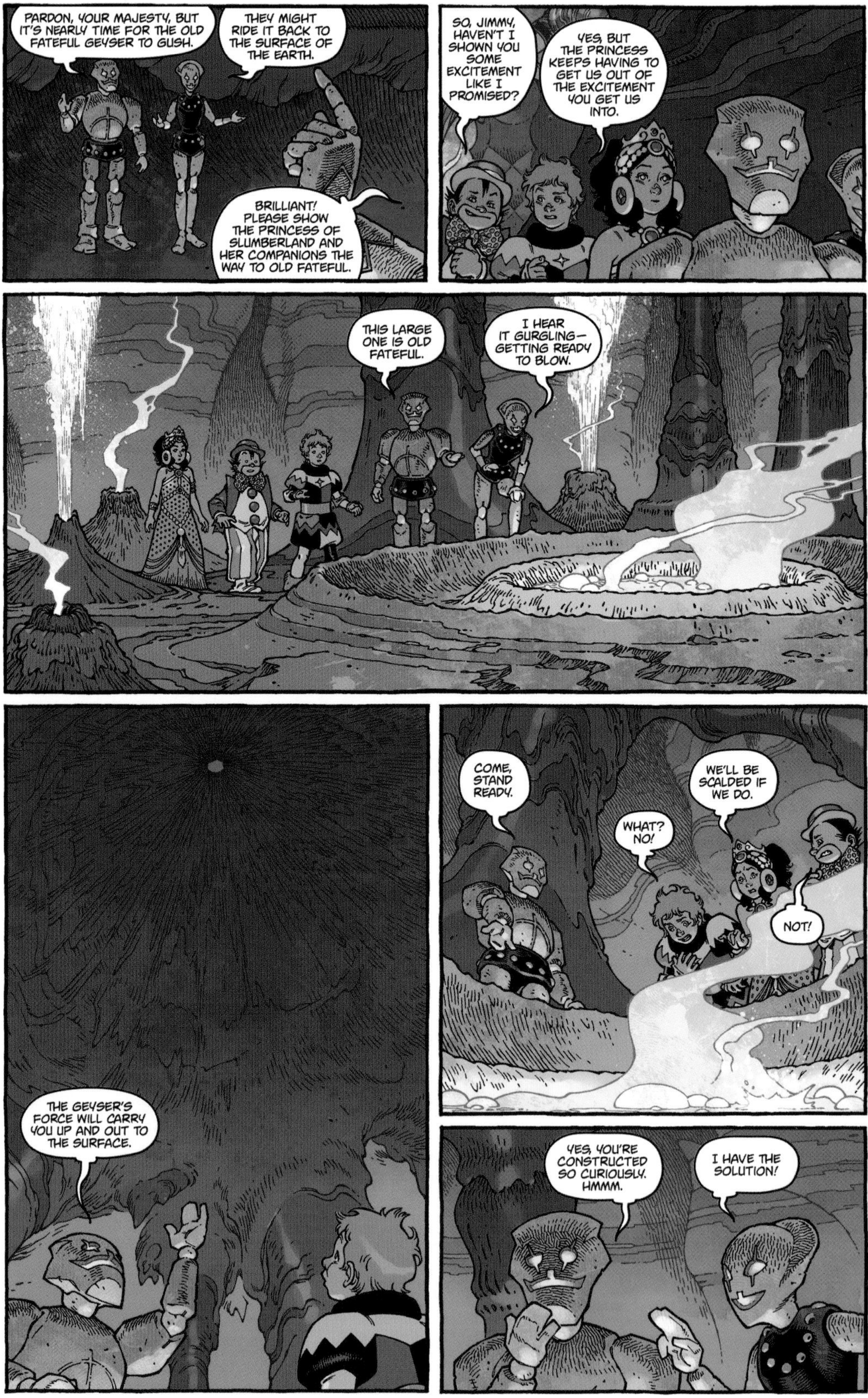
PARDON, YOUR MAJESTY, BUT IT'S NEARLY TIME FOR THE OLD FATEFUL GEYSER TO GUSH.
THEY MIGHT RIDE IT BACK TO THE SURFACE OF THE EARTH.
BRILLIANT! PLEASE SHOW THE PRINCESS OF SLUMBERLAND AND HER COMPANIONS THE WAY TO OLD FATEFUL.
SO, JIMMY, HAVEN'T I SHOWN YOU SOME EXCITEMENT LIKE I PROMISED?
YES, BUT THE PRINCESS KEEPS HAVING TO GET US OUT OF THE EXCITEMENT YOU GET US INTO.
THIS LARGE ONE IS OLD FATEFUL.
I HEAR IT GURGLING— GETTING READY TO BLOW.
THE GEYSER'S FORCE WILL CARRY YOU UP AND OUT TO THE SURFACE.
COME, STAND READY.
WHAT? NO!
WE'LL BE SCALDED IF WE DO.
NOT!
YES, YOU'RE CONSTRUCTED SO CURIOUSLY. HMMM.
I HAVE THE SOLUTION!

THIS STONE BOWL WILL HOLD YOU COMFORTABLY.

COME, LET'S GET IN.

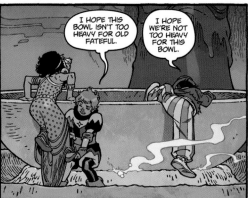

I HOPE THIS BOWL ISN'T TOO HEAVY FOR OLD FATEFUL.

I HOPE WE'RE NOT TOO HEAVY FOR THIS BOWL.

AAA!

WHUUUUUSH-SH-SH-SH...

OLD FATEFUL WILL LOVE THE CHALLENGE, I'M SURE.

THANK YOU FOR YOUR HELP. FAREWELL.

IS IT SUPPOSED TO SHAKE LIKE THIS?

MY QUESTION IS WHAT HAPPENS AFTER WE SHOOT TO THE SURFACE.

SIT TIGHT— I BELIEVE IT'S ABOUT TO—

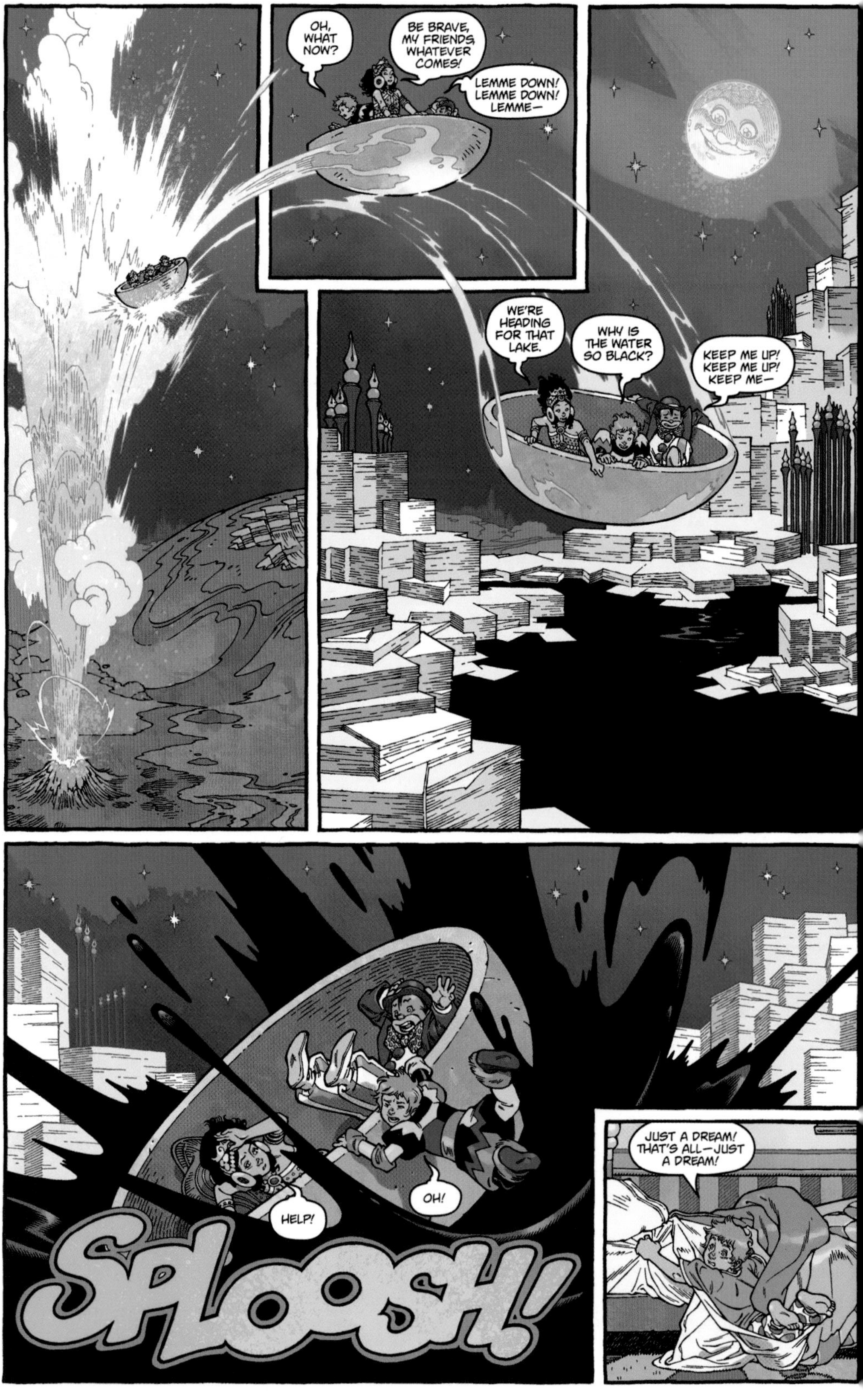
OH, WHAT NOW?
BE BRAVE, MY FRIENDS, WHATEVER COMES!
LEMME DOWN! LEMME DOWN! LEMME—
WE'RE HEADING FOR THAT LAKE.
WHY IS THE WATER SO BLACK?
KEEP ME UP! KEEP ME UP! KEEP ME—
HELP!
OH!
SPLOOSH!
JUST A DREAM! THAT'S ALL—JUST A DREAM!

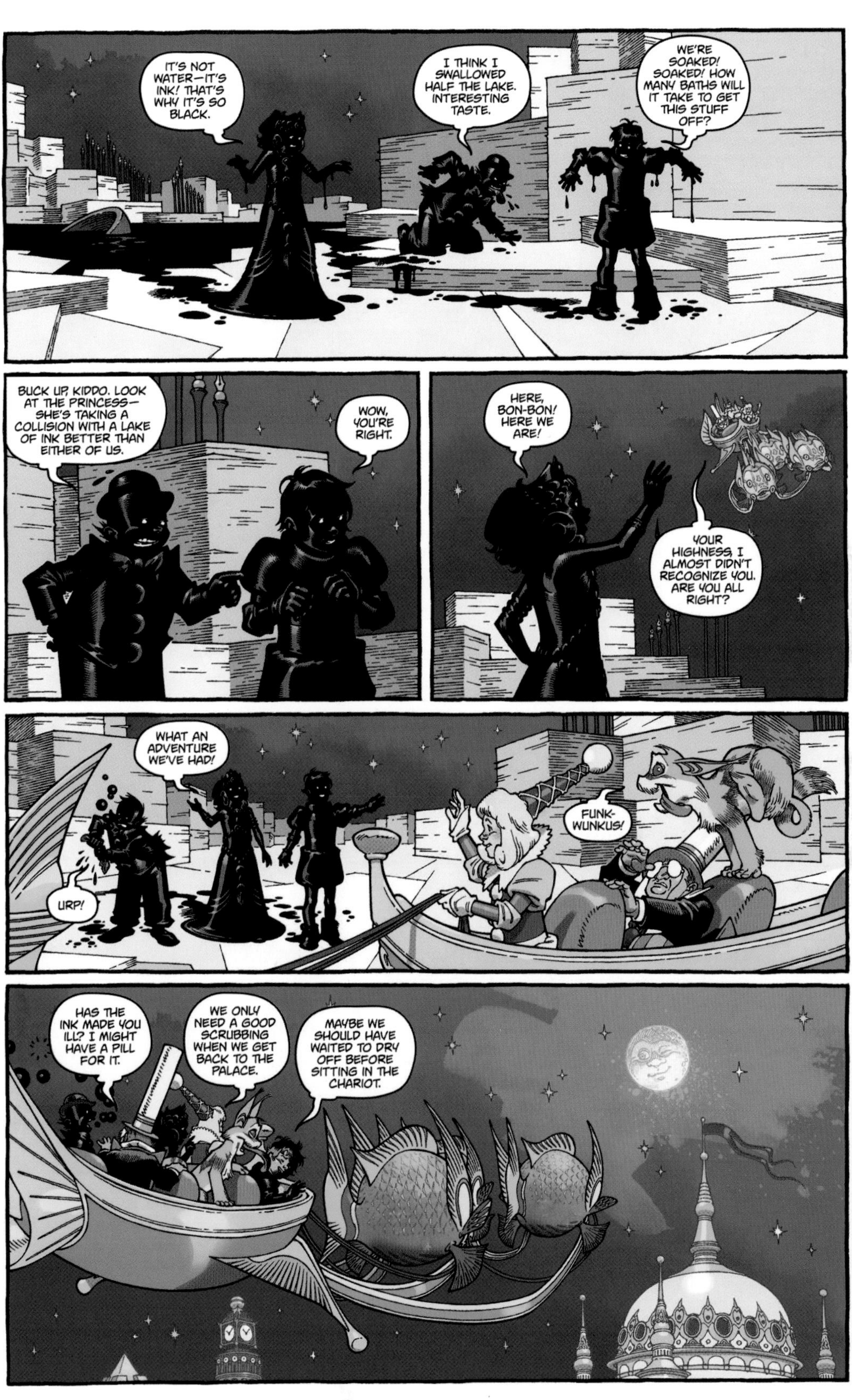
IT'S NOT WATER—IT'S INK! THAT'S WHY IT'S SO BLACK.
I THINK I SWALLOWED HALF THE LAKE. INTERESTING TASTE.
WE'RE SOAKED! SOAKED! HOW MANY BATHS WILL IT TAKE TO GET THIS STUFF OFF?
BUCK UP, KIDDO. LOOK AT THE PRINCESS—SHE'S TAKING A COLLISION WITH A LAKE OF INK BETTER THAN EITHER OF US.
WOW, YOU'RE RIGHT.
HERE, BON-BON! HERE WE ARE!
YOUR HIGHNESS, I ALMOST DIDN'T RECOGNIZE YOU. ARE YOU ALL RIGHT?
WHAT AN ADVENTURE WE'VE HAD!
URP!
FUNK-WUNKUS!
HAS THE INK MADE YOU ILL? I MIGHT HAVE A PILL FOR IT.
WE ONLY NEED A GOOD SCRUBBING WHEN WE GET BACK TO THE PALACE.
MAYBE WE SHOULD HAVE WAITED TO DRY OFF BEFORE SITTING IN THE CHARIOT.

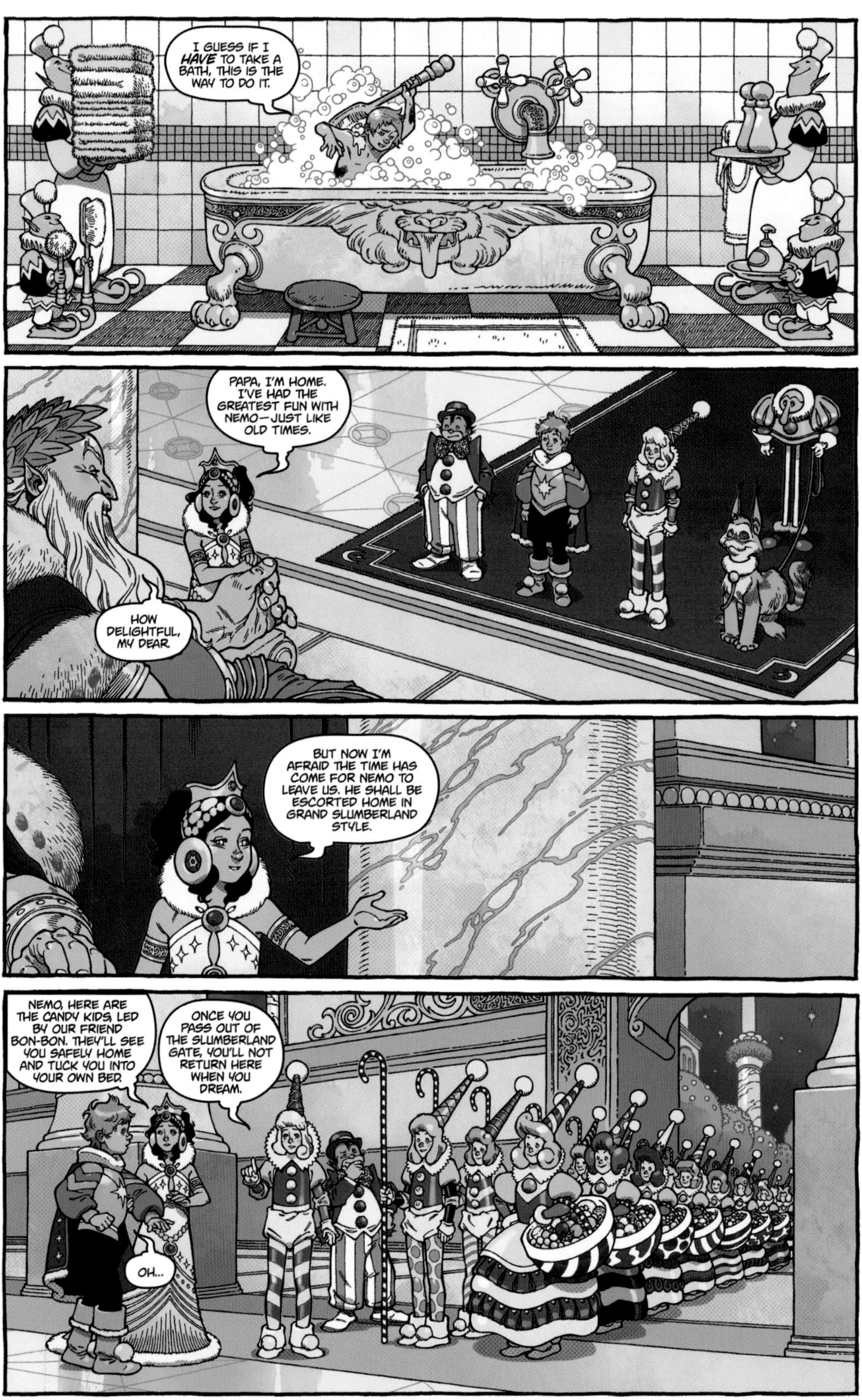
I GUESS IF I *HAVE* TO TAKE A BATH, THIS IS THE WAY TO DO IT.
PAPA, I'M HOME. I'VE HAD THE GREATEST FUN WITH NEMO—JUST LIKE OLD TIMES.
HOW DELIGHTFUL, MY DEAR.
BUT NOW I'M AFRAID THE TIME HAS COME FOR NEMO TO LEAVE US. HE SHALL BE ESCORTED HOME IN GRAND SLUMBERLAND STYLE.
NEMO, HERE ARE THE CANDY KIDS, LED BY OUR FRIEND BON-BON. THEY'LL SEE YOU SAFELY HOME AND TUCK YOU INTO YOUR OWN BED.
ONCE YOU PASS OUT OF THE SLUMBERLAND GATE, YOU'LL NOT RETURN HERE WHEN YOU DREAM.
OH...

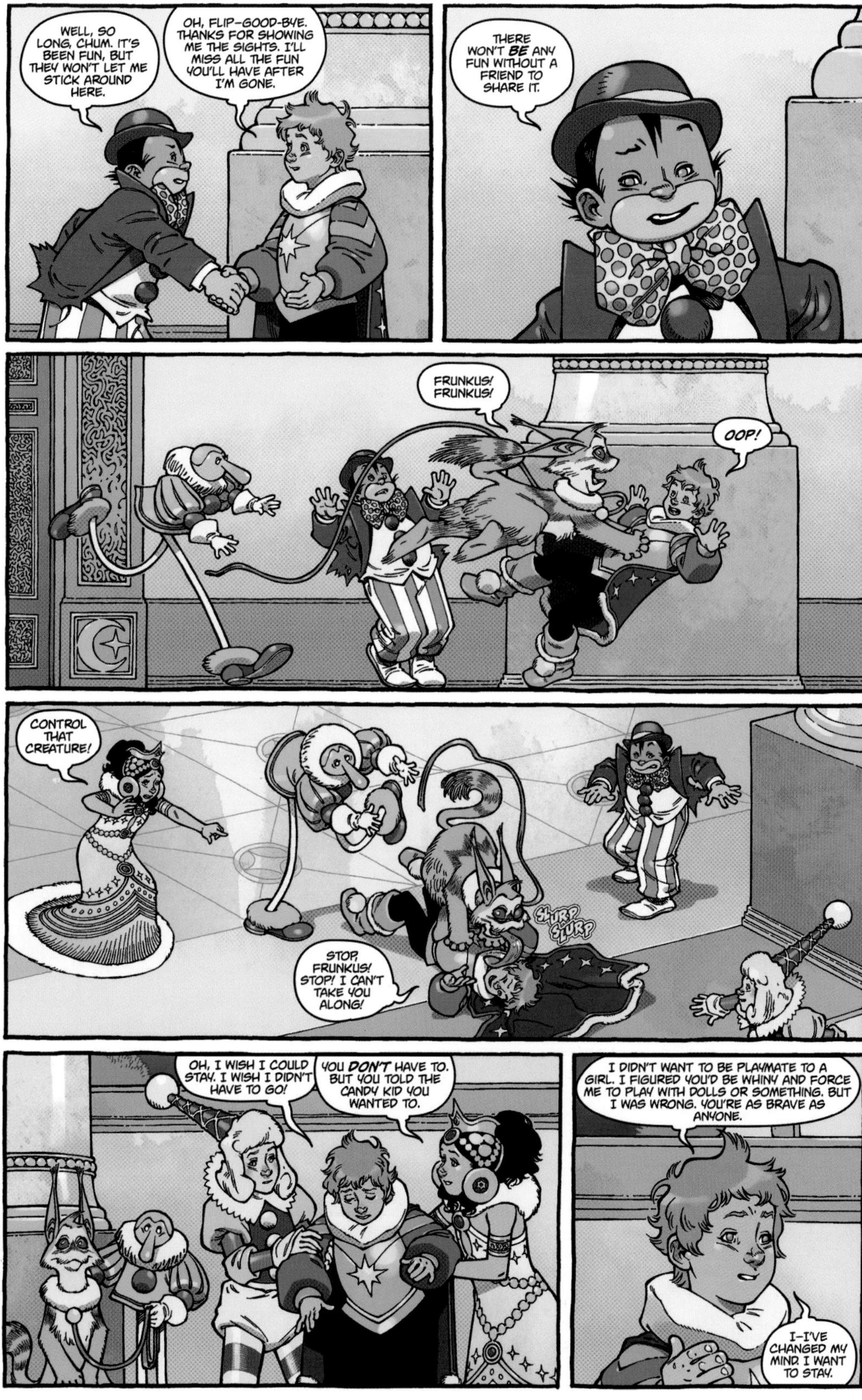

WELL, SO LONG, CHUM. IT'S BEEN FUN, BUT THEY WON'T LET ME STICK AROUND HERE.
OH, FLIP—GOOD-BYE. THANKS FOR SHOWING ME THE SIGHTS. I'LL MISS ALL THE FUN YOU'LL HAVE AFTER I'M GONE.
THERE WON'T BE ANY FUN WITHOUT A FRIEND TO SHARE IT.
FRUNKUS! FRUNKUS!
OOP!
CONTROL THAT CREATURE!
SLURP SLURP
STOP, FRUNKUS! STOP! I CAN'T TAKE YOU ALONG!
OH, I WISH I COULD STAY. I WISH I DIDN'T HAVE TO GO!
YOU DON'T HAVE TO. BUT YOU TOLD THE CANDY KID YOU WANTED TO.
I DIDN'T WANT TO BE PLAYMATE TO A GIRL. I FIGURED YOU'D BE WHINY AND FORCE ME TO PLAY WITH DOLLS OR SOMETHING. BUT I WAS WRONG. YOU'RE AS BRAVE AS ANYONE.
I-I'VE CHANGED MY MIND. I WANT TO STAY.

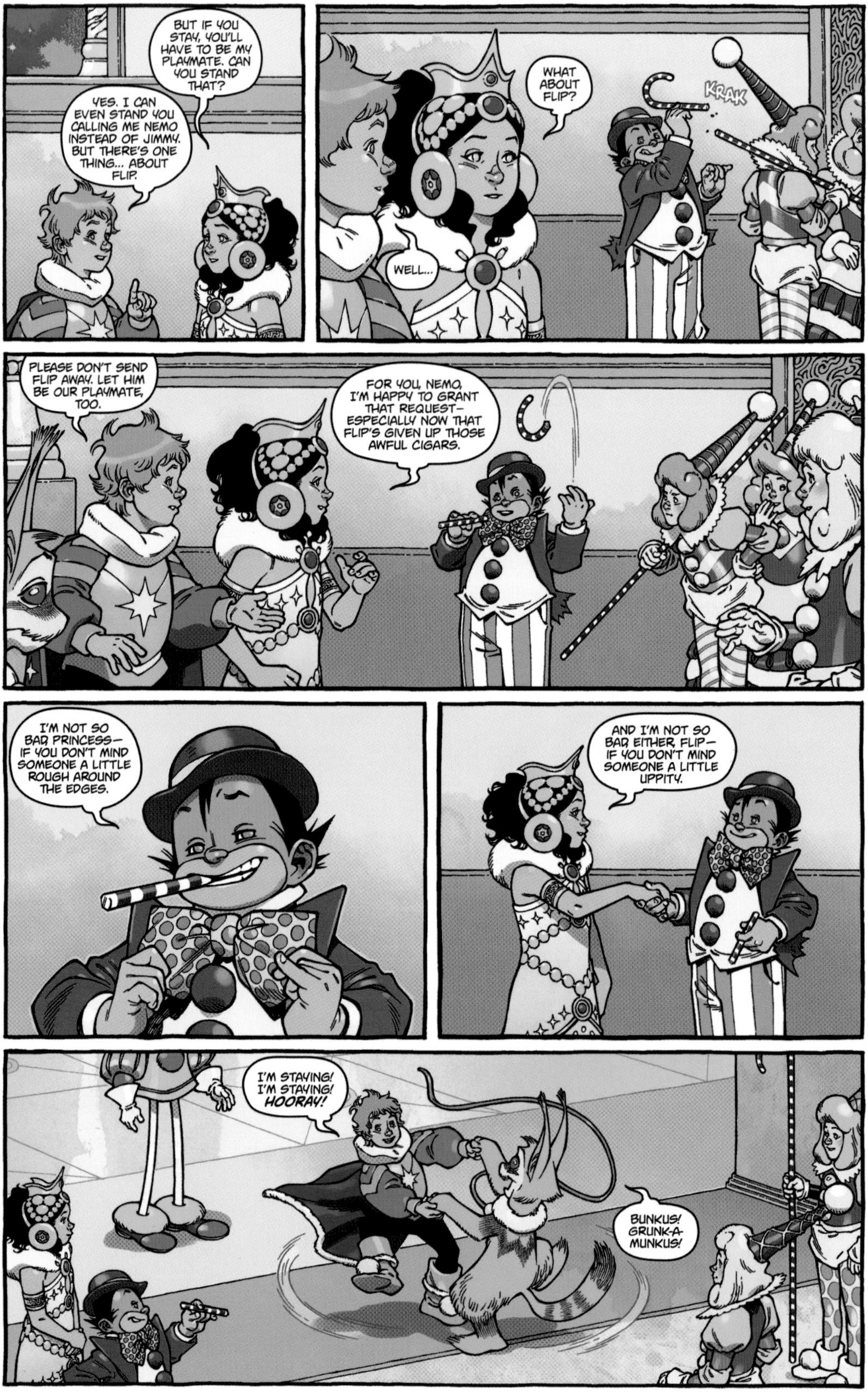
BUT IF YOU STAY, YOU'LL HAVE TO BE MY PLAYMATE. CAN YOU STAND THAT?
YES. I CAN EVEN STAND YOU CALLING ME NEMO INSTEAD OF JIMMY. BUT THERE'S ONE THING... ABOUT FLIP.
WHAT ABOUT FLIP?
WELL...
KRAK
PLEASE DON'T SEND FLIP AWAY. LET HIM BE OUR PLAYMATE, TOO.
FOR YOU, NEMO, I'M HAPPY TO GRANT THAT REQUEST– ESPECIALLY NOW THAT FLIP'S GIVEN UP THOSE AWFUL CIGARS.
I'M NOT SO BAD, PRINCESS– IF YOU DON'T MIND SOMEONE A LITTLE ROUGH AROUND THE EDGES.
AND I'M NOT SO BAD EITHER, FLIP– IF YOU DON'T MIND SOMEONE A LITTLE UPPITY.
I'M STAYING! I'M STAYING! HOORAY!
BUNKUS! GRUNK-A-MUNKUS!

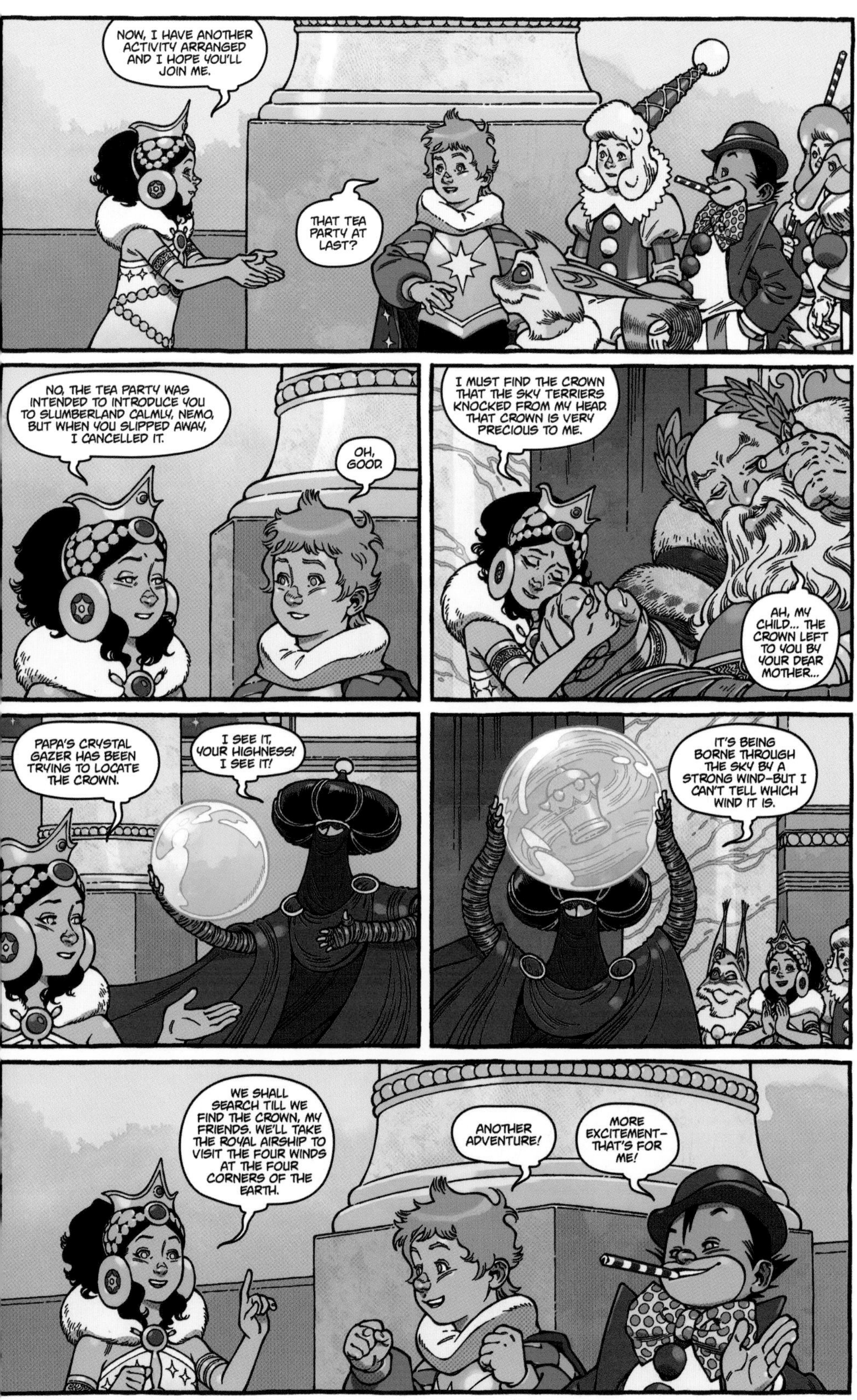
NOW, I HAVE ANOTHER ACTIVITY ARRANGED AND I HOPE YOU'LL JOIN ME.
THAT TEA PARTY AT LAST?
NO, THE TEA PARTY WAS INTENDED TO INTRODUCE YOU TO SLUMBERLAND CALMLY, NEMO, BUT WHEN YOU SLIPPED AWAY, I CANCELLED IT.
OH, GOOD.
I MUST FIND THE CROWN THAT THE SKY TERRIERS KNOCKED FROM MY HEAD. THAT CROWN IS VERY PRECIOUS TO ME.
AH, MY CHILD... THE CROWN LEFT TO YOU BY YOUR DEAR MOTHER...
PAPA'S CRYSTAL GAZER HAS BEEN TRYING TO LOCATE THE CROWN.
I SEE IT, YOUR HIGHNESS! I SEE IT!
IT'S BEING BORNE THROUGH THE SKY BY A STRONG WIND—BUT I CAN'T TELL WHICH WIND IT IS.
WE SHALL SEARCH TILL WE FIND THE CROWN, MY FRIENDS. WE'LL TAKE THE ROYAL AIRSHIP TO VISIT THE FOUR WINDS AT THE FOUR CORNERS OF THE EARTH.
ANOTHER ADVENTURE!
MORE EXCITEMENT—THAT'S FOR ME!

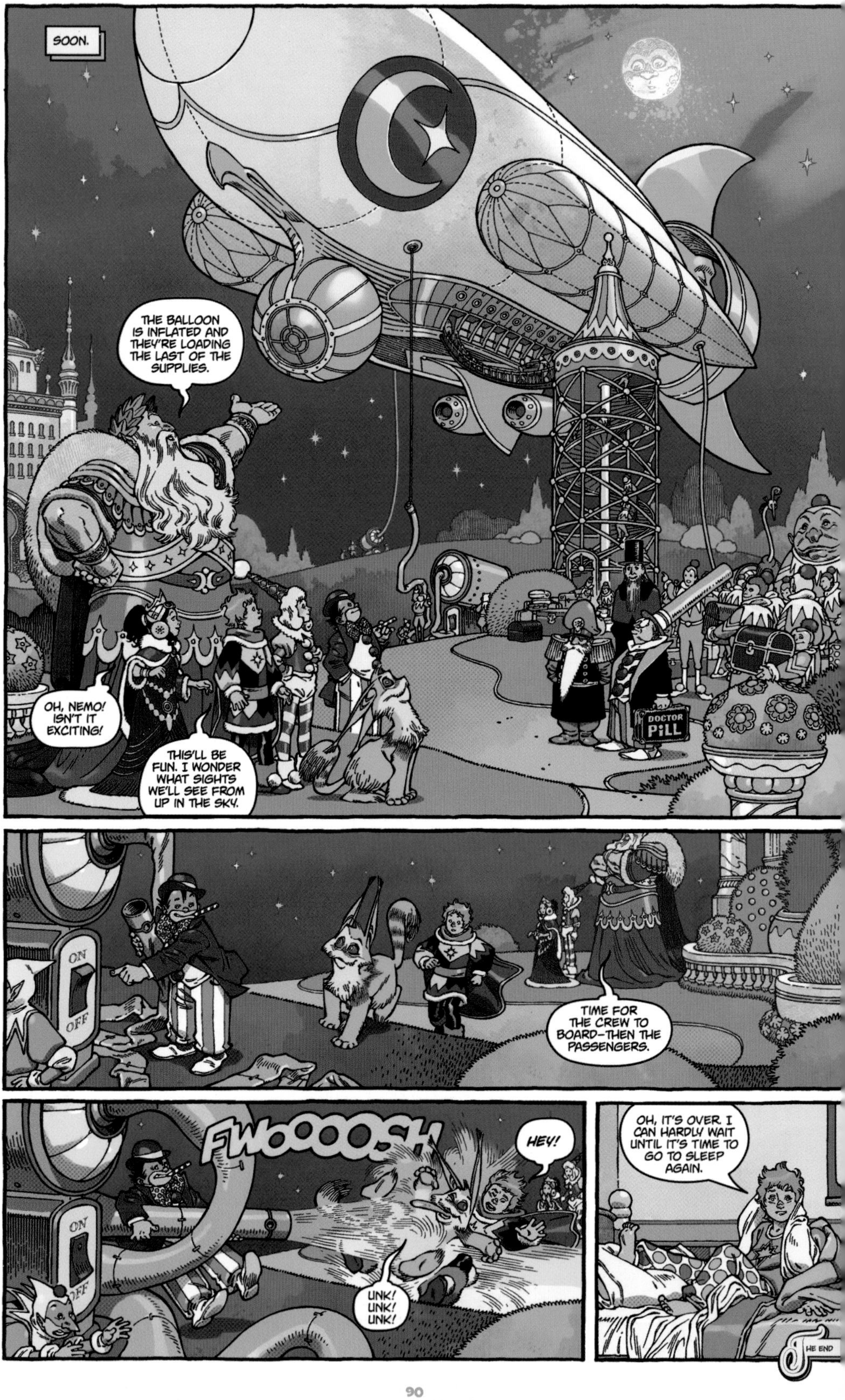
SOON.
THE BALLOON IS INFLATED AND THEY'RE LOADING THE LAST OF THE SUPPLIES.
OH, NEMO! ISN'T IT EXCITING!
THIS'LL BE FUN. I WONDER WHAT SIGHTS WE'LL SEE FROM UP IN THE SKY.
DOCTOR PILL
ON
OFF
TIME FOR THE CREW TO BOARD–THEN THE PASSENGERS.
FWOOOOSH
HEY!
ON
OFF
UNK! UNK! UNK!
OH, IT'S OVER. I CAN HARDLY WAIT UNTIL IT'S TIME TO GO TO SLEEP AGAIN.
THE END

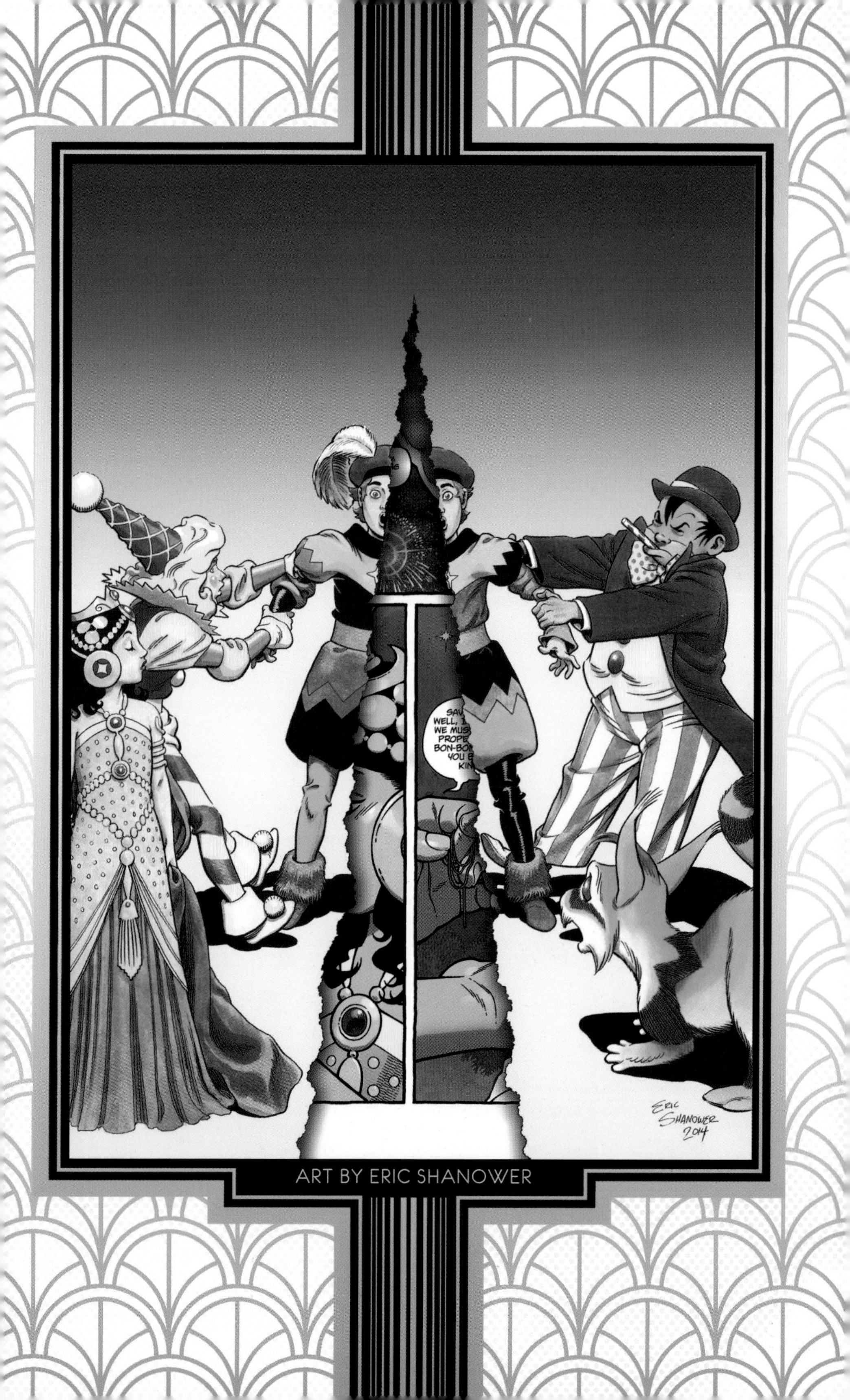
ERIC SHANOWER 2014

ART BY ERIC SHANOWER

CREATOR BIOGRAPHIES

ERIC SHANOWER

Eric Shanower's award-winning graphic-novel series *Age of Bronze* (Image) retells the story of the Trojan War. With cartoonist Skottie Young, he adapted L. Frank Baum's Oz books to *New York Times* best-selling graphic novels (Marvel). Shanower's past comics work includes his own Oz graphic-novel series, published as *Little Adventures in Oz* (IDW), and art for *An Accidental Death* by Ed Brubaker, *The Elsewhere Prince* by Moebius and R-JM Lofficier, and *Harlan Ellison's Dream Corridor*. He has illustrated for television, magazines, and children's books, two of which he wrote himself. He lives in San Diego, California. www.age-of-bronze.com

GABRIEL RODRIGUEZ

Gabriel Rodríguez is a Chilean comic-book artist, and co-creator (with writer Joe Hill) of IDW's award-winning graphic-novel series, *Locke & Key.*

In addition to his current work with Eric Shanower on *Little Nemo*, some of Gabriel's other collaborations with IDW, that span over a decade, include: *Clive Barker's The Great and Secret Show, Beowulf, George Romero's Land Of The Dead, CSI* comics and comic-book covers for *Edward Scissorhands, Transformers, Star Trek, Joe Hill's Wraith, Angel, Astro Boy* and others.

Gabriel has also illustrated for card games, advertising, magazines, and books. He currently lives in Santiago, Chile, with his family, but you can also find him on Twitter: @GR_comics.

NELSON DÁNIEL

Nelson Dániel has worked for over 15 years in film and commercials as an art director, production designer, storyboard and concept artist for films like *Aftershock* and Eli Roth's *Green Inferno*, among others.

In Chile, where Nelson lives, he has published two graphic novels, *Lucca* and *1899.*

He has also worked as a colorist for Marvel and for IDW on series such as *The Cape* and *Wild Blue Yonder*—in fact, it was the artist on both those series, Zach Howard, who first brought Nelson to IDW. Nelson also did all the art and colors on *The Cape: 1969* and the Stephen King/Joe Hill collaboration, *Road Rage: Throttle*. Currently, he draws and colors IDW's monthly *Judge Dredd* series in addition to his ongoing work on *Wild Blue Yonder* and *Little Nemo.*